NEW WAYS TO TRAVEL
THROUGH TIME!

"Those badly addicted to the automobile will never learn or earn the joys of hiking. Similarly, the Time Machine is a little too easy. It's great when urgent business requires that we get there in a hurry, but we are shot into the past, or the future, and the pleasures of the journey have been denied us:

"My intention in putting together this book has been to get, from some of the best science fiction writers alive, their own visions of probing the past *without* Mr. Wells' all too convenient aid."

—Fred Saberhagen

A SPADEFUL
OF SPACETIME

A SPADEFUL
OF SPACETIME

EDITED BY
FRED SABERHAGEN

SF
ace books
A Division of Charter Communications Inc.
A GROSSET & DUNLAP COMPANY
51 Madison Avenue
New York, New York 10010

A SPADEFUL OF SPACETIME

An ACE Book

First Ace printing: February 1981
Published Simultaneously in Canada

2 4 6 8 0 9 7 5 3 1
Manufactured in the United States of America

CONTENTS

INTRODUCTION

Fred Saberhagen

In a world of explosive change, the past seems to offer us a firm handle with which to grip reality, a model, better than the evanescent present, of what the world should be like. We rest on the past, rely on it, and by means of memory, science, and the written record, return to it in search of reassurance and of knowledge.

The Time Machine, popularized as a literary device by H.G. Wells, and used by a thousand writers since, has done much to satisfy the cravings of imagination and nostalgia. By more or less easily returning protagonists and readers to the past, it serves the sense that we ought to be able to participate, or re-participate, in what is gone. But I think the Machine's very effectiveness in this regard has done us all something of a disservice, too.

Those badly addicted to the automobile will never learn or earn the joys of hiking. Similarly, the Time Machine is wont to be a little too easy, for writer and reader alike. It's great when urgent business requires that we get there in a hurry; but we miss something when its routine use becomes a reflex. Whatever the passenger accommodations of a particular model may be, however fancy the controls or innovative the special effects, the travel function is served with sterile ruthlessness. We are shot into the past, or the future, and at once begin to interact with what has become only a different kind of present. The pleasures of the journey have been denied us.

My intention in putting together this book has been to get, from some of the best science fiction writers alive, their own visions on the subject of probing the past without Mr. Wells' all too convenient aid. I have been greatly pleased by the results. And I hope that you, the reader, will share my delight, that print and paper can bridge the gap of time, small or great, that has necessarily grown up between us.

—Fred Saberhagen

1

If there were no such concept as science fiction poetry (science poetry?) it would doubtless have to be invented to accommodate Bob Frazier, whose verse has appeared during the last few years in more than a dozen magazines and anthologies generally devoted to the more conventional prose form of speculative fiction.

DECYPHERED WITH THE POTSHARDS OF TIME

Robert A. Frazier

Sifting through the dust of countless permutations,
gleaning the bones of numberless probabilities,
the Arc 9 Regenerator has visions like an indian shaman.
It imagines in binary
the missing pieces of a jigsawn yesterday.
Like a Navajo at the loom,
from a mere thread,
it weaves a molecular schematic of complete artifacts.
Given enough fragments, bits and runes,
in bondage to a master computer,
it can generate volumes of history,
   colored paintings on the temporal sands,
from a mittful of matter
or a spadeful of spacetime.

It is a truism that what is now our present will become, in our future, someone else's past. What may not be so obvious, as this sharp story by Roger Zelazny illustrates, is that no matter how intensely personal the connection, even unto life and death, the alienation can be vast.

GO STARLESS IN THE NIGHT

Roger Zelazny

Darkness and silence all about, and nothing, nothing, nothing within it.

Me?

The first thought came unbidden, welling up from some black pool. Me? That's all.

Me? he thought. Then, Who? What . . .?

Nothing answered.

Something like panic followed, without the customary physical accompaniments. When this wave had passed, he listened, striving to capture the slightest sound. He realized that he had already given up on seeing.

There was nothing to hear. Not even the smallest noises of life—breathing, heartbeat, the rasping of a tired joint—came to him. It was only then that he realized he lacked all bodily sensations.

But this time he fought the panic. Death? he wondered. A bodiless, dark sentence beyond everything? The stillness . . .

Where? What point in spacetime did he occupy? He would have shaken his head . . .

He recalled that he had been a man—and it seemed that there were memories somewhere that he could not reach. No name answered his summons, no view of his past came to him. Yet he knew that there had been a past. He felt that it lay just below some dim horizon of recall.

He strove for a timeless interval to summon some recollection of what had gone before. Amnesia? Brain damage?

3

Dream? he finally asked himself, after failing to push beyond a certain feeling of lurking images.

A body then . . . Start with that.

He remembered what bodies were. Arms, legs, head, torso . . . An intellectual vision of sex passed momentarily through his consciousness. Bodies, then . . .

He thought of his arms, felt nothing. Tried to move them. There was no sense of their existence, let alone movement.

Breathing . . . He attempted to draw a deep breath. Nothing came into him. There was no indication of any boundary whatsoever between himself and the darkness and silence.

A buzzing tone began, directionless. It oscillated in volume. It rose in pitch, dropped to a rumble, returned to a buzz. Abruptly then, it shifted again, to work-like approximations he could not quite decipher.

There was a pause, as if for some adjustment. Then "Hello?" came clearly to him.

He felt a rush of relief mingled with fear. The word filled his mind, followed by immediate concern as to whether he had actually heard it.

"Hello?"

Again, then. The fear faded. Something close to joy replaced it. He felt an immediate need to respond.

"Yes? Hello? Who—"

His answer broke. How had he managed it? He felt the presence of no vocal mechanism. Yet he seemed to hear a faint echoing of his own reply, feedback-like, tinny. Where? Its source was not localized.

It seemed then that several voices were conversing—hurried, soft, distant. He could not follow the rush of their words.

Then, "Hello again. Please respond one time more. We are adjusting the speaker. How well do you hear us?"

"Clearly now," he answered. "Where am I? What has happened?"

"How much do you remember?"

"Nothing!"

"Panic not, Ernest Dawkins. Do you remember that your

name is Ernest Dawkins? From your file, we have it.''

"Now I do.''

The simple statement of his name brought forth a series of images—his own face, his wife's, his two daughters', his apartment, the laboratory where he worked, his car, a sunny day at the beach . . .

That day at the beach . . . That was when he had first felt the pain in his left side—a dull ache at first, increasing over ensuing weeks. He had never been without it after that—until now, he suddenly realized.

"I—It's coming back—my memory,'' he said. ''It's as if a dam had broken . . . Give me a minute.''

"Take your time.''

He shied away from the thought of the pain. He had been ill, very ill, hospitalized, operated upon, drugged . . . He—

He thought instead of his life, his family, his work. He thought of school and love and politics and research. He thought of the growing world tensions, and of his childhood, and—

"Are you right all, Ernest Dawkins?''

He had lost track of time, but that question caused him to produce something like a laugh, from somewhere.

"Hard to tell,'' he said. ''I've been remembering—things. But as to whether I'm all right— Where the hell am I? What's happened?''

"Then you have remembered not everything?''

He noted odd inflections in the questioning voice, possibly even an accent that he could not place.

"I guess not.''

"You were quite unwell.''

"I remember that much.''

"Dying, in fact. As they say.''

He forced himself to return to the pain, to look beyond it.

"Yes,'' he acknowledged. ''I remember.''

. . . . And it was all there. He saw his last days in the hospital as his condition worsened, passing the point of no return, the faces of his family, friends and relatives wearing this realization. He recalled his decision to go through with an earlier resolution, long since set into motion. Money had never been a problem. It seemed it had always been there, in his family—his, by early inheritance—as ubiquitous as his attitude toward death after his parents' passing. Enough to have himself frozen for the long winter, to drop off dreaming of some distant spring . . .

"I recall my condition," he said. "I know what must finally have occurred."

"Yes," came the reply. "That is what happened."

"How much time has passed?"

"Considerable."

He would have licked his lips. He settled for the mental equivalent.

"My family?" he finally inquired.

"It has been too long."

"I see."

The other gave him time to consider this information. Then, "You had, of course, considered this possibility?"

"Yes. I prepared myself—as much as a man can—for such a state of affairs."

"It has been long. Very long . . ."

"How long?"

"Allow us to proceed in our fashion, please."

"All right. You know your business best."

"We are glad that you are so reasonable a being."

"Being?"

"Person. Excuse we."

"I must ask something, though—not having to do with the passage of time: Is English now spoken as you speak it? Or is it not your native language?"

There was a sudden consultation, just beyond the range of distinguishability. There followed a high-pitched artifact. Then, "Also let us reserve that question," the reply finally came.

"As you would. Then will you tell me about my situation? I am more than a little concerned. I can't see or feel anything."

"We are aware of this. It is unfortunate, but there is no

point in misrepresenting to you. The time has not yet come for your full arouse.''

"I do not understand. Do you mean that there is no cure for my condition yet?''

"We mean that there is no means of thawing you without doing great damage.''

"Then how is it that we are conversing?''

"We have lowered your temperature even more—near to the zero absolute. Your nervous system has become super-conductor. We have laid induction field upon your brain and initiated small currents within. Third space, left side head and those movement areas for talk are now serving to activate mechanical speaker here beside we. We address you direct in the side of brain places for hearing talk.''

There came another wave of panic. How long this one lasted, he did not know. Vaguely, he became aware of the voice again, repeating his name.

"Yes,'' he finally managed. "I understand. It is not easy to accept . . .''

"We know. But this does you no damage,'' came the reply. "You might even take a heart from it, to know that you persist.''

"There is that. I see your meaning and can take it as hope. But why? Surely you did not awaken me simply to dem-onstrate this?''

"No. We have interest in your times. Purely ar-chaeologic.''

"Archaeological! That would seem to indicate the passage of a great deal of time!''

"Forgive we. Perhaps we have chose wrong word, think-ing of it in terms of ruins. But your nervous system is doorway to times past.''

"Ruins! What the hell happened?''

"There was war, and there have been disasters. The rec-ord, therefore, is unclear.''

"Who won the war?''

"That is difficult to say.''

"Then it must have been pretty bad.''

"We would assume this. We are still ourselves learning. That is why we seek to know time past from your cold remains."

"If there was all this chaos, how is it that I was preserved through it?"

"The cold-making units here are powered by atomic plant which ran well untended—save for computer—for long while, and entire establishment is underground."

"Really? Things must have changed quite a bit after my—enrollment—here. It wasn't set up that way at the time I read the prospectus and visited the place."

"We really know little of the history of this establishment. There are many things of which we are ignorant. That is why we want you to tell us about your times."

"It is difficult to know where to begin . . ."

"It may be better if we ask you questions."

"All right. But I would like answers to some of my own afterwards."

"A suitable arrangement. Tell us then: Did you reside at or near your place of employment?"

"No. Actually, I lived halfway across town and had to drive in every day."

"Was this common for the area and the country?"

"Pretty much so, yes. Some other people did use other means of transportation, of course. Some rode on buses. Some car-pooled. I drove. A lot of us did."

"When you say that you drove, are we to understand that you refer to four-wheeled land vehicle powered by internal combustion engine?"

"Yes, that is correct. They were in common use in the latter half of the twentieth century."

"And there were many such?"

"Very many."

"Had you ever problems involving presence of too many of them on trails at same time?"

"Yes. Certain times of day—when people were going to work and returning—were referred to as 'rush hour.' At such times there were often traffic jams—that is to say, so many vehicles that they got in one another's way."

"Extremely interesting. Were such creatures as whales still extant?"

"Yes."

"Interesting, too. What sort of work did you do?"

"I was involved in research on toxic agents of a chemical and bacteriological nature. Most of it was classified."

"What does that indicate?"

"Oh. It was of a secret nature, directed toward possible military application."

"Was war already in progress?"

"No. It was a matter of—preparedness. We worked with various agents that might be used, if the need ever arose."

"We think we see. Interesting times. Did you ever develop any of efficient nature?"

"Yes. A number of them."

"Then what would you do with them? It would seem hazardous to have such materials about during peace."

"Oh, samples were stored with the utmost precaution in very safe places. There were three main caches, and they were well-sheltered and well-guarded."

There was a pause. Then, "We find this somewhat distressing," the voice resumed. "Do you feel they might have survived—a few, some centuries?"

"It is possible."

"Being peace-loving, we are naturally concerned with items dangerous to human species—"

"You make it sound as if you are not yourself a member."

There came another high-pitched artifact. Then, "The language has changed more even than we realized. Apologies. Wrong inference taken. Our desire, to deactivate these dangerous materials. Long have we expected their existences. You perhaps will advise? Their whereabouts unknown to us."

"I'm—not—so sure—about that," he answered. "No offense meant, but you are only a voice to me. I really know nothing about you. I am not certain that I should give this information."

There was a long silence.

"Hello? Are you still there?" he tried to say.

He heard nothing, not even his own voice. Time seemed to do strange things around him. Had it stopped for a moment? Had he given offense? Had his questioner dropped dead?

"Hello! Hello!" he said. "Do you hear me?"

". . . . Mechanical failure," came the reply. "Apologies for. Sorry about yesterday."

"Yesterday!"

"Turned you off while obtaining new speaker. Just when you were to say where best poisons are."

"I am sorry," he stated. "You have asked for something that I cannot, in good conscience, give to you."

"We wish only to prevent damage."

"I am in the terrible position of having no way to verify anything that is told me."

"If something heavy falls upon you, you break like bottle."

"I could not even verify whether that had occurred."

"We could turn you off again, turn off the cold-maker."

"At least it would be painless," he said with more stoicism than he felt.

"We require this information."

"Then you must seek it elsewhere."

"We will disconnect your speaker and your hearer and go away. We will leave you thinking in the middle of nothing. Good-bye now."

"Wait!"

"Then you will tell us?"

"No. I—can't . . ."

"You will go mad if we disconnect these things, will you not?"

"I suppose so. Eventually . . ."

"Must we do it, then?"

"Your threats have shown me what you are like. I cannot give you such weapons."

"Ernest Dawkins, you are not intelligent being."

"And you are not an archaeologist. Or you would do future generations the service of turning me off, to save the other things that I do know."

"You are right. We are not such. You will never know what we are."

"I know enough."

"Go to your madness."

Silence again.

For a long while the panic held him. Until the images of his family recurred, and his home, and his town. These grew more and more substantial, and gradually he came to walk with them and among them. Then, after a time, he stopped reporting for work and spent his days at the beach. He wondered at first when his side would begin to hurt. Then he wondered why he had wondered this. Later, he forgot many things, but not the long days beneath the sun or the sound of the surf, the red rain, the blue, or the melting statue with the fiery eyes and the sword in its fist. When he heard voices under the sand he did not answer. He listened instead to whales singing to mermaids on migrating rocks, where they combed their long green hair with shards of bone, laughing at the lightning and the ice.

If the Zelazny story is intensely personal, this one is broadly human; all the more so, I think, because it reaches out to something that is beyond human, to define humanity by what is at once a boundary and a connection.

Chad Oliver is a professional anthropologist working out of a university in Texas. He's written a lot of fiction, too, though not so much in recent years. One of the reasons I feel good about this book is that the prospectus for it induced Professor Oliver to write one story more.

TO WHOM IT MAY CONCERN

Chad Oliver

Call it a hunt.

If that is too simple, call it a quest.

They were coming.

They had searched through an ocean of darkness, a night sea that floated worlds upon worlds, stars beyond number, universes that began and ended and flowed into yet other universes.

They were after something. Otherwise, they would not have been there.

They needed something. Not technology, certainly. They had plenty of that. They understood technology and respected it, but that was not enough. Endurance was the problem. Call it continuity.

They would know it when they found it. They would know what to do with it. They had a wisdom that went deeper than intelligence. They had other senses.

They were not beyond self-interest. They were driven by their own needs. Otherwise, they would not have been there.

But there was room for others. They knew they were not alone. They knew that it was all linked together.

The seeking was urgent. The journey had been long.

They were ready. They would not quit. They could not afford to miss.

They were coming.

Call it a hunt.

Jerry Hartshorn felt rotten. He wiped the sweat out of his eyes with a sand-streaked hand. He said, "So this is how it ends."

Nobody heard him, of course. He was talking to himself again, which was not a particularly good sign.

He tugged his stained hat down more tightly over his damp hair and squinted into the African sun. It was the same old sun that rolled around the sky everywhere else. Nothing special. It wasn't the sun that was getting to Jerry Hartshorn. It was a bug, despite all the pills and all the shots. He was sick. Not sick enough to go down. Just sick enough to be miserable.

He also did not like what he was seeing.

He swung up his camera, noting that the brown strap across his shoulder was fraying to the danger point. He checked the settings—always the same at this time of the day, but Jerry was a careful man—and snapped a couple of shots. He hated the photography angle; taking pictures made him feel like a tourist. It was a part of his job, but the plain truth was that he was always disappointed with his slides and prints. They were clear enough, barring a disaster here and there, but the magic eluded him. The pictures were flat and literal. The significance and the emotion never got through the camera lens; they stayed behind, locked up in his head and his gut.

In any case, how did you photograph the end of a world? It didn't end with a bang and it didn't end with a whimper. It just stopped.

"Chins up," he said. "Duty and all that. Posterity and tenure."

This is what he photographed:

There was a battered thick-trunked baobab tree that cut the glaring sunlight enough to provide a puddle of shade. There

was the flat rust-red earth of southern Kenya, mottled by
bedraggled flat-topped acacia, the cactus-caricature of
euphorbia, and very ordinary dusty brush.

There was a lot of open country—plains, really—and an
enormous bowl of blue sky. It was as though clouds hadn't
been invented yet.

And there were the people.

They did not seem to be doing anything dramatic. Small,
brown, and leather-tough, they had gathered in the dubious
shade of the baobab. It was the last day, and they were
spending it as they had spent so many others. Waiting.

Most of them were there, clustered near the camp. Jerry
did not have to count them. Fifteen people: old men, women
that ran the gamut from ancient Klu to the young smooth-
skinned Twee, a few children who were blissfully unaware
both of what they were and what they were about to become.

Three men were not present. They had left before dawn,
smearing poison on the foreshafts of their arrows and joking
loudly. They were not likely to find anything, but their spirits
were always good at the start of a hunt. Even the last one.
George Ndambuki, Jerry's African colleague, was with
them.

Taking pictures, Jerry thought ruefully. *Good ones*.

He shut the protective case over his camera and adjusted
the shoulder strap. He had photographed what there was to
see.

Nothing much. Even the clothing would have discouraged
the true devotee of the supposed romance of primitive life.
For the most part, the people were dressed in what might
politely be called contemporary fashion. Torn shorts and
carefully washed undershirts for the men, long cotton dresses
and bandana-turbans for the women. Only the youngest
children had style. They wore nothing at all.

The People. That is what they called themselves, in common with God only knew how many human societies that had
lived and died on this planet. In what was pompously referred
to as the scientific literature, they were the Kwaruma. It was
not the right name. In their own language, the word for

People was Xhagit. The first sound was a click phoneme. However, they had been dubbed the Kwaruma by their Bantu-speaking neighbors, and they were stuck with it.

Tomorrow, the trucks would come. The Kwaruma were going to be "resettled" on farming plots in a development scheme. The television crews would be on hand, because this was no small matter.

As far as anyone knew, the Kwaruma were the last hunters and gatherers left on earth.

A jet smashed through the African sky. The symbolism was so pat that Jerry Hartshorn tried to ignore the racket. He had lived with these people for nearly a year. He did not need a jet aircraft to remind him of what was happening.

He still felt rocky. No matter; a couple of aspirins would get him through the remaining hours. Ah, wonder drugs! The true blessing of civilization. . . .

He checked his field notebook and moved in closer to do what had to be done.

The last camp of the Kwaruma was like most of the camps that Jerry had seen. It had a slapdash quality to it and it had *temporary* written all over it. Compared to the camp, the scarred baobab tree looked eternal.

The structures weren't houses. They were simple lean-tos made of crooked poles and brush. There was almost nothing in them: a few iron pots the Kwaruma had scrounged, some digging sticks, traditional ostrich eggs used as water containers, small cracked hide bundles of treasured heirlooms, a few trade knives and two old wood-pointed spears.

The People lived outside. In any case, when you have to move frequently and do it on foot you get down to essentials. The People did not even have dogs to help them.

Old Klu already had a small fire going. It was partly a sign of confidence and a show of respect for the departed hunters. But Jerry knew that there was another reason. Warm as it was in the African sun, Klu was thinking about the coming night. She suffered from the cold, and it took more than memories to sustain her.

Jerry was working—taking notes—but he found the time to exchange small-talk with everyone. He speculated with the elder men about the possible success of the hunt. He joked with Twee, confining himself to acceptable brother-sister themes. He admired the roots the women had gathered. It made him feel somewhat better. The Kwaruma were a friendly people and they had more or less accepted him. He was proud of that. Who knew? Maybe they even liked him.

If he could help them, later—

Well, he would not forget. But this was not the time. There were so few hours left . . . .

He walked over to Jane's tent, which was pitched a short distance from the camp. He could hear the clicking of the portable typewriter inside.

Not for the first time, he reflected on the percentages. Eighteen Kwaruma and three anthropologists. It was a peculiar world.

The tent was open, of course. There was no breeze, and it was like an oven in there.

"It's Tarzan," he said. "Jane busy?"

Jane Schubauer went right on with her typing. "Come on in," she said.

Jerry picked his way through the clutter and perched on a camp chair that had one slat missing. He removed his hat and used it to fan himself.

Jane finished a paragraph—she always typed up her notes with indecent speed—and turned to face him. Her eyes widened slightly. "You look like a walking corpse," she said.

He shrugged. "Beastly tropical heat. The throb of native drums. You know."

"You can't die now. You're cooking the feast tonight."

"I will not falter. Two aspirins would help the ape-man."

Jane rooted around and produced the aspirin bottle. She handed it to him with a canteen of water. The water was warm and tasted ominous but he got the pills down.

"Just wanted to check," he said. "You go over the life-history with Klu, I measure the amounts of plant foods and meat after the hunters get in, and George writes up the last hunt. Then we eat and kick it around to see if we've forgotten anything. That cover it?''

She nodded. ''Sounds okay to me. We've just run out of time, that's all. Jerry, you do look awful.''

''I'll make it.''

They eyed each other. There were other words to be said between them, but they might never be spoken. They were either beyond that or had never gotten there.

No computer would ever have put them in the same pile, Jerry thought. Jane—she loathed the name—was a tall raw-boned woman who could look attractive when she bothered. She was brilliant and she was difficult. When she laughed, Jerry chalked it up as a triumph.

Jerry was short, wiry, and thin. He had a brownish beard that itched. He had a bad habit of cracking jokes at the wrong times. Even those who knew him well had trouble telling when he was serious—which was all too often—and when he was kidding. He believed in what he was doing.

They were competitors, of course. Back at the University, they were on the Harvard system. Hire six, terminate five, keep one. They were also friends: they liked and respected each other. Once, they had even been lovers. It had been a mutual disaster.

''See you later,'' Jerry said.

Jane went back to the typewriter. The clicking resumed. ''Be careful, Tarzan,'' she said.

The hunters returned in the late afternoon. Jerry could hear them coming, and knew that the hunt had been good. When the hunters had been successful, they made a lot of noise. When they failed, they came silently back to the camp and nobody ever asked them what had happened.

Jerry went to meet them.

They came out of the earth, shadows among shadows. Kwi, still walking lightly after a long day in the bush. Tuwa, who could be spotted at a distance because of his limp. Gsawa, taller than the others, walking a little apart, lost in his private world as usual.

George Ndambuki brought up the rear. Incredibly, he still

had a tie on. He was visibly tired, but he had his camera out
and ready. He was going to photograph the end of the hunt or
perish in the attempt.

The women began to ululate. It was a haunting sound. It
seemed as ancient as humanity itself.

Jerry stayed out of the way until George had his final
pictures. Then he moved in to examine the kill.

Kwi, who was the nearest thing to a leader that the
Kwaruma had, gave him a big smile. Kwi had an upper
incisor tooth missing; he liked to tell the story of how he had
lost it. He also had a safety pin in his ear. He was a delightful
man, solid as a rock but with a consistent good humor that
was contagious. Kwi had pulled Jerry through some difficult
times, just as he had done for the rest of his people.

"See," Kwi beamed. "Did I not tell you? It was Gsawa's
arrow that went home."

The hunters had divided their kill for easier transport and
they had not bothered to bring in the head and horns. Still,
Jerry could identify the animal at a glance. Rather surprisingly, it was a Tommy. They were not common in this part of
Kenya.

"*Gazella thomsonii thomsonii*," Jerry said. He was not
showing off; this was a little running joke he had with Kwi.

"*Swala tomi*," Kwi agreed. He spoke Swahili when he
was having fun with the anthropologist, which was frequently.

Jerry figured it up in his head; he would weigh the meat
later. A Tommy was one of the smaller African antelopes.
This one was a male. It might go sixty pounds, and that meant
something like thirty pounds of edible meat. Close to two
pounds of meat for every adult. Meat was always shared.

"We will provide," Kwi said. He slapped his bow. "No
more Spam."

Jerry nodded gratefully. "No more Spam," he agreed.

George Ndambuki could not stay out of the conversation.
"I timed the poison," he reported. "One hour less thirteen
seconds."

"Great," Jerry said. "I know it wasn't easy." He found it
awkward to talk to George; he felt much closer to Kwi.

George Ndambuki was so impressed with his own Ph.D. that he sometimes forgot to be human. It was understandable—George had sacrificed a great deal for the degree that had come fairly easily for Jerry and Jane—but his everlasting dignity got on Jerry's nerves.

"I will cook," Jerry said to Kwi. "That was the agreement."

Kwi laughed. "The women will cook," he predicted. "You get the beer."

Jerry fell back on a Kwaruma saying. "Friends do not argue."

Kwi laughed again and Tuwa and Gsawa joined in. It paralyzed them to hear Jerry's Kwaruma accent.

"You have much to learn," Kwi said. It was a statement without malice. "I must teach you while I can."

It was a scene not quite as old as time.

The fires were orange and cheerful. There were good smells and the shadows danced. The camp was an island of brightness. The air had cooled and the stars were near.

Jerry Hartshorn chewed on the tough but tasty meat. His head was throbbing but he was strangely content.

He was a part of something.

How many times over how many millions of years had this small ritual been enacted? Fire and food, hunters who had returned and women who had waited, collected, and prepared. Children who watched and listened and dreamed.

It was ancient. It stretched back unbroken to a world older then humanity. Australopithecines and those who had preceded them must have known nights like this.

It was only ten thousand years ago that the human animal had begun the flirtation with agriculture and domesticated animals. Two cheers for the Neolithic! It was only five thousand years since the first cities had stained the earth.

Always, the hunting and gathering peoples had continued. Their numbers had dwindled and they had retreated into remote areas that the manswarm did not covet. But they had survived.

Until now.

The Kwaruma were distant relatives of the San of Bots-
wana and the Kalahari Desert. Once, these people had been
dominant throughout Eastern Africa. They were called the
Bushmen by those who never bothered to learn their proper
name.

The San were finished. They had not been exterminated
physically; there were still plenty of them around. But in
terms of their traditional culture they were extinct. The San
were gold-miners, hired herders, servants, squatters in city
slums. They had adapted.

Only this tiny remnant group of Kwaruma were left. Anywhere. They were anachronisms.

Kwi had been right, or nearly right. The antelope meat had
been broiled by the Kwaruma women; they had allowed Jerry
to weigh it, but they were adamant about the cooking. Jerry
had done his best. He had promised the people a feast and he
delivered after a fashion. He heated up canned corn. He
passed around tins of pineapple. He opened cans of pork and
beans; the Kwaruma preferred it cold. He made coffee and
dumped in cups of sugar.

And he supplied the beer.

He felt at home with the Kwaruma but he did not delude
himself. He was an intruder, along with Jane and George. He
had come from a distant land on his own kind of hunt. When
he had his quarry—information, knowledge—he would go
away again. And then—

Ah yes, that was the question.

Well, save it for tomorrow. Save it for all the tomorrows.

The three of them managed to squeeze into Jane's tent
together. It wasn't much of a conference. George Ndambuki
was out on his feet; he had walked far with the hunters. Jane
Schubauer was having trouble with the wick on her lamp and
she still had notes to type. Jerry Hartshorn was discovering
that the mixture of beer, meat, and fever verged on the lethal.

The camp was anything but festive. They could hear
subdued voices and an occasional rattling of pots and cans
around the dwindling fires. That was all. The Kwaruma had
no drums—just wooden whistles and bows that they tapped

with sticks—and they were not in a mood for dancing. Basically, like all the world that was beyond the reach of electricity, the Kwaruma were a daylight people. The night was for sleeping.

"Well." Jerry spoke because somebody had to do it. "Last chance and all that. Have we forgotten anything?"

"Probably," Jane said. She did not sound unduly worried. She wanted to get back to her notes.

"I think we have done extremely well," George offered. "We have all that there is to get." George's opinion of the Kwaruma was not high. Having made something of a transition himself—his own parents had lived in a thatched hut and sacrificed goats to the ancestors in Ukambani—he viewed primitive lifeways with a slightly jaundiced eye.

"So we have it all." Jerry could not allow himself the luxury of laughter and he didn't feel up to it anyway. "Okay. Meeting is adjourned. See you in the morning."

He ducked out of the tent. The night was chilly and he had to wait a long minute to let his eyes adjust to the darkness. The little fires were not much help now. He shivered and tried to decide what to do.

He went to his own tent and fished out a warm jacket. He retrieved his last bottle of Scotch from under a pile of dirty clothing. He had not exactly been hiding it, but he had been saving it. Scotch was still relatively inexpensive in Kenya—unlike the rare imported bourbons—but it nevertheless put a dent in the budget.

He supplied himself with a tin cup and went outside to sit on a stump.

Jerry had no more questions to ask. This was not because he knew everything there was to know about the Kwaruma. That was George's fantasy. It was because he had gone as far as his educated ignorance would take him.

He looked up at the stars. They were very close and there were lots of them.

He waited.

Jerry was feeling better. The Scotch had something to do

with that, of course. But much more than whisky was involved. Jerry was young. Even with the bug in him, he could handle the Scotch.

He felt like this sometimes. Open, receptive, expectant. Once in a while, you had to relax and get out of your own way. You had to let things happen.

He did not know how long he had been sitting there. He didn't care. The stars had moved. The camp was silent.

Jerry waited.

It happened.

A shadowy form materialized out of the night. A familiar voice spoke.

"Doctor Jerry?"

It was Kwi. The question was a formality. Kwi knew perfectly well who he was; the hunter had eyes like a cat. But a man did not approach another person at night without an invitation.

"Old friend." Jerry replied in Kwaruma. Kwi had just used up most of his English. "I am glad that you have come. Please join me."

Jerry shifted his position on the stump to make room. He should have known better. Kwi dropped down into a squatting position, his heels beneath his body and his elbows on his upper legs. He could sit like that for hours. He had something in his right hand. He did not put it on the ground.

Jerry smiled. He *was* glad that Kwi had come, and that had nothing whatever to do with his work. He enjoyed his company. He could barely see the safety pin in Kwi's ear glinting in the starlight.

Jerry extended the tin cup. "Drink?"

Kwi laughed softly. He liked to show his missing tooth. He took the cup in his left hand, sipped politely and without comment, and returned the cup to Jerry. Kwi did not care for Scotch. They had found that out long ago.

The ensuing silence was long but not uncomfortable. Jerry did not push at it. Kwi would say what he had to say when he was ready.

Jerry studied the man without seeming to look directly at

him. He did not need more light than there was. He knew every wrinkle in that prematurely lined face. He knew every scar on that leather-skinned body. He had photographed his friend hundreds of times; Kwi would be famous one day. He had interviewed him, hunted with him, joked with him.

Oh, he knew all about Kwi. He could tell the story of his life. He knew how Kwi had become the headman of the Kwaruma. (The Kwaruma had no chiefs. Nobody had selected Kwi as headman; "he just got to be that way.") He knew how Kwi had lost the incisor tooth. (Let Kwi tell *that* story.) He knew how Kwi could double as a shaman. ("I can leave my body, Doctor Jerry. It is a gift. When the Others tell me what to do—when the power is right—I can heal.")

And he knew nothing about Kwi. They shared the bond of a common humanity and something in their personalities meshed. But Kwi had lived a life that Jerry could not share. Kwi knew much—and felt much—that he could not communicate to a well-intentioned alien. It worked both ways. Jerry had been unable to explain what a Department of Anthropology was. Somehow, that did not seem very important.

Jerry poured himself a bit more Scotch. He waited. He was very good at that.

Finally, Kwi broke the silence.

"You say that we are the last," he said.

"Yes. It is true."

"That is a hard thing to believe."

"You do not lie to me. I do not lie to you."

Kwi sighed. It was as close as he had come to expressing regret over what was passing. He was not a man given to self-pity. "No," he said. "You do not lie."

The silence came again. Jerry said nothing, prepared to wait it out.

This time, the silence was short.

"There is something I want you to have," Kwi said. "My people have always had it. It will be lost where we are going."

"I will protect it. You honor me with your gift." The

words were Kwaruma. They sounded inadequate. The thoughts that churned in Jerry's head were not Kwaruma. They didn't fit the occasion either.

Kwi rocked forward slightly on his toes. He was more serious than Jerry had ever seen him. "I have listened to the stories you have told me," Kwi said. "I have heard other stories. Understand me. My people have always had it. I do not mean just the Kwaruma. *All* my people."

Very slowly, Jerry put the tin cup down. His hand was shaking. He thought he understood what Kwi was saying. That was the problem.

He picked his words with care. "All of your people? Do you mean all of the hunters and gatherers? Everywhere?"

Kwi smiled his gap-toothed smile and relaxed. Communication had been easier than he had figured. "You have it right. That is what I was told. I have not seen it with my own eyes. Only for some."

Jerry stared at the object in Kwi's right hand. It appeared to be a hide wrapping of some kind. "What is it?" he asked inanely.

"It is yours now," Kwi said. He gave it to Jerry as though ridding himself of a burden.

Jerry took the thing and held it gingerly. It was a skin container; he could tell by the texture. It was small, only a little larger than his hand. There was something hard inside it.

Jerry went into his tent and got a flashlight. He came back and placed the object on the stump.

He unfolded the creased hide and there it was.

He didn't know what he had expected, if anything. But not this.

It was old, chalk-white, and ridged. It had been much used; it had finger smudges on it.

It was the shell of a turtle.

Well, what do you do? Laugh? Cry? Tell shaggy dog stories?

Jerry felt drained. A pragmatic man, he had somehow

believed that he was on the edge of revelation. He should have known better. This was the real world.

A turtle!

The damned thing was not even ancient—certainly not an object handed down from the beginnings of mankind. The shell was dry and brittle, not fossilized. It was at most a century or two old.

Was Kwi joking?

Perhaps sensing his disappointment, Kwi said: "It was given to me by my father. He received it from his father."

No, he was not joking.

Jerry studied the shell. He knew next to nothing about turtles. *Testudo something*. What was the difference between a turtle and a tortoise? Let's see, the upper plates formed the carapace, and the bottom plates were the plastron. . . .

So what?

"It is not clear in my mind," he said. That was putting it mildly. "Your people have always had *this* turtle shell?"

Kwi grunted. He gave Jerry a look reserved for backward children and dim-witted anthropologists. "The shell of the *churi* is not strong when it dries. There is nothing inside. It will break if you drop it. If you put something on top of it, the shell will shatter. This one has lasted a long time. It is lucky. There were many others before this one. That is what I was told."

"So it has been replaced? Many times?"

Kwi did not bother to answer.

"And it is not *this* turtle shell that all of your people—all of the hunters and gatherers—had?"

Kwi stood up. He was getting tired. It may have been that he too was disappointed. Doctor Jerry could be a little slow in the head.

"My meaning was that they all had a *churi*. That is what I was told. I have seen some, long ago. Not this same shell. But like it. They all work the same."

Jerry took a deep breath. They were back in the real world. It was just barely possible—

"Work the same?"

"The *churi* is medicine," Kwi said slowly. "It is power. It connects things."

Jerry did not know how to respond to that. The real world was getting fuzzy again.

"Protect it," Kwi said. "You will see."

The last of the Kwaruma headmen had said all that he cared to say. He had done what he had to do. That was the story of his life.

He turned and vanished into the night.

A great weariness descended over Jerry Hartshorn. The stars seemed heavy. He stumbled into his tent, taking his gear with him.

A half-empty bottle, a tin cup, a flashlight.

And an old turtle shell wrapped in hide.

Sleep would not come.

Tired as he was, Jerry's mind was racing.

It may have been the extraordinary day he had been through. It could have been the illness. It might have been the Scotch.

Who knew? Maybe it was the turtle shell.

He felt it there, right under his cot.

He had made a classic mistake, and he knew it.

He had trapped himself in the real world without asking the key question. *Whose* real world?

His? A world choking with billions of people, a world beset with problems that had no solutions, a world of science that had no room left for miracles?

The world that Kwi had known? Hunters and gatherers had populated the earth, but not harshly. There had been no population explosion. There had been no wars. There had been no destruction of the land. There had been no alienation from other living things. They had killed, yes, but they had not exterminated. They had endured for millions of years. For all Jerry knew, that was a record that had no counterpart in the entire universe. Certainly, as far as mankind was concerned, it had no equal on the planet earth. It was a world that had its own rules: sharing, accommodation, fulfillment. It was a world in which miracles could happen.

The world of the turtles? Well, why not? The turtles were older than humanity, older even than the primates. They were as old as the earliest dinosaurs. Frozen in their shells, they had waddled and paddled down through the eons. They had changed very little; they had developed a mechanism for retracting their heads instead of tucking their necks along the sides of the shells. That was about all. They knew something about endurance. Indeed, they were close to immortality. . . .

Oh yes, the real world.

Did Jerry Hartshorn have a part to play in it?

(*Hartshorn*. Even his name was a link with the past. Was that an accident?)

He could sense the turtle shell under him. *Churi*. What had Kwi said? *"It is power. It connects things."*

Question: Could they have missed something like this? Something crucial? All the anthropologists who had worked with hunting and gathering peoples for more than a century?

Answer: Absolutely. It was precisely the kind of thing that would have been overlooked. Something seemingly without significance. Something that their training never mentioned.

Who asked questions about turtles?

Who listened if the subject came up?

Jerry twisted in his sleeping bag. The cot was singularly uncomfortable.

"Friend," he said aloud, "you've been out here too long. You're headed for the old laughing academy."

The words hung there in the cold night air. They were alien.

He had the sensation that something was trying to get through to him. Something pecking away at the traditional barriers of his mind. . . .

"You're sick, old buddy," he said.

Maybe.

Get out of the way. Let it happen.

He tried. Feeling almost guilty, he even put his hand down and touched the hide container beneath his cot.

Nothing happened. Or had it already happened? Or—

"The hell with it," Jerry said.

He closed his eyes and attempted to sleep.

Dawn was streaking the African sky with color. Inside the little tent, Jerry Hartshorn was neither asleep nor awake. His hand still rested on the skin-wrapped turtle shell.

He had not prayed since he was a child. He was not sure that he was praying now.

His mind seemed clear—unnaturally so—but he had trouble with the proper form of address.

God? No: too culture-bound.

Great Spirit? Never: too corny.

To Whom It May Concern? Not bad. It covered a lot of territory, supernatural and otherwise.

He sent his message, silently. He did not want to be overheard babbling in his tent. Tenure and all that.

I don't know who you are or if you are. I'm new at this game. I have this damned turtle shell and I don't know what it means. If you understand it, if it can help you or it can help us, please find me. The turtle shell and I will be together. We'll be waiting.

There was no answering message. He hadn't expected one.

Just the same, he felt better.

He opened his eyes and examined the pale light.

"Might as well get up," he muttered.

He had a lot to do today.

It was mid-morning before the television crews arrived and Jerry did his best to ignore them. He was in no shape to give interviews. Jane made a perfunctory appearance before the cameras, but George Ndambuki was in his element. He was magnificently glib and he managed to work in all of the proper catch phrases: A Human Tragedy, The Promise of Tomorrow, The Heritage of Mankind, The New Africa, and The Responsibility of Science to Society.

Splendid.

The relocation trucks finally rolled up in the heavy heat of afternoon. Nothing ever happened on time in Kenya. As symbols of The Promise of Tomorrow the trucks did not inspire unlimited confidence. They were coated with dust and they wheezed and clanked like tanks that had been on the wrong side of a tough battle.

The television people insisted on a brief ceremony—a Farewell to Eden kind of thing—and that was the end of the Kwaruma.

The last of the hunters and gatherers were politely herded into the trucks. The adults were very subdued and old Klu was crying. The children were wide-eyed and lively. For them, this was an adventure.

Jerry had said all his farewells and he could not say them again. He walked out into the searing sunlight and stood there with his hat in his hand.

When the trucks pulled away, Jerry waved his hat.

He never saw Kwi again.

The baobab tree that had marked the last camp of the Kwaruma was far behind them now. There was tarmac under the wheels of the Land Rover. After bouncing around in rough country for so long, they seemed to be gliding.

Nairobi was one hundred miles ahead of them: a straight shot. It was still light enough to see but neither Jane nor Jerry gave the scenery so much as a glance. They knew it by heart.

George Ndambuki's vehicle was behind them. It would turn off at Machakos.

"Are you tired?" Jerry asked. "I could drive."

"The hell you say." Jane gripped the wheel until her knuckles whitened. "When we get to the big city, Tarzan is going to the hospital."

"You've been a mess through this whole rotten brick," Jerry said. His voice was so weak that it frightened him a little. His moist hand reached out and touched the hide container that rested between them.

"What is that thing? Why didn't you pack it away with the other gear?"

"It was a gift from Kwi. It's a turtle shell."

"You're kidding."

''Not this time. Neither was Kwi.''

Jane Schubauer didn't know what to say to that. Wisely, she said nothing.

''Jane?''

''I'm here.''

''In case I pass out, I have a favor to ask of you.''

She was really worried now. ''You don't have to ask, Jerry. Just tell me what you want.''

''The *churi*. The turtle shell. I think it's important to us. Keep it for me, will you? It mustn't be lost.''

''Done. Save the explanations for later. Try to get some sleep.''

It was growing dark. The first faint stars dusted the African sky. Jane switched on the headlights.

Jerry closed his eyes. He trusted Jane. He felt good about that.

When you get close to the edge, you do not worry. You just hang on.

Your mind works.

There was a kind of contact.

Jerry knew that he would not die. Not yet. They wouldn't let him.

He was a link. (Missing? No, just a shade fragile.) There was continuity. Something flowed between him and all the countless generations of mankind, those that were gone and those that were yet to be. Something flowed out, touching, connecting . . . .

His own kind of search was ending.

Perhaps he knew what was coming, perhaps not.

He did know that he had found something and that he too would be found.

He was certain enough to smile.

Nairobi was not the end of the trail.

They had searched through an ocean of darkness, a night sea that floated worlds upon worlds, stars beyond number, universes that began and ended and flowed into yet other universes.

They were after something. Otherwise, they would not have been there.

They would know it when they found it. They would know what to do with it.

The seeking was urgent. The journey had been long.

They were ready. They would not quit. They could not afford to miss.

They were coming.

Call it a hunt.

In Orson Scott Card's haunting vision of St. Amy and the Rectifiers, the central idea is not so much a probing of the past as its obliteration and reconstruction on a preferred model. But those who cannot remember the past . . .

ST. AMY'S TALE

Orson Scott Card

Mother could kill with her hands. Father could fly. These are miracles. But they were not miracles then. Mother Elouise taught me that there were no miracles then.

I am the child of Wreckers, born while the angel was in them. This is why I am called Saint Amy, though I perceive nothing in me that should make me holier than any other old woman. Yet Mother Elouise denied the angel in her, too, and it was no less there.

Sift your fingers through the soil, all you who read my words. Take your spades of iron and your picks of stone, dig deep. You will find no ancient works of man hidden there. For the Wreckers passed through the world and all the vanity was consumed in fire; all the pride broke in pieces when it was stricken with God's shining hand.

Elouise leaned on the rim of the computer keyboard. All around her the machinery was alive, the screens displaying information rapidly, as if they knew they were the last of the machines and this the last of the information. Elouise felt nothing but weariness; she was leaning because, for a moment, she had felt a frightening vertigo. As if the world underneath the airplane had dissolved, and slipped away into a rapidly receding star, and she would never be able to land.

True enough, in a way, she thought. I'll never be able to land, not in the world I knew.

"Getting sentimental about the old computers?"

Elouise, startled, turned in her chair and faced her husband, Charlie. At that moment the airplane lurched, but like sailors accustomed to the shifting of the sea they adjusted unconsciously and did not notice the imbalance.

"Is it noon already?" she asked.

"It's the moral equivalent of noon. I'm too tired to fly this thing anymore, and Bill's at the controls."

"Hungry?"

Charlie shook his head. "But Amy probably is."

"Voyeur," said Elouise. Charlie always liked to watch Elouise nurse their daughter. But despite her accusation, Elouise knew there was nothing sexual in it. Charlie liked the idea of Elouise being Amy's mother. He liked the way that Amy's sucking resembled the sucking of a calf or a lamb or a puppy. He had said: "It's the best thing we kept from the animals. The best thing we didn't throw away." Better than sex? Elouise had asked. And Charlie had only smiled.

Amy was playing with a rag doll in the only large clear space in the airplane, near the exit door. "Mommy Mommy Mamommy Mommy-o," Amy said. The child stood and reached to be picked up. Then she saw Charlie. "Daddy Addy Addy."

"Hi," Charlie said.

"Hi," Amy answered. "Ha-ee." She had only just learned to close the diphthong, and she exaggerated it. Amy played with the buttons on Elouise's shirt, trying to undo them.

"Greedy," Elouise said, laughing.

Charlie unbuttoned the shirt for her, and Amy seized on the nipple after only one false grab. She sucked noisily, tapping her hand gently against Elouise's breast as she ate.

"I'm glad we're so near finished," Elouise said. "She's too old to be nursing now."

"That's right, throw the little bird out of the nest."

"Go to bed," Elouise said.

Amy recognized the phrase. She pulled away. "La-lo," she said.

"That's right. Daddy's going to sleep," Elouise said.

Elouise watched as Charlie stripped off most of his clothing and lay down on the pad. He smiled once, then turned over and was immediately asleep. He was in tune with his body; Elouise knew that he would awaken in exactly six hours, when it was time for him to take the controls again. And when he awoke, he would remember all that had been said just before he went to sleep.

Amy's sucking was a subtle pleasure now, though it had been agonizing the first few months, and painful again when Amy's first teeth had come in and she had learned to her delight that by nipping she could make her mother scream. But better to nurse her than ever have her eat the predigested pap that served for food on the airplane. Elouise thought wryly that it was even worse than the microwaved veal cordon bleu that they used to inflict on commercial passengers. Only eight years ago. And they had calibrated their fuel so exactly that when they took the last draught of fuel from the last of their storage tanks, the tank registered empty; they would burn the last of the processed petroleum, instead of putting it back into the earth. All their caches were gone now, and they would be at the tender mercies of the world that they themselves had created.

Still there was work to do; the final work, the final checks. Elouise held Amy with one arm while she used her free hand to slowly key in the last program that her role as commander required her to use. Elouise Private, she typed. Teacher teacher I declare I see someone's underwear, she typed. On the screen appeared the warning she had put there: "You may think you're lucky finding this program, but unless you know the magic words, an alarm is going to go off all over this airplane and you'll be had. No way out of it, sucker. Love Elouise."

Elouise, of course, knew the magic word. Einstein

sucks, she typed. The screen went blank, and the alarm did not go off.

Malfunction? she queried. "None," answered the computer.

Tamper? she queried, and the computer answered, "None."

Nonreport? she queried, and the computer flashed, "AFscanP7bb55."

Elouise had not really been dozing. But still she was startled, and she lurched forward, disturbing Amy, who really had fallen asleep. "No no no," said Amy, and Elouise forced herself to be patient; she soothed her daughter back to sleep before pursuing whatever it was that her guardian program had caught. Whatever it was? Oh, she knew what it was. It was treachery. The one thing she had been sure *her* group, *her* airplane would never have. Other groups of Rectifiers—Wreckers, they called themselves, having adopted their enemies' name for them—other groups had had their spies or their fainthearts, but not Bill or Heather or Ugly-Bugly.

Specify, she typed.

The computer was specific.

Over northern Virginia, as the airplane followed its careful route to find and destroy everything made of metal, glass, and plastic; somewhere over northern Virginia, the airplane's path bent slightly to the south, and on the return, at the same place, the airplane's path bent slightly to the north, so that a strip of northern Virginia a mile long and a few dozen yards wide could contain some nonbiodegradable artifact, hidden from the airplane, and if Elouise had not queried this program, she would never have known it.

But she should have known it. When the plane's course bent, alarms should have sounded. Someone had penetrated the first line of defense. But Bill could not have done that, nor could Heather, really—they didn't have the sophistication to break up a bubble program. Ugly-Bugly?

222222 22 22 22222222222222222 2222222

But she knew it wasn't faithful old Ugly-Bugly. No, not her.

The computer voluntarily flashed, "Override M577b, commandmo4, intwis CtTttT." It was an apology. Someone aboard ship had found the alarm override program, and the overrides for the alarm for improper use of the alarm overrides. Not my fault, the computer was saying.

Elouise hesitated for a moment. Amy was asleep, her face fallen back from the breast, a bubble of milk and saliva almost transparently linking nipple and lip. Elouise looked down at her daughter and moved a curl of red hair away from Amy's eye. Elouise's hand trembled. But she was a woman of ice, yes, all frozen where compassion made other women warm; she prided herself on that, on having frozen the last warm places in her. Frozen so goddam rigid that it was only a moment's hesitation, and then she reached out and asked for the access code used to perform the treachery. Asked for the name of the traitor.

The computer was even less compassionate than Elouise. It hesitated not at all.

The computer did not underline; the letters on the screen were no larger than normal. Yet Elouise felt the words as a shout, and she answered them silently with a scream. Her face screamed, but she made no sound, only read again and again as if the computer were repeating:

Charles Evan Hardy, b24ag61richlandWA

It was Charlie who was the traitor, Charlie her sweet, soft, hard-bodied husband, Charlie who secretly was trying to undo the end of the world.

God has destroyed the world before. Once in a flood, when Noah rode it out in the ark. And once the tower of the world's pride was destroyed in the confusion of tongues. The other times, if there were any other times, those times are all forgotten.

The world will probably be destroyed again, unless we

repent. And don't think you can hide from the angels. They start out as ordinary people, and you never know which ones. Suddenly God puts the power of destruction in their hands, and they destroy. And just as suddenly, when all the destruction is done, the angel leaves them, and they're ordinary people. Just my mother and my father.

I can't remember Father Charlie's face. I was too young.

Mother Elouise told me often about Father Charlie. He was born far to the west in a land where water only comes to the crops in ditches, almost never from the sky. It was a land unblessed by God. Men lived there, they believed, only by the strength of their own hands. Men made their ditches and forgot about God and became scientists. Father Charlie became a scientist. He worked on tiny animals, breaking their heart of hearts and recombining it in new ways. Hearts were broken too often where he worked, and one of the little animals escaped and killed people until they lay in great heaps like fish in the ship's hold.

But this was not the destruction of the world.

Oh, they were giants in those days, and they forgot the Lord; but when their people lay in piles of moldering flesh and brittling bone, they remembered they were weak.

Mother Elouise said, "Charlie came weeping." This is how Father Charlie became an angel. He saw what the giants had done, by thinking they were greater than God. At first he sinned in his grief. Once he cut his own throat. They put Mother Elouise's blood in him to save his life. This is how they met: in the forest where he had gone to die privately, Father Charlie woke up from a sleep he thought would be forever, to see a woman lying next to him in the tent, and a doctor bending over them both. When he saw that this woman gave her blood to him whole and unstintingly, he forgot his wish to die. He loved her forever. Mother Elouise said he loved her right up to the day she killed him.

When they were finished, they had a sort of ceremony, a sort of party. "A benediction," said Bill, solemnly sipping at the gin. "Amen and amen."

"My shift," Charlie said, stepping into the cockpit.

Then he noticed that everyone was there, and that they were drinking the last of the gin, the bottle that had been saved for the end. "Well, happy us," Charlie said, smiling.

Bill got up from the controls of the 787. "Any preferences on where we set down?" he asked. Charlie took his place.

The others looked at one another. Ugly-Bugly shrugged. "God, who ever thought about it?"

"Come on, we're all futurists," Heather said. "You must know where you want to live."

"Two thousand years from now," Ugly-Bugly said. "I want to live in the world the way it'll be two thousand years from now."

"Ugly-Bugly opts for resurrection," Bill said, "I, however, long for the bosom of Abraham."

"Virginia," said Elouise. They turned to face her. Heather laughed.

"Resurrection," Bill intoned, "the bosom of Abraham, and Virginia. You have no poetry, Elouise."

"I've written down the coordinates of the place where we are supposed to land," Elouise said. She handed them to Charlie. He did not avoid her gaze. She watched him read the paper. He showed no sign of recognition. For a moment she hoped that it had all been a mistake—but no. She would not let herself be misled by her desires.

"Why Virginia?" asked Heather.

Charlie looked up from the paper. "It's central."

"It's east coast," Heather said.

"It's central in the high survival area. There isn't much of a living to be had in the western mountains or the plains. It's not so far south as to be in hunter-gatherer country, and not so far north as to be unsurvivable for a high proportion of the people. Barring a hard winter."

"All very good reasons," Elouise said. "Fly us there, Charlie."

Did his hands tremble as he touched the controls?

Elouise watched very carefully, but he did not tremble. Indeed, he was the only one who did not. Ugly-Bugly suddenly started to cry, tears coming from her good eye and streaming down her good cheek. Thank God she doesn't cry out of the other side, Elouise thought; then she was angry at herself, for she had thought Ugly-Bugly's deformed face didn't bother her anymore. Elouise was angry at herself, but it only made her cold inside, determined that there would be no failure. Her mission would be complete. No allowances made for personal cost.

Elouise suddenly started out of her contemplative mood to find that the other two women had left the cockpit—their sleep shift, though it was doubtful they would sleep. Charlie silently flew the plane, while Bill sat in the copilot's seat, pouring himself the last drop from the bottle. He was looking at Elouise.

"Cheers," Elouise said to him.

He smiled sadly back at her. "Amen," he said. Then he leaned back and sang softly:

"Praise God, from whom all blessings flow.
Praise him, ye creatures here below.
Praise him who slew the wicked host.
Praise Father, Son, and Holy Ghost."

Then he reached for Elouise's hand. She was surprised, but let him take it. He bent to her, kissed her palm tenderly. "For many have entertained angels unaware," he said to her.

"You get maudlin when you're drunk, Bill."

"Hallelujah."

A few moments later he was asleep. Charlie and Elouise sat in silence. The plane flew on south as darkness overtook them from the east. At first their silence was almost affectionate. But as Elouise sat and sat, saying nothing, she felt the silence grow cold and terrible, and for the first time she realized that when the airplane landed, Charlie would be her—Charlie, who had been half her life for these last few years, Charlie whom she had never lied to and who had never lied to her—would be her enemy.

I have watched the little children do a dance called Charlie-El. They sing a little song to it, and if I remember the words it goes like this:

"I am made of bones and glass
Let me pass, let me pass.
I am made of brick and steel.
Take my heel, take my heel.
I was killed just yesterday.
Kneel and pray, kneel and pray.
Dig a hole where I can sleep.
Dig it deep, dig it deep.
Will I go to heaven or hell?
Charlie-El. Charlie-El."

I think they are already nonsense words to the children. But the poem first got passed word of mouth around Richmond when I was little, and living in Father Michael's house. Will I go to heaven or hell? Who is good, and who is evil? The children are very wise. They do not try to answer their song. They just sing it, and do a very clever little dance while they sing. They always end the song with all the children falling down on the ground, laughing. That is the best way for the song to end.

Charlie brought the airplane straight down into a field, great hot winds pushing against the ground as if to shove it back from the plane. The field caught fire, but when the plane had settled upon its three wheels, foam streaked out from the belly of the machine and overtook the flames. Elouise watched from the cockpit, thinking: Wherever the foam has touched, nothing will grow for years. It seemed symmetrical to her. Even in the last moments of the last machine, it must poison the earth. Elouise held Amy on her lap, and thought of trying to explain it to the child. But Elouise knew Amy would not understand or remember.

"Last one dressed is a sissy-wissy," said Ugly-Bugly in her husky, ancient-sounding voice. Yet it was not so incongruous. They had dressed and undressed in front of each other for years now, but today as the old plastic-polluted clothing came off and the homespun went on, they felt and acted like schoolkids on their first day in coed gym. Amy caught the spirit of it and kept yelling at the top of her lungs. No one thought to quiet her. There was no need. This was a celebration.

But Elouise, long accustomed to self-examination, forced herself to realize that there was a strain to her frolicking. She did not believe it, not really. Today was not a happy day, and it was not just from knowing the confrontation that lay ahead. There was something so final about the death of the last of the engines of mankind. Surely something could be—but she forced the thought from her, forced the coldness in her to overtake that sentiment. Surely she could not be seduced by the beauty of the airplane. Surely she must remember that it was not the machines, but what they inevitably did to mankind that was evil.

They looked and felt a little awkward, almost silly as they left the plane and stood around in the blackened field. They had not yet lost their feel for stylish clothing, and the homespun was so lumpy and awkward and rough. It didn't look right on any of them.

Amy clung to her doll, awed by the strange scenery. In her life she had only been out of the airplane once, when she was an infant. She watched as the trees moved unpredictably. She winced at the wind in her eyes. She touched her cheek, where her hair moved back and forth in the breeze, and hunted through her vocabulary for a word to name the strange invisible touch on her skin. "Mommy," she said. "Uh! Uh! Uh!"

Elouise understood. "Wind," she said. The sounds were still too hard for Amy, and the child did not attempt to say the word. Wind, thought Elouise, and immediately thought of Charlie. Her best memory of Charlie was in the wind. It was during his death wish time, not long after his suicide attempt. He had insisted on climbing a mountain, and she knew that he meant to fall. So she had climbed with him, even though there was a storm coming up. Charlie was angry all the way. She remembered a terrible hour clinging to the face of a cliff, held only by small bits of metal forced into cracks in the rock. She had insisted on remaining tied to Charlie. "If one of us fell it would only drag the other down too," he kept saying. "I know," she kept answering. And so Charlie had not fallen, and they made love for the first time in a shallow cave, with the wind howling outside and occasional sprays of rain coming in to dampen them. They refused to be dampened. Wind. Damn.

And Elouise felt herself go cold and unemotional; and they stood on the edge of the field in the shade of the first trees. Elouise had left the Rectifier near the plane, set on 360 degrees. In a few minutes the Rectifier would go off, and they had to watch, to witness the end of their work.

Suddenly Bill shouted, laughed, held up his wrist. "My watch!" he cried.

"Hurry," Charlie said. "There's time."

Bill unbuckled his watch and ran toward the rectifier. He tossed the watch. It landed within a few feet of the small machine. Then Bill returned to the group, jogging and shaking his head. "Jesus, what a moron. Three years wiping out everything east of the Mississippi, and I almost save a digital chronograph."

"Texas Instruments?" asked Heather.

"Yeah."

"That's not high technology," she said, and they all laughed. Then they fell silent, and Elouise wondered if they were all thinking the same thing: that jokes about brand names will be dead within a generation, if they were not already dead. They watched the Rectifier in silence, waiting for the timer to finish its delay. Suddenly there was a shining in the air, a dazzling not-light that made them squint. They had seen this many times before, from the air and from the ground, but this was the last time, and so they saw it as if it were the first.

The airplane corroded as if a thousand years were passing in seconds. But it wasn't true corrosion. There was no rust—only dissolution as molecules separated and seeped down into the loosened earth. Glass became sand; plastic corrupted to oil; the metal also drifted down into the ground and came to rest in a vein at the bottom of the Rectifier field. Whatever else the metal might look like to a future geologist, it wouldn't look like an artifact. It would look like iron. And with so many similar pockets of iron and copper and aluminum and tin spread all over the once-civilized world, it was not likely that they would suspect human interference. Elouise was amused, thinking of the treatises that would someday be written, about the two states of workable metals—the ore state and the pure-metal vein. She hoped it would retard their progress a little.

The airplane shivered into nothing, and the Rectifier also died in the field. A few minutes after the Rectifier disappeared, the field also faded.

"Amen and amen," said Bill, maudlin again. "All clean now."

Elouise only smiled. She said nothing of the other Rectifier, which was in her knapsack. Let the others think all the work was done.

Amy poked her finger in Charlie's eye. Charlie swore and set her down. Amy started to cry and Charlie knelt by her and hugged her. Amy's arms went tightly around his neck. "Give Daddy a kiss," Elouise said.

"Well, time to go," rasped Ugly-Bugly's voice. "Why the hell did you pick this particular spot?"

Elouise cocked her head. "Ask Charlie."

Charlie flushed. Elouise watched him grimly. "Elouise and I once came here," he said. "Before Rectification began. Nostalgia, you know." He smiled shyly and the others laughed. Except Elouise. She was helping Amy urinate. She felt the weight of the small Rectifier in her knapsack, and did not tell anyone the truth: that she had never been in Virginia before in her life.

"Good a spot as any," Heather said. "Well, bye."

Well, bye. That was all, that was the end of it, and Heather walked away to the west, toward the Shenandoah Valley.

"Seeya," Bill said.

"Like hell," Ugly-Bugly added.

Impulsively Ugly-Bugly hugged Elouise, and Bill cried, and then they took off northeast, toward the Potomac, where they would doubtless find a community growing up along the clean and fish-filled river.

Just Charlie, Amy, and Elouise left in the empty, blackened field where the airplane had died. Elouise tried to feel some great pain at the separation from the others, but could not. They had been together every day for years now, going from supply dump to supply dump, wrecking city and town, destroying and using up the artificial world. But had they been friends? If it had not been for their task, they would never have been friends. They were not the same kind of people.

And then Elouise was ashamed of her feelings. Not her kind of people? Because Heather liked what grass did to her and had never owned a car or had a driver's license in her life? Because Ugly-Bugly had a face hideously deformed by cancer surgery? Because Bill always worked Jesus into the conversation, even though half the time he was an atheist? Because they just weren't in the same social circles? There were no social circles now. Just people trying to survive in a bitter world they weren't bred for. There were only two classes now—those who would make it, and those who wouldn't.

Which class am I? thought Elouise.

"Where should we go?" Charlie asked.

Elouise picked up Amy and handed her to Charlie. "Where's the time capsule, Charlie?"

Charlie took Amy and said, "Hey, Amy, baby, I'll bet

we find some farming community between here and the Rappahanock."

"Doesn't matter if you tell me, Charlie. The instruments found it before we landed. You did a damn good job on the computer program." She didn't have to say, Not good enough.

Charlie only smiled crookedly. "Here I was hoping you were forgetful." He reached out to touch her knapsack. She pulled abruptly away. He lost his smile. "Don't you know me?" he asked softly.

He would never try to take the Rectifier from her by force. But still. This was the last of the artifacts they were talking about. Was anyone really predictable at such a time? Elouise was not sure. She had thought she knew him well before—yet the time capsule existed to prove that her understanding of Charlie was far from complete.

"I know you, Charlie," she said, "but not as well as you do. Don't try to stop me."

"I hope you're not angry," Charlie said.

Elouise couldn't think of anything to say to that. Anyone could be fooled by a traitor, but only I am fool enough to marry one. She turned from him and walked into the forest. He took Amy and followed.

All the way through the underbrush, Elouise kept expecting him to say something. A threat, for instance: You'll have to kill me to destroy that time capsule. Or a plea: You have to leave it, Elouise, please, please. Or reason, or argument, or anger, or something.

But instead it was just his silent footfalls behind her, just his occasional playtalk with Amy. Just his singing as he put Amy to sleep on his shoulder.

The capsule had been well hidden. There was no surface sign that men had ever been here. Yet, from the Rectifier's emphatic response, it was obvious that the time capsule was quite large. There must have been heavy earth-moving equipment. Or was it all done by hand?

"When did you ever find the time?" asked Elouise, when they stood over the spot.

"Long lunch hours," he said.

She set down her knapsack, and then stood there, looking at him.

Like a condemned man who insists on keeping his composure, Charlie smiled wryly and said, "Get on with it, please."

"Oh, God," Elouise said. But she got on with it.

After Father Charlie died, Mother Elouise brought me here to Richmond. She didn't tell anyone that she was a Wrecker. The angel had already left her, and she wanted to blend into the town, be an ordinary person in the world she and her fellow angels had created. And she wanted to raise me in peace.

Yet she was incapable of blending in. Once the angel touches you, you cannot go back, even when the angel's work is done. She first attracted attention by talking against the stockade. There was once a stockade around the town of Richmond, when there were only a thousand people here. The reason was simple. People still weren't used to the hard way life was without the old machines. They had not yet learned to depend on the miracle of Christ. They still trusted in their hands, yet their hands could work no more magic. So there were tribes in the winter that didn't know how to find game, that had no reserves of grain, that had no shelter adequate to hold the head of a fire.

"Bring them all in," said Mother Elouise. "There's room for all. There's food for all. Teach them how to build ships and make tools and sail and farm, and we'll all be richer for it."

But Father Michael and Uncle Avram knew more than Mother Elouise. Father Michael had been a simple priest before the destruction, and Uncle Avram had been a professor at a university. They had been nobody. But when the angels of destruction finished their work, the angels of life began to work in the hearts of men. Father Michael threw off his old allegiance to Rome and taught Christ simple, from his

memory of the Holy Book. And Uncle Avram plunged into
his memory of ancient metallurgy, and taught the people who
gathered at Richmond how to make iron hard enough to use
for tools.

And weapons.

Father Michael forbade the making of guns, and forbade
that anyone teach children what guns were. I will also not
teach you what guns were, for they were terrible. But for
hunting there had to be arrows, and what will kill a deer will
also kill a man.

Many people agreed with Mother Elouise about the stockade. But then in the worst of winter a tribe came from the
mountains and threw fire against the stockade and against the
ships that kept trade alive along the whole coast. The archers
of Richmond killed most of them, and people said to Mother
Elouise, "Now you must agree we need the stockade."

But Mother Elouise said, "Would they have come with
fire if there had not been a wall?"

How can anyone judge the greatest need? Just as the angel
of death had come to plant the seeds of a better life, so that
angel of life had to be hard and endure death so the many
could live. Father Michael and Uncle Avram held to the laws
of Christ simple, for did not the Holy Book say, "Love your
enemies, and smite them only when they attack you; chase
them not out into the forest, but let them live as long as they
leave you alone"?

I remembered that winter. I remember watching as they
buried the dead tribesmen. Their bodies had stiffened quickly, but Mother Elouise brought me to see them and said,
"This is death, remember it, remember it." What did
Mother Elouise know? The cold corpse is not death. Death is
only our passage from flesh into the living wind, until Christ
brings us forth into flesh again. Christ will bring forth Mother
Elouise, and she will find Father Charlie again, and every
wound will be made whole.

Elouise knelt by the Rectifier and carefully set it to go
off in half an hour, destroying itself and the time capsule
buried a hundred feet under the ground. Charlie stood

near her, watching, his face nearly expressionless; only a faint smile broke his perfect repose. Amy was in his arms, laughing and trying to reach up to pinch his nose.

"This Rectifier responds only to me," Elouise said quietly. "Alive. If you try to move it, it will go off early and kill us all."

"I won't move it," Charlie said.

And Elouise was finished. She stood up, reached for Amy. Amy reached back, holding out her arms to her mother. "Mommy," she said.

Because I couldn't remember Father Charlie's face, Mother Elouise thought I had forgotten everything about him. But that is not true. I remember very clearly one picture of him. But he is not in the picture.

This is very hard for me to explain. I see a small clearing in the trees, with Mother Elouise standing in front of me. I see her at my eye level, which tells me that I am being held. I cannot see Father Charlie, but I know that he is holding me. I can feel his arms around me. But I cannot see his face.

This vision has come to me often. It is not like other dreams. It is very clear, and I am always very afraid, and I don't know why. They are talking, but I do not understand their words. Mother Elouise reaches for me, but Father Charlie will not let me go. I feel afraid that Father Charlie will not let me go with Mother Elouise. But why should I be afraid? I love Father Charlie, and I never want to leave him. Still I reach out, reach out, reach out, and still the arms hold me and I cannot go.

Mother Elouise is crying. I remember that also. I see her face twisted in pain. I want to comfort her. "Mommy is hurt," I say, again and again. I have been told that I say these words aloud during the dream.

And then, suddenly, at the end of this vision I am in my mother's arms and we are running, running up a hill, into the trees. I am looking back over her shoulder. I see Father Charlie then, I see him—but I do not see him. I know exactly where he is, in my vision, I could tell you his height, I could

tell you where his left foot is, and where his right foot is, but
still I can't *see* him. He has no face, no color, he is just a
man-shaped emptiness in the clearing, and then the trees are
in the way and he is gone.

Elouise stopped only a little way into the woods. She
turned around, as if to go back to Charlie. But she would
not go back. If she returned to him, it would be to
disconnect the Rectifier. There would be no other
reason to do it.

"Charlie, you son of a bitch!" she shouted.

There was no answer. She stood, waiting. Surely he
would come to her. He would see that she would never
go back, never turn off the machine. Once he realized it
was inevitable, he would come running from the
machine, into the forest, back to the clearing where the
787 had landed. Why would he want to give his life so
meaninglessly? What was in the time capsule, after all?
Just history—that's what he said, wasn't it? Just history,
just films and metal plates engraved with words and
microdots and other ways of preserving the story of
mankind. "How can they learn from our mistakes, unless we tell them what they were?" Charlie had asked.

Sweet, simple, naive Charlie. It is one thing to pre-
serve a hatred for the killing machines and the soul-
destroying machines and the garbage-making
machines. It was another thing to leave behind detailed,
accurate, unquestionable descriptions. History was not
a way of preventing the repetition of mistakes. It was a
way of guaranteeing them. Wasn't it?

She turned and walked on, not very quickly, out of the
range of the Rectifier, carrying Amy and listening, all the
way, for the sound of Charlie running after her.

What was Mother Elouise like? She was a woman of
contradictions. Even with me, she would work for hours
teaching me to read, helping me make tablets out of river clay
and write in them with a shaped stick. And then, when I had

written the words she taught me, she would weep and say, "Lies, all lies." Sometimes she would break the tablets I had made. But whenever part of her words was broken, she would make me write it again.

She called the collection of words The Book of the Golden Age. I have named it The Book of the Lies of the Angel Elouise, for it is important for us to know that the greatest truths we have seem like lies to those who have been touched by the angel.

She told many stories to me, and once I asked her why they must be written down. "For Father Charlie," she would always say. "Is he coming back, then?" I would ask. But she shook her head, and finally one time she said, "It is not for Father Charlie to read. It is because Father Charlie wanted it written."

"Then why didn't he write it himself?" I asked.

And Mother Elouise grew very cold with me, and all she would say was, "Father Charlie bought these stories. He paid more for them than I am willing to pay to have them left unwritten." I wondered then if Father Charlie was rich, but other things she said told me that he wasn't. So I do not understand except that Mother Elouise did not want to tell the stories, and Father Charlie, though he was not there, constrained her to tell them.

There are many of Mother Elouise's lies that I love, but I will say now which of them she said were most important:

1. In the Golden Age, for ten times a thousand years men lived in peace and love and joy, and no one did evil one to another. They shared all things in common, and no man was hungry while another was full, and no man had a home while another stood in the rain, and no wife wept for her husband, killed before his time.

2. The great serpent seems to come with great power. He has many names: Satan, Hitler, Lucifer, Nimrod, Napoleon. He seems to be beautiful, and he promises power to his friends and death to his enemies. He says he will right all wrongs. But really he is weak, until people believe in him

and give him the power of their bodies. If you refuse to
believe in the serpent, if no one serves him, he will go away.

3. There are many cycles of the world. In every cycle, the
great serpent has arisen and the world has been destroyed to
make way for the return of the Golden Age. Christ comes
again in every cycle, also. One day when he comes men will
believe in Christ and doubt the great serpent, and that time
the Golden Age will never end, and God will dwell among
men forever. And all the angels will say, come not to heaven
but to Earth, for Earth is heaven now.

These are the most important lies of Mother Elouise.
Believe them all, for they are true.

All the way to the airplane clearing, Elouise deliber-
ately broke branches and let them dangle, so that Charlie would have no trouble finding a straight path out of
the range of the Rectifier, even if he left his flight to the
last second. She was sure Charlie would follow her.
Charlie would bend to her as he had always bent,
resilient and accommodating. He loved Elouise, and
Amy he loved even more. What was in the metal under
his feet that would weigh in the balance against his love
for them?

So Elouise broke the last branch and stepped into the
clearing, and then sat down and let Amy play in the
unburnt grass at the edge while she waited. It is Charlie
who will bend, she said to herself, for I will never bend on
this. Later I will make it up to him, but he must know that
on this I will never bend.

The cold place in her grew larger and colder until she
burned inside, waiting for the sound of running feet
crashing through the underbrush. The damnable birds
kept singing, loudly, so that she could not hear the
footsteps.

Mother Elouise never hit me, or anyone else so far as I
knew. She fought only with her words and silent acts, though

she could have killed easily with her hands. I saw her physical power only once. We were in the forest, to gather firewood. We stumbled upon a wild hog. Apparently it felt cornered, though we were weaponless; perhaps it was just mean. I have not studied the ways of wild hogs. It charged, not Mother Elouise, but me. I was five at the time, and terrified. I ran to Mother Elouise, tried to cling to her, but she threw me out of the way and went into a crouch. I was screaming. She paid no attention to me. The hog continued rushing, but seeing I was down and Mother Elouise was erect, he changed his path. When he came near, she leaped to the side. He was not nimble enough to turn to face her. As he lumbered past, Mother Elouise kicked him just behind the head. Just kicked him. It broke his neck so violently that his head dropped and he rolled over and over and when he was through rolling he was already dead.

Mother Elouise did not have to die.

She died in the winter when I was seven. I should tell you how life was then, in Richmond. We were only two thousand souls by then, not the large city of ten thousand we are now. We had only six finished ships trading the coast, and they had not yet gone so far north as Manhattan, though we had run one voyage all the way to Savannah in the south. Richmond already ruled and protected from the Potomac to Dismal Swamp. But it was a very hard winter, and the town's leaders insisted on hoarding all the stored grain and fruits and vegetables and meat for our protected towns, and let the distant tribes trade or travel where the would, they would get no food from Richmond.

It was then that my mother, who claimed she did not believe in God, and Uncle Avram, who was a Jew, and Father Michael, who was a priest, all argued the same side of the question. It's better to feed them than to kill them, they all said. But when the tribes from west of the mountains and north of the Potomac came into Richmond lands, pleading for help, the leaders of the town turned them away and closed the gates of the towns. An army marched then, to put the fear, as they said, of God into the hearts of the tribesmen. They did not know which side God was on.

Father Michael argued and Uncle Avram stormed and fumed, but Mother Elouise silently went to the gate at moonrise one night and alone overpowered the guards. Silently she bound them and gagged them and opened the gates to the hungry tribesmen. They came through weaponless, as she had insisted. They quietly went to the storehouses and carried off as much food as they could bear. They were only discovered as the last few got away. No one was killed.

But there was an uproar, a cry of treason, a trial, and an execution. They decided on beheading, because they thought it would be quick and merciful. They had never seen a beheading.

It was Jack Woods who used the axe. He practiced all afternoon with pumpkins. Pumpkins have no bones.

In the evening they all gathered to watch, some because they hated Mother Elouise, some because they loved her, and the rest because they could not stay away. I came also, and Father Michael held my head and would not let me see. But I heard.

Father Michael prayed for Mother Elouise. Mother Elouise damned his and everyone else's soul to hell. She said, ''If you kill me for bringing life, you will only bring death on your own heads.''

''That's true,'' said the men around her. ''We will all die. But you will die first.''

''Then I'm the luckier,'' said Mother Elouise. It was the last of her lies, for she was telling the truth, and yet she did not believe it herself. For I heard her weep. With her last breaths she wept, and cried out, ''Charlie! Charlie!'' There are those who claim she saw a vision of Charlie waiting for her on the right hand of God, but I doubt it. She would have said so. I think she only wished to see him. Or wished for his forgiveness. It doesn't matter. The angel had long since left her by then, and she was alone.

Jack swung the ax and it fell, more with a smack than a

thud. He had missed her neck and struck deep in her back and shoulder. She screamed and screamed. He struck again, and this time silenced her. But he did not break through her spine until the third blow. Then he turned away, spattered with blood, and vomited and wept and pleaded with Father Michael to forgive him.

Amy stood a few feet away from Elouise, who sat on the grass of the clearing, looking toward a broken branch on the nearest tree. Amy called, "Mommy! Mommy!" Then she bounced up and down, bending and unbending her knees. "Da! Da!" she cried. "La la la la la." She was dancing, and wanted her mother to dance and sing, too. But Elouise only looked toward the tree, waiting for Charlie to appear. Any minute, she thought. He will be angry. He will be ashamed, she thought. But he will be alive.

In the distance, however, the air was suddenly shining. Elouise could see it clearly because they were not far from the edge of the Rectifier field. It shimmered in the trees, where it caused no harm to plants. Any vertebrates within the field, any animals that lived by electricity passing along nerves, were instantly dead, their brains stilled. Birds dropped from tree limbs. Only stupid insects droned on.

The Rectifier field lasted only a few minutes.

Amy watched the shining air. It was as if the empty sky itself were dancing with her. She was transfixed. She would soon forget the airplane, and already her father's face was disappearing from her memories. But she would remember the shining. She would see it forever in her dreams, a vast thickening of the air, dancing and vibrating up and down, up and down. In her dreams it would always be the same, a terrible shining light that would grow and grow and grow and press against her in her bed. And always with it would come the sound of a voice she loved saying, "Jesus. Jesus. Jesus." This dream would come so clearly once when she was twelve that she would tell it to her adopted father, the priest named Michael. He told her that it was the voice of an angel, speaking the name of the source of all light. "You must not fear the light," he said. "You must embrace it." It satisfied her.

But at the moment she first heard the voice, in fact and not in dream, she had no trouble recognizing it. It was the voice of her mother, Elouise, saying, "Jesus." It was full of grief that only a child could fail to understand. Amy did not understand. She only tried to repeat the word. "Deeah-zah," she said.

"God," said Elouise, rocking back and forth, her face turned up toward a heaven she was sure was unoccupied.

"Dog," Amy repeated. "Dog dog doggie." In vain she looked around for the four-footed beast.

"Charlie," Elouise screamed as the Rectifier field faded.

"Daddy," Amy cried, and because of her mother's tears she also wept. Elouise took her daughter in her arms and held her, rocking back and forth. Elouise discovered that there were some things that could not be frozen in her. Some things that must burn: Sunlight. And lightning. And everlasting, inextinguishable regret.

My mother, Mother Elouise, often told me about my father. She described Father Charlie in detail, so I would not forget. She refused to let me forget anything. "It's what Father Charlie died for," she told me, over and over. "He died so you would remember. You cannot forget."

So I still remember, even today, every word she told me about him. His hair was red, like mine was. His body was lean and hard. His smile was quick, like mine, and he had gentle hands. When his hair was long or sweaty, it kinked tightly at his forehead, ears, and neck. His touch was so delicate he could cut in half an animal so tiny it could not be seen without a machine; so sensitive that he could fly, an art that Mother Elouise said was not a miracle—it could be done by many giants of the Golden Age, and they took with them many others who could not fly alone. This was Charlie's gift, Mother Elouise said.

Mother Elouise also told me that I loved him dearly.

But for all the words that she taught me, I still have no picture of my father in my mind. It is as if the words drove out the vision, as so often happens.

Yet I still hold that one memory of my father, so deeply hidden that I can neither lose it nor fully find it again. Sometimes I wake up weeping. Sometimes I wake up with my arms in the air, curved just so, and I remember that I was dreaming of embracing that large man who loved me. My arms remember how it feels to hold Father Charlie tight around the neck, and cling to him as he carries his child. And when I cannot sleep, and the pillow seems to be always the wrong shape, it is because I am hunting for the shape of Father Charlie's shoulder, which my heart remembers though my mind cannot.

I believe that this is Jesus. Surely he is a shining light; but just as surely, his is the shoulder against which every face may comfortably press; surely all arms will fit tight around his neck, to cry into his loving kiss.

God put angels into Mother Elouise and Father Charlie, and they destroyed the world, for the cup of God's indignation was full, and all the works of man were an abomination. All the works of men become dust; but out of dust God makes men, and out of men and women, angels.

Where will you hear my words, you who believe? Will you sit in a stone church to hear a priest read aloud? Will you have the books in your own home, and will you read the words to each other? Outside it is raining, raining on all the world except you, for you are warm and dry. Stand up and walk out into the rain, you who believe; do not watch the ground, do not try to keep your feet clean. Look up, look up, and see the clouds moving on the face of heaven. Look up and see the rainbow. It is the promise that however much the sun might hide from us, it is still there, still waiting, and those who look for light will always find it, shining in the air like a vision of God, so bright that even the birds don't sing.

I know little about David Langford except that he's British. And has a firm grasp on how to make a powerful short political statement that transcends all current politics, all local names and slogans.

THE FINAL DAYS

David Langford

It was under the hot lights that Harman always felt most powerful. The air throbbed and sang with dazzlement and heat, wherein opponents—Ferris merely the most recent— might shrivel and wilt; but Harman sucked confidence from cameras, glad to expose something of himself to a nation of watchers, and more than a nation. Just now the slick, machine-stamped interviewer was turned away, towards Ferris; still Harman knew better than to peer surreptitiously at his own solid, blond and faintly smiling image in the monitor. Control was important, and Harman's image was imperturbable: his hands lay still and relaxed, the left on the chair-arm, the right on his thigh, their stillness one of the many small negative mannerisms which contributed to the outward Harman's tough dependability.

Gradually the focus was slipping away from Ferris, whose mere intelligence and sincerity should not be crippling his handling of the simplest, the most hypothetical questions.
"What would be *your* first act as President, Mr. Ferris?"
"Well, er . . . it would depend on . . ."
And the monitor would ruthlessly cut back to Harman in relaxed close-up, faintly smiling. One of the tricks was to be always the same. Ferris, alternately tense and limp, seemed scarcely camera-trained. Why? Ferris did not speak naturally toward the interviewer, nor oratorically into the camera which now pushed close, its red action-light ablink; his gaze wavered as he assembled libertarian platitudes, and his attention was drawn unwillingly beyond the arena's heat and

58

light, to something that troubled him. Harman glanced easily about the studio, and followed Ferris's sick fascination to his own talisman, the magic box which traced the threads of destiny. (Always to be ready with a magniloquent phrase; that was another of the tricks.)

He could have laughed. Ferris, supposedly a seasoned performer and a dangerous opponent, could not adapt to this novelty. Four days to go, and his skill was crumbling under the onslaught of a gigantically magnified stage-fright. Posterity was too much for him.

Looking up from the box, the technician intercepted Harman's tightly relaxed gaze and held up five fingers; and five more; and four. Harman's self-confidence and self-belief could hardly burn brighter. Fourteen watchers. Favoured above all others, he had never before scored higher than ten. The wheel still turned his way, then. *Ecce homo*; man of the hour; man of destiny; he half-smiled at the clichés, but no more than half.

The interviewer swivelled his chair to Harman, leaving Ferris in a pool of sweat. His final questions had been gentle, pityingly gentle; and Ferris with flickering eyes had fumbled nearly all.

"Mr. Ferris has explained his position, Mr. Harman, and I'm sure that you'd like to state yours before I ask you a few questions."

Harman let his practised voice reply at once, while his thoughts sang *fourteen . . . fourteen . . .*

"I stand, as I have said before, for straight talking and honest action. I stand for a rejection of the gutless compromises which have crippled our economy. I want a fair deal for everyone, and I'm ready to fight to see they get it."

The words were superfluous. Harman's followers had a Sign.

"I'll tell you a true story about something that happened to me a while ago. I was walking home at night, in a street where vandals had smashed up half the lights, and a mugger came up to me. One of those scum who will be swept from the streets when our programme of police reform goes through.''

(He detected a twitch of resentment from Ferris; but Ferris was off-camera now.)

''He showed me a knife and asked for my wallet, the usual line of talk. Now I'm not a specially brave man, but this was what I'd been talking about when I laid it on the line about political principles. You just don't give in to threats like that. So I said damn you, come and try it, and you know, he just crumpled up. There's a moral in that story for this country, a moral you'll see when you think who's threatening us right now—''

(It was a true story. As it happened, the security man on Harman's tail had shot the mugger as he wavered.)

''A few questions, then,'' said the interviewer. ''I think we're all waiting to hear more about the strangest gimmick ever included in a Presidential campaign. A lot of people are pretty sceptical about these scientists' claims, you know. Perhaps you could just briefly tell the viewers what you yourself think about these eyes, these watchers—?''

When you're hot, you're hot. Harman became still chattier.

''It's not a gimmick and it's not really part of my campaign. Some guys at the Gravity Research Foundation discovered that we—or some of us—are being watched. By, well, posterity. As you'll know from the newspapers, they were messing about with a new way of picking up gravity waves, which is something a plain man like me knows nothing about; and instead their gadget spotted these (what did they call them?) little knots of curdled space. The nodes, they called them later, or the peepholes. The gadget tells you when they're looking and how many are looking. It turns out that ordinary folk ''—he suppressed the reflexive *like you and me*—''aren't watched at all; important people might get one or two or half-a-dozen eyes on them . . .''

At a sign from the interviewer, a previously dormant camera zoomed in on the technician and the unremarkable-looking Box. ''Can you tell us how many—eyes—are present in this studio, sir?''

The technician paused to make some minor adjustment, doubtless eager for his own tiny share of limelight. He looked up after a few seconds, and said: ''Fifteen.''

Ferris shuddered very slightly.

''Of course,'' said Harman smoothly, ''some of these will be for Mr. Ferris.'' Ferris, he knew, had two watchers; intermittently; and it seemed that he hated it. The interviewer, giant of this tiny studio world, was never watched for his own sake when alone. He was marking time now, telling the tale of Sabinnen, that artist whom they tagged important in earlier tests of the detectors. Sabinnen was utterly obscure at that time; that ceased when they tracked the concentration of eight eyes, and his cupboardful of paintings came to light, and did it not all hang together, this notion of the Future watching the famous before their fame?

Harman revelled in the silent eyes which so constantly attended him. It recalled the curious pleasure of first finding his home and office bugged; such subtle flattery might dismay others, but Harman had nothing to hide.

''But I must emphasize that this is only a pointer,'' he said, cutting in at the crucial moment. ''The people have this hint of the winning side, as they might from newspaper predictions or opinion polls—but the choice remains theirs, a decision which we politicians must humbly accept. Of course I'm glad it's not just today's voters who have faith in me—'' He was full of power; the words came smoothly, compellingly, through the final minutes—while Ferris stared first morosely at his shoe and then bitterly at Harman, while the interviewer (momentarily forgetful of the right to equal time, doubtless reluctant to coax the numbed Ferris through further

hoops) listened with an attentive silence which clearly said
In four days you will be President.

Then it was over, and Harman moved through a triumphal
procession of eager reporters, scattering bonhomie and predictions of victory, saluted again and again by electronic
flashes which for long minutes burnt green and purple on his
retinas; and so to the big, quiet car with motorcycles before
and behind, off into the anonymous night. He wondered idly
whether any reporter had been kind enough to beg an opinion
or two from Ferris.

He refused to draw the car's shades, of course, preferring
to remain visible to the public behind his bullet proof glass.
There was a risk of assassination, but though increasing it
was still small. (How the eyes must have hovered over JFK,
like a cloud of eager flies. But no-one could wish to assassi-
nate Harman . . . surely.) He settled in the rear seat, one
hand still and relaxed upon the leather, the other resting
calmly on his own right thigh. The outline of the chauffeur's
head showed dimly through more impervious glass. . . . In
four days he would rate six motorcyclists before and behind;
with two only to supplement the eye-detector's van and this
purring car, he felt almost alone. Better to recall the seventeen watchers (the number had been rising still, the Argus
eyes of destiny marking him out); or the eye of the camera,
which held within it a hundred million watchers here and
now. The show had gone well. He felt he might have succeeded without the silent eyes, the nodes of interference born
of the uncertainty principle which marked where information
was siphoned into the years ahead. How far ahead? No-one
knew; and it did not matter. Harman believed in himself and
knew his belief to be sincere, even without this sign from
heaven to mark him as blessed of all men.

And *that* was strangely true, he knew. The princes and
powers of the world had been scanned for the stigmata of

lasting fame (not the Soviets, of course, nor China); politicians—Harman smiled—often scored high, yet none higher than eight or nine. *Seventeen* showed almost embarrassing enthusiasm on the part of the historians, the excellent, discriminating historians yet to be.

I shall deserve it, Harman told himself as his own home came into view, searchlights splashing its pale walls and throwing it into due prominence. In a brief huddle of guards he passed within to the theoretical privacy of his personal rooms, sincere and knowing again that he was sincere. He would fulfil his promises to the letter, honest and uncompromising, ready to risk even his reputation for the good of Democracy. He paced the mildly austere bedroom (black and white, grey and chrome); he fingered the chess-set and *go*-board which magazines had shown to the nation. The recorders whirred companionably. His clothes were heavy with sweat, inevitable under the hot lights; the trick was not to look troubled by heat, not ever to subside and mop oneself like Ferris, poor Ferris.

This room had no windows, for sufficient reasons; but Harman knew of six optical bugs at the least. Naked in the adjoining shower, he soaped himself and smiled. Seventeen watchers—or perhaps nineteen or twenty, for the power was still rising within him—the bugs and the watchers troubled him not at all. That, he was certain, was his true strength. He had nothing to hide from the future, nor from the present; in all his life, he believed there was no episode which could bring shame to his biography. Let the eyes peer! The seedy Ferris might weaken himself with drink, with women, but Harman's energies flowed cool and strong in a single channel, which for convenience he called The Good Of The Nation.

He fumbled into pajamas, his erection causing some small discomfort. Four days. Only four days and then: no compromise. The hard line. Straight talk, nation unto nation. He would give them good reason to watch him, Harman, the ultimate politician. He felt, as though beneath his fingers, the Presidential inheritance of red telephones and red buttons.

The eyes of time were upon him. He knew he would not fail them.

*In thinking about a seeking of the past, another idea
arises: that the past, or pasts, might begin to converge upon
the unwitting and perhaps unwilling seeker . . .*

RECESSIONAL

Fred Saberhagen

From the window of his high hotel room, sixty dollars a
day at convention rates, he could look between other build-
ings to see a small piece of the ocean. Within the mirror
where he looked when shaving there was another window
with another square of sea, and an hourly newscast came on
that morning just as he was starting to shave. Razor in hand
he listened while the voice of the woman announcer went
through a few details of what she called the grisly discovery.
The thing somehow got to him, enough to keep him from
concentrating properly either on shaving or on what he ought
to say when he appeared on the panel in a couple of hours.
Not only that, it stayed with him after he finished getting
ready and left the room.

The radio really hadn't given many facts. The body of a
woman of indeterminite age had been washed up on a beach
somewhere down in the Keys, which put it, he supposed,
almost a hundred miles to the southwest of Miami Beach. An
unnamed authority was quoted to the effect that the body
might have been in the water as long as several years. He
thought at first that the newscaster had probably got that
garbled somehow, but then mention was made of pockets of
cold, uncirculating water to be found in certain depths, in
which unusual preservative action could be expected.

One reason for the grisly discovery remaining with him all
morning, he supposed, was that his panel topic was "Science
in Science Fiction," and he hoped to be able to work that
"unusual preservative action" into what he had to say. He
felt a little uncomfortable about this panel, as he really was

no scientist, though he read the professional journals fairly often and popularizations a lot, and his stories tended to be thick with scientific jargon. He thought some of the readers liked the jargon better than the stories, and he loved it himself, really, which was why long ago he had begun to use so much of it. For him it had always made a kind of poetry.

Some of the other people on the panel were not only real scientists, but were writers as well. They talked quantum mechanics. They talked epistemology. He wasn't sure at first that he remembered what that meant. He wondered for a little while if he was going to have to sit there like a dummy for long minutes at a time. So as soon as the chance came, he got in a few words that shifted the subject to alternate universes. Anybody could talk about that.

Suppose, he thought to himself, looking out over the heads of the audience in the far last row while some argument between two other panelists droned on, just suppose that body could have been five years in the sea. How far could a body drift in five years? Well, certainly not through the Panama Canal. When, in the early afternoon, he got back to his room, he looked out at what little he could see of the one great ocean that went all the way around the world, and thought about that body again. They hadn't said what, if anything, the woman had been wearing. He couldn't quite shake the subject, it seemed to have set up a resonance of some kind inside his head. Time passed, what seemed like a lot of time as he sat waiting in his room, but the phone call from another hotel room that he was expecting failed to come.

So he left the convention earlier than he had planned, left it that very afternoon, driving north through summer Florida. Going to the convention, he told himself, had been more trouble than it was worth. In the old days, the cons ran three days, no more, and were relaxed and friendly. Now each one he went to seemed like some damned big business in itself. Just getting away on his own was something of a relief.

A day and a half later, waking up early in his motel room in

Atlanta, he put in a call to his agent in New York. The agent would be back in the office in half an hour, the girl thought, and would call him back then. Waiting for the agent to call back, he took a shower, and when he came out of the shower, dripping, turned on the radio.

Listening, he experienced an inward chill.

". . . thought to have been in her early twenties, recovered from the Cattahoochie some twenty miles north of Atlanta. The condition of the body made it impossible to determine immediately if there were any marks of violence. Sheriff's officers said that the body might have been in the water for as long as several months. Attempts at identification . . ."

The phone rang. It was the agent, for once communicating even earlier than expected. And with good news: money was coming through, even more money than they had been looking for, and he could afford a trip, a wander across the country, if he felt like one. He hadn't really felt like one for several years, not since he had been living alone, but he felt like one now, before he went home and got back to work. Not that New York or any place else was really home. He had reached the stage of being down to mailing addresses.

The Interstate impelled him west. He liked driving his car, he usually liked machines. Quantum mechanics. Epistemology. That was what they talked about on panels nowadays. In the old days they had talked about relativity sometimes, but then you could figure that almost no one knew what they were talking about. He should have taken the time, before coming to the convention, to read up a little more on current work. That way he could have at least sounded a little more intelligent. He would settle in for a day or two of reading when he got home.

A feeling was growing in him that the convention he had just left had marked some kind of turning point, a new departure in his life. Something had changed. Whether it was for better or worse had yet to be discovered. For richer, for poorer. He was never going to get married again, that much he felt pretty sure about, not even when his status as a

widower became finally and fully legal and official, as one of
these years it would. Was it two years now, or three? Conventions were still good for providing a little fun in bed, and
that was all he needed. Then next day he waited in his room
and the phone refused to ring as scheduled. Well, maybe it
was just as well.

He didn't really know where he was driving now, he just
wanted to get off for a few days. On a new course. Alternate
universe. When he had brought up that hoary old science
fiction concept on the panel, one of the real scientists, almost
condescending though he was trying not to sound that way,
had admitted aloud that some experiments in particle physics
carried out within the last ten years even suggest that physical
reality may depend in some sense, to some extent, on human
consciousness. If that was true, the writer had thought,
listening, if that could be true, how was it possible for
everybody to remain so calm about it? But thus spake a real
life quantum mechanic. The Bell inequality, whatever the
hell that was. The spin of elementary particles . . .

The car radio assured him that gas supplies were good
everywhere across the country, though prices showed no sign
of coming down. Tourist business was suffering. He was
going to have no trouble finding a motel room, wherever he
went.

At Birmingham he decided to head on west for a while,
and stayed with Interstate 20 going southwest to Jackson.
Hell of a country to be driving through in the summer in
search of fun or relaxation. But the car was nicely air con-
ditioned, a space capsule whose interior guarded its own
sounds and atmosphere, keeping noise and dust and rain and
heat all nicely sealed outside. What showed on the windows
could almost be no more than pictures from outside, computer presentations.

In Vicksburg he located a bottle of bourbon and took it to
bed with him. A lot less trouble than a woman. But then to his
own surprise he discovered that he didn't feel like drinking
much, even after the long drive. He took a couple of sips,
then let the bottle sit. He turned on the television, got some

local talk show. Talk shows were usually his favorite, they provided humanity at just about the right distance. They proved that the human race was still around somewhere, alive, not too terribly far away. But when you wanted, you could turn them off.

". . . for your research at the battlefield cemeteries?" the host was asking.

"Well, the opportunity came about because of some new road construction in the park." The speaker was a well-dressed man in the prime of life, mustached, relaxed, superior. He enjoyed talking like this. He was reminiscent of some of the people on the convention panel. "In the process of excavation for the road, some previously unknown 1863 military burials came to light, and we applied for permission to use some of the skulls in our tests, the same kind of tests we had been developing for the archaeological work on Indian sites. There were twenty-seven of the Civil War skulls altogether, all completely unidentified. We think they were divided about evenly between Union and Confederate."

"And you got the same results with these, as with the older subjects, that had been in the ground for maybe thousands of years?"

"Better, in many cases. The bone frequently was much better preserved than in the older specimens. We were able to get some very interesting results indeed. The trace elements in the bone that resonate with the NMR . . ."

Jargon, of any scientific field, could still soothe him like poetry. Better than poetry. He sipped at his bottle and set it back on the table and got ready to drift toward sleep.

" . . . beauty of the whole thing, you see, is that the visual cortex of the brain need not be intact, or even present."

"That's the real discovery, then."

"That's part of it. Apparently what no one had suspected all along was that the hard bone of the skull itself has another purpose besides that of mere protection."

They had him drifting toward wakefulness again. Why hadn't he heard anything about any of this before? It sounded revolutionary. He wanted to hear it now.

" . . . bone perhaps serves as a kind of backup memory storage system, at least in human skulls. We don't know yet if it works the same way in other mammals."

"Then there should be applications of this outside the field of archaeology, wouldn't you say?"

"Oh, yes, definitely. Police work, for instance. Medicine. X-rays will still have their place, of course. But in medicine the NMR is soon going to replace the X-ray for most purposes, because it doesn't involve ionizing radiation; X-ray always presents some element of risk. Anyway, a police laboratory, say, can set up an unidentified skull and obtain from it images of scenes that the person actually saw when alive."

"That's spooky. Would you get, maybe, the last thing they saw before they died? Wasn't there some nineteenth-century theory that by photographing a dead person's eyes the image of the last thing they saw in life could be recovered?"

"Yes. There's a Kappling short story about it. But that's all sheer superstition. This is something entirely different."

Not *Kappling,* you numbskull, you mean Kipling. But the word had been so clear and deliberate. Some affected pronunciation? Some in-joke? No one was laughing.

" . . . a thing like this to be acceptable as legal evidence, I wonder."

"I'm no lawyer, but I do know that police all over the country are already trying it out. I think that sooner or later it's bound to be accepted fully. The weight of accumulated evidence is going to silence the objections."

"What objections are there? If you can obtain a good picture, as you say you can, doesn't that prove you're right?"

"Well, a few pretty bright people were worried, at first, when they realized what we were doing. There were arguments that what we were doing could start to unravel the whole fabric of physical reality. There's a kind of resonance factor operating, and the more people you have doing similar experiments—especially on similar subjects—the more likely it seems to be that there will be a concentration, a focusing of the effects of many separate experiments upon one subject.''

''How can that be?''

''We don't know. But if reality can depend in some sense upon human consciousness, then maybe the existence, the form, of an individual human consciousness depends also upon the reality surrounding it. Or the realities, if you prefer.''

''You said there was no harmful radiation, though.''

''Right. All the physical objections have now been pretty well taken care of. The main objection now is to the fact that our best pictures are partially subjective. That is, we obtain the best readings from a human skull when we use another skull, the observer's own, as a kind of resonator.''

''The observer's own skull? Give me that again, will you?''

''All right.'' But there ensued a thoughtful pause. The scientist chewed his mustache.

The host, avoiding dead air time if nothing else, interjected: ''With NMR you *do* project waves of some kind into the body, into whatever's being examined—?''

''Yes. NMR scans are a proven means of probing inside matter. They've been used now for thirty years.''

''And, tell me again, NMR stands for—?''

''Nuclear magnetic resonance. All that we actually project into the body, the specimen, or whatever, is a strong magnetic field. This causes the nuclei of certain atoms inside the specimen to line up in certain ways. Then, when the imposed field is removed, the nuclei flip back again. When a nucleus flips back it emits a trace of radiation that registers on our detectors, and from all these traces our computer can form a picture.''

''No harmful radiation, though.''

The scientist smiled. ''Do you have a sort of a *thing* about radiation?''

''Most people do, these days.''

''Well, no, it's not harmful. Now what we've discovered

is that when the observer's own skull is used as a kind of magnetic resonator, then pictures, images, are actually induced in the observer's own visual cortex. He sees a finer, sharper version of what the computer can otherwise extract from the specimen and put up on a stage in the form of a holographic projection. But we can't yet repeat the results as consistently as we'd like. When you scan a specimen skull more than once, you're likely to get a different picture every time. So the question is, is what the human experimenter claims to see really the same as the blurry picture that the computer puts up on the hologram stage?''

''I wish you could have brought some pictures along to show our audience.''

''By the time I photographed the hologram, and then you ran it through your cameras and so on here, onto their sets at home, they would be seeing a picture of a picture of a not very good picture.''

''Maybe next time?''

''Maybe next time. But as I say, it's not really all that informative when the first image is blurry.''

''And you can't get the same picture twice?''

''The structure of the skull, the specimen, is changed minutely by the very act of reading it. There are various interpretations of why and how this whole thing works at all. It surprised the hell out of a lot of us when we first began to realize what was happening. And even worried a few people, as I say: can time and space become unraveled? Do we tend to get different readings each time because we are reaching for similar atoms, similar skulls, in adjoining universes? The theoretical physicists think it has to do with coupling through electron spin resonance, that's ESR. The ligand field of each particle expands indefinitely, they say now, which is going to open up a whole new field of research.''

''Superhyperfine splitting,'' commented the host, nodding sagely, and got a laugh in the studio. He was obviously harking back to something that had earlier snowed him and the audience as well.

The scientist shook his head and smiled tolerantly. He murmured something that was lost in the subsiding laughter.

"I see," added the host. He continued to nod in a way that meant he had given up on trying to see, especially after that ligand field. "But do you think you'd be able to help the police discover, for instance, who this young woman is whose body came down the Mississippi today? They say she might have been in the water for several weeks. Wearing a yellow bikini and—"

His jerking hand at last found the right switch on the unfamiliar set. The picture died, in an erratically shrinking white dot-spark, that lashed about for a moment as if trying to escape its glassy prison.

The departure of the voices left a hollowness in the air of the dark motel room. Other murmurings came in from other rooms not far away. The carpet under his knees felt rough and dusty. He might have just got up calmly and walked over to the set to turn it off, if he wanted it off. But there had been a bad moment there, bad enough to make him lunge and crawl.

He stood up, stiffly. On the bedside table the bottle waited, hardly started. No. He was all right. No, just a moment of panic there, such as sometimes came when he was drifting off to sleep. He had thought that at last, after months of learning to sleep alone again, he was all through with midnight panics. Just one small sip now, and even without that he was tired enough to sleep. Then, tomorrow, he would drive again. He could drive anywhere he wanted to. Things were all right . . .

In the morning he knew that he was not going to follow the great river north, up to the Great Lakes. Yesterday the plan in the back of his mind, as well as he could remember it, had been to do something along that line. But enough of water, and watery places. He would go on west, and put the big rivers and the lakes behind him.

In Shereveport he sat in a plastic booth, eating plastic-tasting food, and abruptly realizing that in the booth next to him sat two state police officers. Whether it was more nearly impossible that they had already been there, unseen by him, when he sat down, or that they had walked in past him without his knowing it, he couldn't estimate.

". . . she mighta been from way upstream somewheres.

The Doc, he says days in the water. White gal. Just a lil ol bathing suit on. No wounds, nothing like that.''

"Well, the Red can be worse'n the Mississippi even, when it rains enough. It's been like pourin' piss out'n a boot up there in Oklahoma.''

Back in his car, moving on the highway, he realized that somehow he must have paid the restaurant cashier. Otherwise the two state troopers would already be in hot pursuit.

Fifty-five was the law, and maybe in some places they cared about that. But once he got to Texas he felt sure that nobody was going to give a damn. He opened her up.

Greenery and rivers dried up and blew away in the hot wind of his passage. Signs indicated where to turn to get to Midland, Odessa, Corsicana, Nazareth. If a name existed in the universe, if a name was even conceivable, and maybe sometimes if it was not, it could be found somewhere in the vastness of Texas, applied to a small town.

He slept in a motel somewhere, in a room where he turned on no radio or television. And sometime after that he crossed a border that lay invisibly athwart the unfamiliar lunar landscape and found that he was in New Mexico. Maybe he had never come exactly this way before. He couldn't remember things being quite this barren even here.

Signs told him he was nearing Carlsbad. The highway topped a stark rise to disclose an unexpected wall of greenery waiting for him, not far ahead. Pecos River, a small sign added. He drove across a highway bridge over the river, which was for this part of the country so wide and full that he was astonished by it until he saw the dam.

If he tried to go any farther tonight he was going to drive right off the road somewhere in exhaustion. And yet, once settled in the Carlsbad Motel, he couldn't sleep. He had to know first what was happening. No, not quite right. He had to know if he was going to have to admit to himself that something was happening. Maybe he was just going a little crazy from being alone too much in summer heat. If that was all, he should just stay in one cool room for a day and a night and sleep.

He forced himself to turn on the ten PM television news, and he listened to the whole half hour attentively, and there was not a word about drowned bodies anywhere. He started to relax, to feel that whatever had started to happen to him was over. When the news was over, he found a talk show, on another channel that came in by cable from the west coast. Show biz people and famous lawyers sat around a table. During the first commercial he roused himself and went out to get half a pint of good bourbon. To hell with being so careful, you could probably drive yourself crazy that way. Tonight he was going to drink. He had the feeling that things were going to be all right after all.

He thought he had turned off the television set, but the voices were busy when he came back with the whisky. The same host, but evidently a new segment of the show, for the guests were different.

The scientist had no mustache, but he was certainly a scientist, and he even looked a little like that one on the other show. Well-entrenched in the world and imperturbable.

". . . from Cal Tech, going to talk with us a little about nuclear physics, quantum mechanics, the nature of reality, all kinds of good stuff like that there." Laughter in the studio followed, febrile and feeble at the same time, predictable as the outcome of a lab demonstration.

"The nature of reality," said another panelist. "You left that out." But it hadn't been left out. Didn't they even listen to each other's words?

Someone else on the panel said something else, and they all laughed again.

"Speaking of reality, we'll be right back, after this."

The cable brought in a good many channels. Here was Atlanta. Who knew where they all came from? But he knew that he would have to switch back.

". . . pretty well accepted now by everyone in the field that it can't have any effect on the general perception of reality, what people generally experience as reality, no matter how many of these experiments you have going on around the world at the same time, or how many of them are concen-

trated on the same type of subject. The concentration effect,
if there is one, sort of goes off somewhere; we can't even
trace where it goes.''

''You're saying that in effect you fire a volley off over the
fields . . .''

''. . . and it could possibly hit someone, but the chance is
very small.''

''Endor, did you say a moment ago?''

''The Witch of Endor?'' another guest put in, archly, oh
they were sharp out there on the coast, and there was more
reflexive laughter, from people who recognized their cue,
even if they didn't know what they were laughing about.

''ENDOR is an acronym,'' the scientist with no mustache
was explaining, ''for Electron-nuclear double resonance.
You see, it seems now that resonance is set up not only in the
real atoms but in virtual atomic particles in nearby time-
frames. The implications are enormous. Someday, theoreti-
cally, we could each have our own personal universe to carry
around with us, tuned to our own skulls, our own percep-
tions. The original idea was only to measure the hyperfine . . .''

Flying a little high on bourbon now, and getting doses of
jargon like that one, he needed only a few more sips from the
bottle before he drifted off. To wake up, as it seemed, almost
at once, with daylight coming in around the motel drapes.
The air conditioner was humming already, the television had
somehow been turned off. He lay there feeling better than he
had dared to expect. Jargon is the thing, he thought. Jargon is
definitely in. Where the hell have I been the last few days,
anyway? But it seemed to be over now, whatever it had been.

He thought: I'm going to have to have to try to get on some
talk show myself.

Taking his time in the warm morning, he listened without
much apprehension to what scraps of news the radio was
willing to give up. No drowned bodies anywhere. He went
out and breakfasted. As far as he could tell from looking out
across the landscape away from town, he might still have

been in Texas. But in town there were trees, and lawns, though the grass when he looked at it closely was of an unfamiliar variety.

Driving away from the motel, he was still unsure about whether to head north, east, or west. South—Mexico—he didn't want. On impulse he drove a couple of blocks toward the massed trees, the river. Above the dam it looked like an eastern river, wide and full and slow-moving, and there for some distance the banks were lined with expensive-looking houses. There was the sound of a motorboat, and in a moment a crack in the green wall showed a skier passing on the brown water. Nearby was a city park; he entered and drove through it slowly. There was a small sand beach, already in use in the day's heat.

There was also a police car, and a small but steadily growing crowd, fed by running children who were not interested just now in swimming. Between the standing bodies he caught a single glimpse of brown hair, yellow cloth. Bare, tanned arms being worked up and down by arms in blue policeman's sleeves.

He remembered to gas up the car and have the oil checked before heading on west. He was worried. But somehow he didn't seem to be as worried as he ought to be. He had the feeling that he was forgetting, putting behind him, a lot, an awful lot of recent happenings. Nothing essential, though. Excess baggage. Part of the feeling of strangeness was no doubt due to the fact that he was just coming out of a bad time. Even if he hadn't been on good terms with her lately, it was only to be expected that such a loss would leave him in a shocked condition for several weeks. But he was starting to come out of it now.

Later that day, he was almost at Tucson where he realized where he was going.

At home in San Diego, he watched the sun go down into the one great ocean, just as once, long ago, he had watched it rise. On the Atlantic horizon, he could remember, there had been pink-gray nothingness, and then, instantly out of nowhere, a spark. Now at the last instant of sunset the shrinking sun became what looked like that identical same, long-remembered spark. And then, then night.

This house was his, this house right on the beach, only a hundred feet from water at high tide. Decades ago his parents had first rented then bought it, and he had hung onto it as an investment. This afternoon as soon as he got into town he had driven past the place on an impulse. It had looked unoccupied, though he had been sure that it was rented. He was going to have to talk to the agent about that in the morning.

The place had looked completely deserted from the outside, but when he had let himself in with the key he always kept, it was hard to be sure whether it was currently being lived in or not. There were furnishings, not all of them unfamiliar. Pictures on the walls, some of which he could remember.

He turned on a couple of lights after watching the sunset. A little food in the kitchen cabinets, a little in the refrigerator. As if some people might just have moved out, not bothering to take everything or use it up.

He went out again, through the French windows, to sit in a lawn chair on the patio overlooking the sea. The ocean, never quite silent, was now almost invisible in the gathering darkness. The smell of it brought back to him no memories that were peculiar to this place. He had looked at and smelled the sea in too many other, different places for that. The one great ocean that went on and on.

Through low clouds there came suddenly the half-familiar, half-surprising sound of a slow Navy plane from the air station not far away. One of the search and rescue craft, and it sounded like it was heading out. Would they commence a search at night? That seemed unlikely, but there were always new devices, new techniques. Anyway, they wouldn't be using a plane to look for her, she hadn't gone out in a boat. And if they hadn't started to look for her last night, when she walked out, they wouldn't be starting now.

He paused, trying to clear his thoughts. How could they

have started any search last night? He still, up to this minute, hadn't told anyone how she had gone. Not yet . . .

If you can't stand your own life, he had said to her, *then I suggest you put an end to it. I have an interesting life of my own that's going to take all my time.* The room seemed still to echo with the words.

The waves were getting a little louder now, rolling invisibilities up the invisible beach.

He went into the house and turned up the volume of the television slightly; he could not really remember having turned it on. The voices from the talk show came with him as he went outside again, onto the seaward patio. The hyperfine and superhyperfine splittings could now be measured accurately, but that was only the start. Police forces all over the country were using the technique on unidentified bodies every day, with great success. Nobody worried anymore that the technique might offer any danger to the fabric of the world. The implications were really vast. The ligand fields expanded without limit. The voices continued to follow as he opened the gate in the low wall and walked down a slope of sand to meet the still invisible burden of the waves.

ENCASED IN THE AMBER OF TIME

Robert A. Frazier

Snakeskin exfoliations of history
creep back in particle waves like lemmings,
laminating themselves to an ancient artifact
within the golden glowing projection field.
The Arc 9 Rejuvenator can only offer snapshots,
peeks through a keyhole in time,
stage sets for an archaeologist's musings,
relative to the era of its dial's reading.
Shifting the setting once each day,
up and down the harmonic scales of decades,
provides a slide show.
Does the machine physically replicate matter like DNA,
knead time as malleable as potter's clay,
or merely offer a chameleon's illusion?
We do not know,
for no human can cleave to its field;
it runs off like water on a goose's oily down.
But sometimes in the right circumstance,
of light in the desertion of late night,
its inventor sees human wraiths
like pencil smudges
racing forever down the highways of their destinies.

In modern cosmology, time and distance are inextricably entangled. The following tale by Connie Willis is concerned with this fact. Also with the Romser lenses, and the Stories, and the heavy light years; and, in intimate contact with them all, the human heart.

THE CHILD WHO CRIES FOR THE MOON

Connie Willis

Most of the staff blame me. I have never been their favorite patient. My ugliness is an affront to their pretty faces. So is my talent for doing myself in under their very noses. Some of them have nearly lost their jobs over me. I can hear Dr. Ann, trying to sound administrative and calm:

"Isn't it kept locked?"

"Yes, doctor. Of course, doctor."

"And where are the keys?"

"Right here in my pocket, doctor. I swear they never left there. She must have . . .''

"Then would you mind telling me why she's in intensive at this very minute? From now on the silvrynadryl will be in the vault. If you need it, you will go through degreed personnel." It is no wonder they aren't sympathetic. I am doing myself in under their very noses again, and this time they can't stop me.

Nurse Fetter is the worst. Why are guilty people always cruel like that? She has taken to coming in when Ann is asleep, her hands still holding mine. Fetter whispers to me across Ann, "Selfish. Selfish." She sounds a little like my father.

I say coldly, "It is your fault." To get her out of the room. It is her fault. She was not authorized to tell me anything. She should have taken me to my room and then called for Dr. Ann. She knew better than to give any information to somebody like me. I already held some kind of hospital record for

81

suicide attempts. And now I am even more of a celebrity as my heart catches, coughs, and inevitably yields to the crack. They have come up with all so.ts of diagnoses, but the truth is it can't beat properly because it's broken. And who broke it? Nurse Fetter? Dr. Ann?

It hardly matters. Fetter will lose her job when all this is over. Ann has lost hers already. She will not hold case histories in her pretty hands again, tapping her slender finger on a crucial line, saying, "Her comments about her father indicate a deep rejection trauma basic to her self-image." Her hands do nothing now but hold mine.

She doesn't look at me, although as it turns out, I will have a presentable death after all. She looks into her lap or out the window or sometimes at our hands. Even I feel sorry for her.

I can remember her with her pretty hands in her lab coat pockets. Daily session time with me in intensive again for the third time. I had gotten hold of enough silverwine to nearly make it.

"Do you know what I think?" This was her shock question. Her hands were making fists inside the pockets. "I think you don't really want to kill yourself."

It was hard to come up with an answer to that one. I had been brought here after my ninth attempt outside. I had managed to get hold of silverwine three times since then. My success was a hospital disgrace. I waited for more of her peculiar reasoning.

"It's such a slow way to die. And so painful. A real suicide would choose some fast, painless way. Like phedrine maybe. And she'd succeed." Ann is very young. I am her first case and she is making a lot of mistakes. Never give a suicide suggestions.

Anyway, she's wrong about the silverwine. I don't use it because it's slow and painful. I'm not a complete fool. I use it because it's pretty. And that is something Ann, with that face, with those hands, could never understand in two million years.

Do you know the kind of faces people make when they have to look at me? Even the nurses. Even the other patients, who don't look any better than I do. They are disgusted by the sight of me. Do you think I would add exploded brains to the mess? Or streams of staining brown blood? Phedrine kills you fast all right, but your tongue swells and your face turns a nice bloated purple. Are you kidding me? I look bad enough as it is.

Silverwine, on the other hand, is a lovely way to die. The poison starts to glow silver in your veins and you have time to fold your hands on your breast, time to protect your face from showing the pain that is coming. It's easy to get, too. The mental hospitals can't do without it. They call it the sanity drug. In little doses it's lethal against paranoia. But too much of the truth can kill you, so they sell it on the streets to those of us who need it. Silverwine, the pretty poison.

I didn't tell her that, of course. It was my policy not to tell her anything. She didn't mean it about the suicide anyway. She was just trying to get me angry enough to talk to her. I looked up at her and smirked. "I don't know, silverwine's just *me*, I guess. What's your favorite method of suicide, doctor?" Her hands clenched and unclenched in the pockets. In those days it didn't occur to me to take pity on her.

"I am going to try a Story on you," she said angrily. "I don't know what else to do." It was two weeks later. Still in intensive, and I had done it again. With silverwine.

Her voice had been soft at the beginning of the session, and the hands out of the pockets, gently entreating. "Why do you keep trying to kill yourself?"

"I'll bet it's because I want to die."

"And why do you want to die?"

She had put me through this three times in one week, and I didn't feel like playing anymore. "You know why."

"Because you're ugly."

"See!" I said triumphantly. "Even you admit it. Only that's a very unethical practice, telling the patient the truth. Didn't they teach you that in medical school? If you tell a suicide the truth, it may just kill her."

"Do you want to hear the truth?" Her hands were on my shoulders, shaking me. "Do you? All right. Here is the truth.

You are sixteen years old and it is not too late to change things.''

"Look, doctor dear, next time you catch me with the silverwine, why don't you both save us a lot of trouble? Why don't you just give me a little more time? That's the problem with silverwine. I never have quite enough time.''

Oh, can you hear me saying that? I never had any time at all. My father was right. He read his newspaper and didn't look at me. He didn't have to look. Me with my little suitcase in my hand, fresh from the Mayo Clinic, covered with all sorts of beneficial new scar tissue. Still ugly.

"We will try something new," Mama said, desperately. "There's a new place in Rio.''

My father rattled his newspaper and said, in the flat voice that takes on depth and muddiness with every year till I can no more see through it than through a phial of silverwine, "It's too late.''

I stood there, suitcase and scars. Seven years old.

Surely he did not say that. Surely the rustling paper blurred the words some way. But Mama's voice was clear. "We must not abandon hope.''

Her choice of words was perfect. Because I had already entered the gates of hell and could speak with the authority of one inside. Oh, Mother, people don't abandon hope. They are abandoned by it. Without warning.

I used to hate my mother for hoping. For Rio and Phoenix and all the rest of it. But I was wrong about her. She never really had any hope at all. When I told her that I was quitting school, not going to any more clinics, that I was giving up, she said, "You have broken my heart.''

"How idiotic, mother," I said. "Hearts don't break.''

When she found me with the silverwine that last time, already nearly gone, she stood for a long time by my bed before she called my father. It was him that called the hospital.

I didn't try silverwine for nearly two years after I quit school, even though I knew about it. Oh, no, for two years I went to the movies and sat in the dark and ate popcorn. Dr.

Ann calls that self-destructive behavior. Maybe she's right. It was stupid to hope in the first place. I should have started on the silverwine immediately. But I hadn't given up hope, and it was dark in the movies, and nobody could see my face.

"It's dark in your room at home." Therapy session nine. Patient's childhood experiences.

"I didn't have a popcorn machine in my room."

"But why the movies? What did you think you'd find there?"

"I told you. Popcorn."

"Did you think you would be beautiful some day like the people on the screen?"

Are you kidding me? I could see the handwriting on the wall when I was seven years old. I didn't understand why then, but I would have had to be an idiot not to see that I'd been born at the wrong time. Not to see that everybody was obsessed with physical beauty and that there was no place right then for even a moderately homely child, let alone a real disaster like me. When I got older I thought it was because of the competition man was up against, that the Romser lenses were the reason for my being miserable. I was still wrong, but I was getting warmer.

We used a set of Romser lenses once in second grade to look at subatomics. The teacher said they were a fluke discovery, that we were terribly lucky to have made because now we didn't have to ever worry about magnification again. Actually, we had a lot of other things to worry about, but probably she didn't know about them either. Their use was closely regulated, so closely in fact that I had never seen a Story until the one Dr. Ann used. I didn't know that there was a time when they had all been watching Stories, when they had showed them in the movies to audiences as grateful for the dark as I was.

I used to think people made up those awful stories about monsters in outer space to scare themselves. When I found out what the Romser lenses had done I decided people liked the universe that way, full of tentacles and bugging eyes so that man would come off looking good. That wasn't the way the universe was. It was full of rainbow people, flower people, creatures with skin like watered silk and golden eyes. Man looked like something that had just crawled out from under a rock, peering eagerly at the beautiful people through his telescope. Just like me at the movies.

I figured that was why they restricted the use to mental hospitals and scientific laboratories. They didn't like looking at them. They liked being the fairest one of all, so they locked up the Romser films in good old government controls and went on pretending they were, that that whole universe of beautiful people wasn't even out there. Defense mechanism, I figured Dr. Ann would call it. She'd tell me how I was a threat to it because I represented man's real subconscious image of himself. She'd explain the emotional reasons for the cosmetic surgery clinics and the mirrors on every floor of the hospital and why it was so hard to be ugly just now. Well, if she knew so much about it, why didn't she just stand there like my mother and watch while the silverwine made me pretty for just a little while. If she knew so much about it, why couldn't she figure out my defense mechanisms? Why couldn't she figure out that I went to the movies to find somebody to love me?

I went to the movies for two years, and only once did I even come close. The movies were a poor excuse for beauty after the Romsers. I didn't know that until I saw the Story, of course, but even I could see that they went for the cheap, flashy effect. Sequins on everything, costumes that would blind you, plastic sets. Only once in a great while did the movies come up with something truly beautiful. When they did I was caught off guard, vulnerable, my heart lying carelessly in the aisle to be stepped on. Like now.

They were doing something about young lovers, a dark blue twilight sky with little light bulb stars, a lavender hill, I had seen it all before. But I was not prepared for what came next. The moon walked slowly over the blue arch of sky, a lady in a white dress and silver shoes. I half-rose in my chair, half-started for the screen. They did a full shot of her face, a face that would wither somebody like me to nothing, and I sat down again and put my coat over my face.

I had gotten an idea that I found I could not shake afterwards, not even to get at whatever the Story was supposed to be telling me. I don't think I thought the moon was a beautiful lady who would save me. It was not that simple. It was an idea that came from the little that I knew about Romser lenses and all the silly romantic movies I had watched and the way my face hurt when people looked at me on the street. Somewhere, I thought, somewhere in all that beautiful universe is a lady like that, distant and kind as the moon, who will look at me as you look at an oddly-shaped shell, and think, "How pretty, how strange!"

You can see I had not exactly given up hope, Dr. Ann. I only took the silverwine because I did not think I would ever find the moon.

I didn't tell Ann that charming little heartbreaker. Would it have helped if I had? She was very young and I was her first case and she was making a lot of mistakes. Could she have put that story about the moon and my ignorance of the universe together and said, "Not this one." Would she have pressed her fragile fingertips together and decided against a Story altogether? It doesn't matter. I didn't tell her. So she said, all unknowing, "You are scheduled for tomorrow morning." And I went, all unknowing, to my death.

I thought until I saw one that the Stories must be some kind of galactic Rorschach, with everything so alien that we would see inkblots and make them into ourselves. They are more like a bright dream that you accept, no matter how strange it seems, so long as you are in it.

You cannot hear anything, of course. There are subtitles, but those are the names of the characters written below so that in therapy you can say, "I would have loved Eajiph. Why did he go away?" Subtitles and screen and curtain. No popcorn, but anybody who had been to the movies as much as I had can recognize a movie. I had gone to the movies to find somebody so far away that they could love me. And here was the movie.

Dr. Ann could not have chosen worse if she had tried. Dark blue sky and stars that were not light bulbs, everything. Even the moon. It was a creature in a white dress and silver

shoes. Afterwards I couldn't remember what name they had
printed under her silver feet for therapy. She was the moon.
She turned her head toward the camera and raised her hand,
and oh, she was made of glass! She splintered the twilight
and the glitter of the early stars like crystal. My heart
stopped, and then started again in light breathless beats.

She was holding out her hand to someone at the edge of the
forest. A dark forest where no light would come, I thought,
as dark as a movie house. He stood in it, and I read the
subtitle before I even saw him. Eajiph. He took a step
forward out of the shadow toward the light of the girl. He was
ugly. Jagged and dark as the stones you pick up on cold days
and skip across the water. Slate perhaps, solid and beautiful
to the touch. He was ugly and not ugly. Did I think he could
love me because of that? Did I think because I thought,
"How beautiful," standing on the edge of my own dark
forest, that he would think the same of me? Ann would have a
fancy name for it. Rejection fantasy maybe. I didn't care. I
had gone to the movies to find somebody to love me. And
here was the movie. And here was Eajiph.

He took another step toward the moon, a faltering step, as
if he was afraid she would put up that crystal hand to stop
him. But she was holding it out to him. I can see that, the
small transparent hand, the white sleeve falling down and
away from the diamond wrist in angled softness. An offer of
beauty, of love, of everything. That image is strongest of all.
"Take it," I whispered. "'Take her hand."

He turned and walked back into the forest. I started after
him, my hand outstretched. "Eajiph!" I said aloud,
"Eajiph, no, wait!"

Nurse Fetter heard that. I had my hand out to an empty
screen. There was a whirr of rewinding. "Eajiph!" I yelled,
and then sat down again. I could not be hysterical or Fetter
would not tell me anything. She had to tell me where the
Story was from. She had to tell me so I could go find Eajiph
before it was too late, before he was lost in that dark forest. I
needed to get to him and take his hand and show him that
somebody loved him. Surely after the Romsers had shown

the scientists the beauty out there they had built spaceships to get to it. I would have to buy a ticket. I would have to tell my father so he would give me the money. I would have to tell him some way so he would not think I was buying silverwine with it, so he would not say, "too late" and rustle his newspaper. I would have to convince Dr. Ann that I was all right so I could get out to go see my father.

Dr. Ann was in emergency. Nurse Fetter came to tell me that and take me back to my room.

"Wait, please," I said. "Please tell me about the Stories."

She looked frightened. Never tell a suicide anything.

"I thought it was wonderful. It made me want to get well, just seeing it. But my doctor isn't here, and I'm afraid I'll forget my questions before the therapy session."

"We can show it again," she said. "I've showed that one lots of times."

"Where's it from?"

"Oh, I don't know the names of all those places. Clear out of the galaxy. Andromeda, I think."

It is not so much losing him. Can you really imagine me in a spaceship with my suitcase on my lap and the dark stars flashing past the horrible face I have pressed to the glass? Me at seven. Flying down to Rio. What hurt the worst was being caught, after so much careful building up of scar tissue out of the open wound of my face, totally vulnerable. To find that hearts do break is bad enough, but who would have thought I would be so stupid as to leave mine lying there for anyone to step on.

The staff is not sorry I'm dying. Why should they be? Who is ever really touched by the child who cries for the moon? "You can't have it and that's that," Nurse Fetter said when she saw my face go blank with the shock of what she had told me. "There's no good crying about it."

I don't cry. I did at first, even though the tears made my face red and swollen. I don't know what my face looks like now. There are no mirrors. They say that Ann went out and smashed all the mirrors on the floor. I can believe that.

The first thing she said, coming in to Nurse Fetter's alarm, was, blankly, "What happened?" And then, shaking poor guilty frightened Fetter, "What happened?"

But she already knew from the first sight of me, crushed and dying. She knows everything she will know: that the Story destroyed me, that it was somehow a mistake, a terrible, fatal mistake. That she has, after all these patient months of rescuing my life, led me to my death. "What did you do to her?" she yelled at Fetter.

She told me the truth. Too much truth can kill you, Dr. Ann. I had it all wrong. Man didn't put the Romser lenses away because he hated the universe, but because he loved it. Just like me. He packed his suitcases of desire and started off in all directions, too. But there was no place to go. All he could hear, over the muddy rustling of the newspaper, was, "Too late."

"Andromeda?" I said to Nurse Fetter. "Where is it?"

"You have to keep in mind that the Romser lenses are only a camera, of course. It doesn't matter where things are, you just point it at them and that's what you see. But it can only photograph the light that hits the lenses, and light only travels at a certain speed. Light years. You know about those, I suppose."

I shook my head.

"That's how far light can travel in a year. It took that Story there two million years to get here from Andromeda."

I am not listening. "How can I get there?"

"Why would you want to go there, even if you could?"

"To see . . . all those beautiful people made of glass, of course. How can I get there?"

"It took that light two million years to get here. All those people are dead. They have been for two million years. And there's nothing closer in, don't think they haven't tried. Just think, a whole beautiful universe that we can see but that isn't really there. All those beautiful people, dead and gone."

Long dusty ages ago Eajiph turned and lost himself in the dark forest. Abandoned by hope as all of us are here. There is no such thing as a light year. They are heavy, heavy. They descend upon the heart with the weight of planets. I am dying, Eajiph, dying, and you were always dead. Even silverwine didn't hurt as much as this.

Too much truth can kill you, Dr. Ann, didn't you know that? No, of course not, young and pretty and your first patient. How would you know that? Listen, someday you'll have patients again, and I really hope they're better than I was and tell you things and not die like I did. But don't make the same mistakes with them. Don't tell them it isn't too late unless you know for sure what you're talking about, and don't show them Stories that look like movies they saw when they were younger, and don't show them Stories about somebody who could love them, because they might, if they're really stupid, think they had a chance and they just get their hearts broken and it gives the hosptial a terrible reputation. It would help your patients if you weren't so beautiful, too, but I know you can't help that. You can't help anything, sitting there holding onto my hands for dear life, least of all me.

I know you'd have some fancy name for what happened to me if you weren't so upset. I know you'd be able to figure out why I forgot the moon's name and saw only Eajiph and why I thought he'd love me when it was the girl he was supposed to love and why I was so sure he'd be able to take my hand and not hers and what the hands meant, and whether after all they could have saved him.

Your hands do not seem to be saving me. What was I supposed to see in the story, dear Dr. Ann? Whose hand was I supposed to take? And how come the moon, distant and beautiful and kind, how come she looked just like you?

*How does one deal with the new problems brought on by a
new probing of the past? It is only to be expected that some of
these difficulties will be very grim. And others not what one
expects at all.*

GRAIN OF TRUTH

Charles Spano, Jr.

Klaus Memorial Primate Research Center
April 1, 1990

My dear sister Virginia,

I want to thank you for the wonderful week you allowed
me at your home last month. Your cooking is truly delightful;
Mother would have been pleased. I can only hope my
brother-in-law appreciates what a fine woman you are. On
the subject of him, dear sister, please accept my apologies for
the scene at the table. It was rude of me to call him a mentally
undisciplined, credulous cretin.

I make no apologies for my position, however, and you
must understand that. Easter bunnies, fairies, leprechauns
and UFO's (it makes my pressure rise just to write these
words!) are utter bunk and wish my nephew and niece
weren't exposed to such sloppy thinking!

I am glad our mutual inheritance makes us more able than
the average to see through that trash.

Anyway, Virginia, my main reason for writing is to give
you some good news. Remember that proposal I told you I
was presenting to the Director? Well, they approved it!

Tonight I pack and tomorrow I shall be going to the Brooks
Range in Alaska to choose sites. The expedition will follow
next week. It was tough getting them to go along with the
idea that if ancient man crossed the Bering Strait some groups
may have adapted to the environment and left traces, perhaps

near extinct volcanoes. The data from the Burmese ape find in '79 was what convinced them, I'm sure.

I'm off then and will be incommunicado for some time. I'll send the children something.

Your brother,
Josh

VIDEOFAX INSTAMESSAGE—VIDEOFAX INSTAMESSAGE—VIDEOFAX INSTAMESSAGE
subsidiary of Western Union
Anchorage, Alaska

31 May 1990
Ginny

Great news made find stop Pithicene skull type with flesh adhering stop New species says anthropologist As geneticist have brilliant idea good for Nobel at least end

Josh

Klaus Memorial Primate Research Center
June 4, 1990

Dear Virginia,

By now you've no doubt seen all the media coverage of our find but there is one thing we did not release which I alluded to in my previous letter (by the way, I hope you don't mind my using 'Ginny', I was very excited. Still am.).

My idea hit me as soon as I saw that flesh. If you remember what I told you when I saw you last, I've been pushing recombinant DNA techniques to their limits. I've always felt like a fifth wheel here at Klaus being a geneticist among so many non-geneticists that I had to have something to do with my time.

I've gotten terrific results with plasmid splicing and production of very long synthetic DNA. Fragments so far, but

I've worked out a technique to make a full chain of DNA that won't break up.

You're probably ahead of me now. Yes, I intend to use my techniques to reproduce the DNA in that frozen flesh. I will implant the molecule into a chimpanzee ovum and in a few months the first borealipithicene in half a million years will again walk the earth.

We haven't released that bit of news because if the experiment fizzles the Director doesn't want the Center embarrassed. I think he was never happy with me and is a little leery of my project.

When we dug up that Northern ape skull we found a lot of grains and spores. The biologists and climatologists are reconstructing the Alaskan environment from them as it must have been back then.

We plan to build a compound here to house the creatures and study them. Obviously the scientific data will be tremendous and I see myself picking up a Nobel in less than the usual time.

I'll stop now. I have a lot of work to do just identifying the fragments of DNA and attempting to learn their proper order before I let the *E. coli* do their work. Write soon.

Your brother,
Josh

Klaus Memorial Primate Research Center
July 4, 1990

Dear Virginia,

It's good to hear from you again. I'm glad the children liked the books on Alaskan geohistory and biology but they really should read them not just look at the pictures. I did not send any totem poles as you wrote me they asked about because you know very well what my feelings are about such fetishes. Mere artifacts of superstition.

Speaking of superstition, I suppose I should offer congratulations to your husband on his doctorate in comparative social belief. I suppose it did involve some work on his part but I fail to comprehend the nature of the subject.

We're making excellent progress on the DNA synthesis. The *coli* are having no trouble at all producing the proper links in the proper order and we shall soon have a large amount of viable DNA ready for implantation. As for creatures, plural, which I did mention in my last letter, as you've guessed, I've managed to alter the sex of the original sample.

It was a brilliant inductive effort on my part, if I do say so myself, and I'll send you the reports since you're interested. Our first sample was female, by the way, which made it easier to convert the sex though with additional effort a male could have been converted with my technique.

I have to close now, my assistant just called me into the lab. They've found something unusual in the gene makeup they say but if they've fouled up I'll have their heads.

Brother Josh

Klaus Memorial Primate Research Center
July 20, 1990

Dear Virginia,

I suppose I should have expected you and your husband to discuss what I've been telling you ahead of the mass media consumers but I really must ask that he not worry over such sentimental considerations such as fairness to our growing subjects. Fairness doesn't enter into it at all. This is scientific research of the highest order. We will learn what one form of early man was like. It will revolutionize thinking!

If he needs assurance then let him know that our experts will make every effort to simulate the Alaskan environment of five hundred millenia ago and the boreals will have no contact with our civilization. Our monitors are quite well hidden.

Corrupt them, indeed! And another thing, though I did not mean to imply interest in comparative social belief, I am grateful for the dissertations your husband sent me.

Jungian Archetypes in Selected Episodes of Laverne and Shirley; A Comparative Analysis of the Evolution and Characteristics of Demons of Polynesia and North European Little People; Quantification of Belief Incidence in Extrapolation of Afternoon Videocast Personae; and his own, and of course my favorite, *The Correlation of Cognitive Structures, Belief, and the Prevailing Personification of Santa Claus!*

He sounds a bit conservative to me there! Who would have suspected it! I got great amusement from them and it broke the tension and excitement of our latest discovery which I referred to last time.

The boreals have extra chromosomes (the DNA has been dividing nicely but were checking it out before implanting) and our early results indicate some unusual abilities. I'll let you know more later.

Your brother,
Josh

P.S. Watch the videocast this weekend. I'm on "Science Speaks" and the Director has consented to let me hint about our work.

Josh

Klaus Memorial Primate Research Center
October 1, 1990

Dear Virginia,

I must apologize for not having written sooner but as you may surmise the reaction to my appearance last July was astounding! We've had to triple the guard and the State Police are having a hard time with tourists.

It occurs to me that some people still are attracted to the lure of good science and haven't been swept up in this end of the millenia hysteria. I also think those dissertations are a sad indication of imminent breakdown and I certainly hope you are not letting your husband infect my dear niece and nephew with his ridiculous ideas about belief making reality. It's as if he were saying wishes come true when, manifestly, they do not. Please, Virginia, stand as a bulwark for rationality in your own family. But enough of that. I'm sure I can count on you.

Our boreals are progressing very well. We implanted the ova with the fully assembled DNA by the end of July. The chimpanzee host-mothers are doing excellently. We were worried for a while about primitive hormones being produced which would terminate the host-mothers but that problem seems to have never existed, the placental filtration is better than modern females, or so our obstetrician thinks. I feel there has been a slight devolution in filtration quality, therefore, as witness the harmful things which pass to embryos.

The obstetrician also believes the boreals will be born very soon. An evolved survival trait, no doubt. Rapid fetal growth and early birth leading to higher population would help insure survival especially in the northern environment which by the way is finished. It is cold in there!

The chromosomes you asked about in your August letter carry, I think, instinctive patterns which we as later evolved beings have naturally lost. We'll see in six weeks which is the time left before birth.

Your brother,
Josh

P.S. I have it on good authority from a friend of mine on the Nobel committee that if this project succeeds the committee will consider speeding up the awarding process for me, possibly in as little as two years.

Josh

Klaus Memorial Primate Research Center
November 6, 1990

Dear Virginia,

Great news! They're born! Twenty-four healthy boreals,
twelve of each sex, averaging four kilos with two, a male and
female, hitting close to five kilos. They will be the dominant
members of the troop obviously. Have to go.

                                              Brother Josh

                    Klaus Memorial Primate Research Center
                                        November 8, 1990

Dear Virginia,

I have more time today. I wrote my last letter at 2:30 A.M.
as the boreals were being born. You will get a chance to see
them in a day or so after we're certain they're fit in all
respects but I shall describe them to you so you are ahead of
the mass media.

Each borealipithicene looks much like the representations
of australopithicene. They have a chunky torso with a good
deal of fat covering the abdomen, short sturdy legs and apish
arms. They are covered with long smooth reddish-brown fur
fringed with white at anatomically significant areas: hands,
feet and waist.

Their faces are smooth-skinned and round as are their
heads. At the rate their brains are developing they will
average 1000 ccs, one-third more than the australs but of
course these are a different species. Their faces are fringed
with white, too, looking much like beards. They have a
topknot of reddish fur ending in white that grows fairly long
in the two largest but much less in the rest. Obviously a sign
of dominance. Their feet are black and smooth-skinned on
top but roughly calloused on the sole and layered with fat.

Even in their extreme youth they seem very friendly,
peering around with bright brown eyes. We expect they
won't grow over one and a half meters tall, if that much.
They will be let into their environment before the videocast
and we will feed the pickup right onto the network and cable
hookups.

This is reality, Virginia, not that speculative nonsense your husband teaches. Share this with him, by all means, and I would be very interested to know his reaction. Perhaps it will wake him up.

Your brother,
Josh

Klaus Memorial Primate Research Center
November 23, 1990

Dear Virginia,

What nerve! So your husband thinks I don't sound much like a "stuffed shirt". Much! I am a scientist. I see things logically, using inductive reasoning from the evidence before my senses. If I have no patience with your husband's brand of nonsense, it is because there isn't any evidence for it.

If he shows me properly verified and verifiable evidence for his fairies and elves and ghosts and whatnot then I shall consider it. Naturally, such proof is impossible. And as for his contention that all legends and social fables or myths have some basis in reality, a grain of truth, I say it is impossible to show without ambiguity any connection. The same with that ancient astronauts stuff back in the sixties and seventies, remember?

Take the boreals, for example. I had solid bases for speculating on their existence. Investigation proved me right.

Speaking of the boreals, we put them into their environment a few days ago and they are thriving. Their intelligence is totally unexpected for brains that small. One of my assistants believes they use more of their brain capacity than we moderns do. With the evidence of your husband and his ilk, I'm inclined to agree.

They forage very efficiently on the short grain-like plants we found buried with them and they get along very well with the caribou.

One will approach a caribou and sit down in a direct line with its vision. They will stare at each other unmoving for a few minutes then, amazingly, the caribou will let the boreal milk it!

Then they do something unbelievable if you haven't seen it (and we'll have to videocast that!), they mix the milk with pounded grain and cook it! That's right, they have fire. I believe it's some ancestral memory locked in the genes of the sample we found in the Brooks Range. It was in a volcano's cave after all, as I had suspected there may have been traces.

The food they make is flat and round. One of my technicians was so carried away with that discovery that she crept into the environment after the troop was asleep and took a sample. She also discovered something we had not seen. The boreals make cups out of small branches woven together with caribou fur and lined with clay. They drink caribou milk from those cups. That find is the only reason I didn't fire that technician, it shows advanced toolmaking ability.

Oh, one other thing, the technician tasted the bread-like food and said it was like an oatmeal cookie. I tasted a bit but find no such similarity. Subjective reports make poor science anyhow.

These boreals constantly move. They look very heavy with their abdominal bulges of fat but they move with characteristic primate agility. The smaller ones seem to do the bidding of the larger but that must be due to the dominance factor though we have never observed any fighting or even dominance displays. They seem a completely peaceful, gentle race. I find it calming to watch them after a hard day.

Your brother,
Josh

Klaus Memorial Primate Research Center
November 30, 1990

Dear Virginia,
I must protest! Your husband completely misunderstood my last sentences in my previous letter.

I was not reporting scientific data as such but merely remarking on the quality of the lives of boreals. It had no real effect on me. I only meant after struggling with incompetents and hassling with the Director that it was pleasant to watch a cooperative society.

By the way, does your husband know any of the staff here? One of my assistants made a strange remark yesterday that sounded as if your husband could have written it. I overheard the assistant mumble some nonsense about how "elfin" the boreals look. I made certain he would think twice before ever saying something like that again. Elfin! Bah!

The boreals continue to thrive and have extended their toolmaking behavior. Several of them weave small pouches of moss, caribou fur and tiny feathers from the birds we placed inside. They forage berries and crush them to make a crude dye and smear it on the pouches. They make use of the snow to get different shades of dye. It is fascinating to watch. They are demonstrating highly advanced techniques. Several ethologists have remarked how similar the boreals' behavior is to much modern day activities. I can't accept that, not fully. I believe our science has placed us several notches above the boreals as has our technology. I think we've left their culture behind as well.

I'll be busy the next few days. The boreals are demonstrating new behavior even more complex. I must go.

Your brother,
Josh

Klaus Memorial Primate Research Center
December 6, 1990

Dear Virginia,

Why is it every time I respond to one of your letters I must include some reaction to your husband? It's getting to be annoying beyond tolerance. I will not even comment on his analysis of the boreals, their markings and their behavior. What does he know? Imagine believing the boreals are the true basis for the . . . no, I can't even write it! I will not

show the Director, either. And he better not write to the
Director and tell him what he thinks, though thinks is too
strong a word for what your husband does. I will not put up
with that humiliation.

Furthermore, not even the latest behavior can be twisted to
fit your husband's . . . analysis, for want of a more accurate
word.

The gift-giving behavior they now show is quite common
to certain species of penguins in the Antarctic. The boreals
have a refinement. They place small "gifts" of food or
woven dyed fur into the small pouches and they give them to
each other. The two largest, now almost fully grown, have
made a very large sack and pile the majority of the "gifts"
into it. I believe this was common among larger troops
though this group of boreals isn't aware they are the only
troop.

The big ones also seem to be able to dominate the caribou
and have even tamed eight. They (the two boreals) lead the
caribou around with long woven reins. The boreal troop
guards the herd but naturally there are no predators.

I am puzzled by one thing though. The boreals don't seem
to have a language though, as I've said before, they do
communicate. They stare into each other's eyes and some
message passes. The same technician who took the cookies
and milk claims one of their genes gave them extrasensory
perception.

There is a degree of evidence for ESP, I know, but it is so
sketchy. Of course, there are those extra genes which we
have lost.

There have been unexplained movements in the environment which this same technician claims could be evidence of
telekinesis. Several huge boulders have been moved and
muscle mass calculations we've made show the boreals
couldn't have lifted them. There aren't any drag marks so the
caribou didn't help, either. We will test them by putting a
large wall in the middle of their camp tonight. I'll hold off on
this letter until after that so I can tell you about the results.

December 7, 1990: It must be true, though I can hardly
believe it! What a shock it is to see how they surprised us. We

placed the partition late last night and left the video cameras recording. They jumped over the wall! Incredible. They went straight up at least thirty feet, as high as an average house. We're not certain really if they all have this ability because it was the tall male who went over the wall carrying his share of the smaller ones. The visual evidence shows he apparently stimulated a growth on the side of his nose. We think it may be similar to electric sensing organelles in sharks. This calls for great investigation.

I'll write as soon as I can.

Your brother,
Josh

Klaus Memorial Primate Research Center
December 20, 1990

Dear Virginia,

Did you see it? Did you see that nauseating videocast yesterday? That sentimental fool of a reporter. I wonder why the Director let him in? Do you think it's true that some vidcasters pay for transmission rights to news events? Ugly thought. The things he said were utterly revolting.

"Cute elfin creatures" "Giving gifts out of peace and charity" ". . . with their holiday fur coats and swinging tassled caps and jolly round bellies just as"—no, I won't write it. You heard it. Rather, I hoped you were spared the trauma. Did your husband have anything to do with that script? I was so sickened I couldn't finish watching. Did he? It sounded like some nonsense he would dream up. Totally contrary to all our evidence and interpretations.

The only thing that idiot got right was the fact that the boreals are up to something. For the last few weeks they have been working ever harder on their, well, I won't call them gifts anymore, let's say their courtship offerings which is much closer to the truth anyhow. The large male has a bulging sack of offerings which is natural. Curiously, the smaller males have given him an equal share of offerings.

Another curious fact is the lack of sexual distinction among the small boreals as compared to the larger two who are easily distinguished. Could we have erred in making two sexes? It doesn't seem possible.

We'll have to get tissue samples soon and analyze them. There may be some genetic changes which will explain the sex and size discrepancy.

Your brother,
Josh

Klaus Memorial Primate Research Center
December 23, 1990

Dear Virginia,

They do talk! At least they make noises. Late last night I was observing them. I'm sure they didn't know I was there though the big male gave me the feeling he was looking right at me and winking at me, too.

I saw their mouths moving and turned up the volume on the output panel. We had it low but audible in case they ever made noise. Now, I heard it.

They sat in a circle, legs crossed and hands together. A peculiar sound came out of them like a deep throated grunting or coughing sound. The big male led them and it sounded as if he was clearing his throat.

I played the tape back later that day and that same technician made the absurd suggestion that they were laughing.

Virginia! The Director just was in my office and showed me an "analysis" sent to him, directly to him, by your husband! I thought I asked you to not allow him to do that!

What an embarrassment. I had all my reports laid out and was organizing them for the conference in January where I will spell out all our findings and here the Director shows me this ten page package of drivel that I'm supposed to acknowledge in some way.

I tell you I almost laughed in the Director's face. I did repudiate your husband's puerile assertion that the borealipithicene represents the grain of truth in the Santa Claus tale. I will not defend that nor will I acknowledge it!

Josh

Klaus Memorial Primate Research Center
Office of the Director
December 24, 1990

Dear Ms. Santonicoli,

I am writing to inform you that your brother, Dr. Joshua Hand, was taken ill early this morning though he is in no danger now. He told me he has written to you many times of his work here so I feel it incumbent on me to inform you of the circumstances of his collapse.

It was his habit of late to rise about midnight and check on the borealipithicene compound. This morning he did so and what he found was shocking. Indeed, it shocked everyone though our youngest staffers made the quickest recovery.

You see, the boreals have vanished. The domed roof of the environmental compound was shattered though no one heard any noise.

The only things missing beside the roof and the boreals were the eight small caribou over which they had apparently had some control.

We tried to find out if your brother had seen anything but all he said was "He can't be right. Ho, ho, ho."

We're not sure if that means anything and if you can help us we will pay all your expenses down here.

We are beginning a search for the boreals but have no leads. Our best guess is that they are heading North.

Oh, by the way, is your husband free to address our conference next month? His paper was most enlightening.

Season's Greetings,
Peter C. Plummer, Director

The short story of less than a thousand words has long been an especially powerful science fiction mode, despite the fact that in such small compass the writer must create—or at least convincingly suggest—a whole world alien to the reader's experience. The hands of Steve Rasnic Tem have here produced one of the best examples that I can remember reading in a long, long time.

FORWARD

Steve Rasnic Tem

"Susa, Memphis, Athens may crumble: but an ever more highly organized awareness of the universe is passed on from hand to hand and increases with each successive stage in clarity and brilliance."

—Pierre Teilhard de Chardin

1   The sun was hot; it rained every day. He discovered that hard stone was better for tearing the hide of the large gray leaper. He dimly remembered a time when the leaper had been a brother to him, when his hands and legs had been closer to his thinking, and he hadn't been so alone. He raised the hard stone, began pounding the meat.

2   Rome's soldier was nearing his spot behind the tree. He hefted the shaft of his spear. When the soldier was only a foot or so away he leapt in front of the startled man, plunging the shaft into his abdomen. He tightened the grip with his hands, and pushed. He was fascinated by the look of the soldier, his face betraying surprise, then a sense of loss shared only between the two of them. He prodded the body with his foot when it fell, got down on his knees and rifled the clothing with trembling hands.

3 He leapt out of the foxhole, suddenly realizing his foolishness, and wanting to dive back in. But the German was on him at once. He barely had time to squeeze off one shot with his cold-numbed finger. The corpse knocked him back into the hole, and lay on him, pressing the side of his face, his hands into the mud.

4 The enemy had broken through into sector seven. He pushed Y-7, R-9, Q-5-20. Red switch. Green switch. Yellow. A haze of dots washed over the blips on the screen. When it passed, most of the blips had disappeared. He clenched and unclenched his wet hands.

5 He opened his hands as wide as possible, stretching thumbs and little fingers painfully. He danced them about the shimmering column of heat in proscribed movements. He watched his middle fingers, dipping them carefully into their proper, invisible positions. The complex rose on plasteel shafts, iridescent ramps, corruscating lines. At the end of the day he collapsed in exhaustion, but the city was done.

6 The man in the multi-layered robe clapped his hands once, twice, then floated two feet off the floor. He waved a hand to his pupils, and one, now three, now a dozen were following him out of the opening in the middle of the ceiling. The sun was warm that day, so several pulled on their hoods.

7 The complex of circuits was light in his palm. He examined it gingerly. Under the scanner it was a seamless piece, both inside and out. To the untrained eye it appeared to be nothing more than an ordinary stone.

8 He stroked her cheeks lightly with his fingertips, whispering the syllables low, and without hurry. She began to growl, then mewl, then emitted a sharp rasping sound. Her eyelids were fluttering. She was a bird now, wondering what could be holding her down.

9 It is hot today; it has rained every day for months. He slides down the hard edge of rock, landing on two feet, then four points. Looking out on the plain he spies more movements of himself. The grass is low. The plain is almost empty except for distant stone ridges. He yawns and stretches back

into dust that also seems himself. He is content to be cat, bovine, grass, and sun. His hands sleep when he sleeps. They grow larger in his dreams, become flatlands, streams, and mountain where animals hide, deeply within themselves.

I've been told that people who write grim, mean stories may give no indication of that fact in their personal demeanor. Ed Bryant is a gentleman from Colorado, a frequent toastmaster and master of ceremonies at science fiction conventions, a literate and witty speaker, and a fine young writer. He looks nothing at all like a shark.

The human feeling of this story, above and beyond its sense of brooding menace, is what really sold me on it.

STRATA

Edward Bryant

Six hundred million years in thirty-two miles. Six hundred million years in fifty-one minutes. Steve Mavrakis traveled in time—courtesy of the Wyoming Highway Department. The epochs raveled between Thermopolis and Shoshoni. The Wind River rambled down its canyon with the Burlington Northern tracks cut into the west walls, and the two-lane blacktop, U.S. 20, sliced into the east. Official signs driven into the verge of the highway proclaimed the traveler's progress:

DINWOODY FORMATION
TRIASSIC
185-225 MILLION YEARS

BIG HORN FORMATION
ORDOVICIAN
440-500 MILLION YEARS

FLATHEAD FORMATION
CAMBRIAN
500-600 MILLION YEARS

The mileposts might have been staked into the canyon rock under the pressure of millennia. They were there for those who could not read the stone.

Tonight Steve ignored the signs. He had made this run many times before. Darkness hemmed him. November clawed when he cracked the window to exhaust Camel smoke from the Chevy's cab. The CB crackled occasionally and picked up exactly nothing.

The wind blew—that was nothing unusual. Steve felt himself hypnotized by the skiff of snow skating across the pavement in the glare of his brights. The snow swirled only inches above the blacktop, rushing across like surf sliding over the black packed sand of a beach.

Time's predator hunts.

Years scatter before her like a school of minnows surprised. The rush of her passage causes eons to eddy. Wind sweeps down the canyon with the roar of combers breaking on the sand. The moon, full and newly risen, exerts its tidal force.

Moonlight flashes on the slash of teeth.

And Steve snapped alert, realized he had traversed the thirty-two miles, crossed the flats leading into Shoshoni, and was approaching the junction with U.S. 26. Road hypnosis? he thought. Safe in Shoshoni, but it was scary. He didn't remember a goddamned minute of the trip through the canyon! Steve rubbed his eyes with his left hand and looked for an open cafe with coffee.

It hadn't been the first time.

* * *

All those years before, the four of them had thought they were beating the odds. On a chill night in June, high on a mountain edge in the Wind River Range, high on more than mountain air, the four of them celebrated graduation. They were young and clear-eyed: ready for the world. That night they knew there were no other people for miles. Having learned in class that there were 3.8 human beings per square mile in Wyoming, and as *four,* they thought the odds outnumbered.

Paul Onoda, eighteen. He was Sansei,—third-generation Japanese-American. In 1942, before he was conceived, his parents were removed with eleven thousand other

Japanese-Americans from California to the Heart Mountain Relocation Center in northern Wyoming. Twelve members and three generations of the Onodas shared one of four hundred and sixty-five crowded, tar-papered barracks for the next four years. Two died. Three more were born. With their fellows, the Onodas helped farm eighteen hundred acres of virgin agricultural land. Not all of them had been Japanese gardeners or truck farmers in California, so the pharmacists and the teachers and the carpenters learned agriculture. They used irrigation to bring in water. The crops flourished. The Nisei not directly involved with farming were dispatched from camp to be seasonal farm laborers. An historian later laconically noted that "Wyoming benefited by their presence."

Paul remembered the Heart Mountain camps only through the memories of his elders, but those recollections were vivid. After the war, most of the Onodas stayed on in Wyoming. With some difficulty, they bought farms. The family invested thrice the effort of their neighbors, and prospered.

Paul Onoda excelled in the classrooms and starred on the football field of Fremont High School. Once he overheard the president of the school board tell the coach, "By God but that little Nip can run!" He thought about that; and kept on running ever faster.

More than a few of his classmates secretly thought he had it all. When prom time came in his senior year, it did not go unnoticed that Paul had an extraordinarily handsome appearance to go with his brains and athlete's body. In and around Fremont, a great many concerned parents admonished their white daughters to find a good excuse if Paul asked them to the prom.

Carroll Dale, eighteen. It became second nature early on to explain to people first hearing her given name that it had two r's and two l's. Both sides of her family went back four generations in this part of the country and one of her bequests had been a proud mother. Cordelia Carroll had pride, one daughter, and the desire to see the Hereford Carrolls retain *some* parity with the Angus Dales. After all, the Carrolls had

been ranching on Bad Water Creek before John Broderick
Okie illuminated has Lost Cabin castle with carbide lights.
That was when Teddy Roosevelt had been President and it
was when all the rest of the cattlemen in Wyoming, including
the Dales, had been doing their accounts at night by kerosene
lanterns.

Carroll grew up to be a good roper and a better rider. Her
apprenticeship intensified after her older brother, her only
brother, fatally shot himself during deer season. She
wounded her parents when she neither married a man who
would take over the ranch nor decided to take over the ranch
herself.

She grew up slim and tall, with ebony hair and large, dark,
slightly oblique eyes. Her father's father, at family Christmas dinners, would overdo the whisky in the eggnog and
make jokes about Indians in the woodpile until her paternal
grandmother would tell him to shut the hell up before she
gave him a goodnight the hard way, with a rusty sickle and
knitting needles. It was years before Carroll knew what her
grandmother meant.

In junior high, Carroll was positive she was eight feet tall
in Lilliput. The jokes hurt. But her mother told her to be
patient, that the other girls would catch up. Most of the girls
didn't; but in high school the boys did, though they tended to
be tongue-tied in the extreme when they talked to her.

She was the first girl president of her school's National
Honor Society. She was a cheerleader. She was the valedic-
torian of her class and earnestly quoted John F. Kennedy in
her graduation address. Within weeks of graduation, she
eloped with the captain of the football team.

It nearly caused a lynching.

Steve Mavrakis, eighteen. Courtesy allowed him to be
called a native despite his birth eighteen hundred miles to the
east. His parents, on the other hand, had settled in the state
after the war when he was less than a year old. Given another
decade, the younger native-born might grudgingly concede
their adopted roots; the old-timers, never.

Steve's parents had read Zane Grey and *The Virginian*,

and had spent many summers on dude ranches in upstate New York. So they found a perfect ranch on the Big Horn River and started a herd of registered Hereford. They went broke. They refinanced and aimed at a breed of inferior beef cattle. The snows of '49 killed those. Steve's father determined that sheep were the way to go—all those double and triple births. Very investment-effective. The sheep sickened, or stumbled and fell into creeks where they drowned, or panicked like turkeys and smothered in heaps in fenced corners. It occurred then to the Mavrakis family that wheat doesn't stampede. All the fields were promptly hailed out before what looked to be a bounty harvest. Steve's father gave up and moved into town where he put his Columbia degree to work by getting a job managing the district office for the Bureau of Land Management.

All of that taught Steve to be wary of sure things.

And occasionally he wondered at the dreams. He had been very young when the blizzards killed the cattle. But though he didn't remember the National Guard dropping hay bales from silver C-47s to cattle in twelve-foot deep snow, he did recall for years after, the nightmares of herds of nonplussed animals futilely grazing barren ground before towering, slowly grinding, bluffs of ice.

The night after the crop-duster terrified the sheep and seventeen had expired in paroxysms, Steve dreamed of brown men shrilling and shaking sticks and stampeding tusked, hairy monsters off a precipice and down hundreds of feet to a shallow stream.

Summer nights Steve woke sweating, having dreamed of reptiles slithering and warm waves beating on a ragged beach in the lower pasture. He sat straight, staring out the bedroom window, watching the giant ferns waver and solidify back into cottonwood and boxelder.

The dreams came less frequently and vividly as he grew older. He willed that. They altered when the family moved into Fremont. After a while Steve still remembered he had had the dreams, but most of the details were forgotten.

At first the teachers in Fremont High School thought he

was stupid. Steve was administered tests and thereafter was
labeled an underachiever. He did what he had to do to get by.
He barely qualified for the college-bound program, but then
his normally easy-going father made threats. People asked
him what he wanted to do, to be, and he answered honestly
that he didn't know. Then he took a speech class. Drama
fascinated him and he developed a passion for what theater
the school offered. He played well in *Our Town* and *Arsenic
and Old Lace* and *Harvey*. The drama coach looked at
Steve's average height and average looks and average brown
hair and eyes, and suggested at a hilarious cast party that he
become either a character actor or an FBI agent.

By this time, the only dreams Steve remembered were
sexual fantasies about girls he didn't dare ask on dates.

Ginger McClelland, seventeen. Who would blame her for
feeling out of place? Having been born on the cusp of the
school district's regulations, she was very nearly a year
younger than her classmates. She was short. She thought of
herself as a dwarf in a world of Snow Whites. It didn't help
that her mother studiously offered words like "petite" and
submitted that the most gorgeous clothes would fit a wearer
under five feet, two inches. Secretly she hoped that in one
mysterious night she would bloom and grow great, long legs
like Carroll Dale. That never happened.

Being an exile in an alien land didn't help either. Though
Carroll had befriended her, she had listened to the president
of the pep club, the queen of Job's Daughters, and half the
girls in her math class refer to her as "the foreign exchange
student." Except that she would never be repatriated home;
at least not until she graduated. Her parents had tired of living
in Cupertino, California, and thought that running a Coast to
Coast hardware franchise in Fremont would be an adventur-
ous change of pace. They loved the open spaces, the mountains and free-flowing streams. Ginger wasn't so sure. Every
day felt like she had stepped into a time machine. All the
music on the radio was old. The movies that turned up at the
town's one theater—forget it. The dancing at the hops was
grotesque.

Ginger McClelland was the first person in Fremont—and perhaps in all of Wyoming—to use the adjective "bitchin'." It got her sent home from study hall and caused a bemused and confusing interview between her parents and the principal.

Ginger learned not to trust most of the boys who invited her out on dates. They all seemed to feel some sort of perverse mystique about California girls. But she did accept Steve Mavrakis's last-minute invitation to the prom. He seemed safe enough.

Because Carroll and Ginger were friends, the four of them ended up double-dating in Paul's father's old maroon DeSoto that was customarily used for hauling fence posts and wire out to the pastures. After the dance, when nearly everyone else was heading to one of the sanctioned after-prom parties, Steve affably obtained from an older intermediary an entire case of chilled Hamms. Ginger and Carroll had brought along jeans and Pendleton shirts in their overnight bags and changed in the restroom at the Chevron station. Paul and Steve took off their white jackets and donned windbreakers. Then they all drove up into the Wind River Range. After they ran out of road, they hiked. It was very late and very dark. But they found a high mountain place where they huddled and drank beer and talked and necked.

They heard the voice of the wind and nothing else beyond that. They saw no lights of cars or outlying cabins. The isolation exhilarated them. They *knew* there was no one else for miles.

That was correct so far as it went.

* * *

Foam hissed and sprayed as Paul applied the church key to the cans. Above and below them, the wind broke like waves on the rocks.

"Mavrakis, you're going to the university, right?" said Paul.

Steve nodded in the dim moonlight, added, "I guess so."

"What're you going to take?" said Ginger, snuggling close and burping slightly on her beer.

"I don't know; engineering, I guess. If you're a guy and in the college-bound program, you end up taking engineering. So I figure that's it."

Paul said, "What kind?"

"Don't know. Maybe aerospace. I'll move to Seattle and make spaceships."

"That's neat," said Ginger. "Like in *The Outer Limits*. I wish we could get that here."

"You ought to be getting into hydraulic engineering," said Paul. "Water's going to be really big business not too long from now."

"I don't think I want to stick around Wyoming."

Carroll had been silently staring out over the valley. She turned back toward Steve and her eyes were pools of darkness. "You're really going to leave?"

"Yeah."

"And never come back?"

"Why should I?" said Steve. "I've had all the fresh air and wide open spaces I can use for a lifetime. You know something? I've never even seen the ocean." *And yet he had* felt *the ocean*. He blinked. "I'm getting out."

"Me too," said Ginger. "I'm going to stay with my aunt and uncle in L.A. I think I can probably get into the University of Southern California journalism school."

"Got the money?" said Paul.

"I'll get a scholarship."

"Aren't you leaving?" Steve said to Carroll.

"Maybe," she said. "Sometimes I think so, and then I'm not so sure."

"You'll come back even if you do leave," said Paul. "All of you'll come back."

"Says who?" Steve and Ginger said it almost simultaneously.

"The land gets into you," said Carroll. "Paul's dad says so."

"That's what he says." They all heard anger in Paul's voice. He opened another round of cans. Ginger tossed her empty away and it clattered down the rocks, a noise jarringly out of place.

"Don't," said Carroll. "We'll take the empties down in the sack."

"What's wrong?" said Ginger. "I mean, I . . ." Her voice trailed off and everyone was silent for a minute, two minutes, three.

"What about you, Paul?" said Carroll. "Where do you want to go? What do you want to do?"

"We talked about—" His voice sounded suddenly tightly controlled. "Damn it, I don't know now. If I come back, it'll be with an atomic bomb—"

"What?" said Ginger.

Paul smiled. At least Steve could see white teeth gleaming in the night. "As for what I want to do—" He leaned forward and whispered in Carroll's ear.

She said, "Jesus, Paul! We've got witnesses."

"What?" Ginger said again.

"Don't even ask you don't want to know." She made it one continuous sentence. Her teeth also were visible in the near-darkness. "Try that and I've got a mind to goodnight you the hard way.'"

"What're you talking about?" said Ginger.

Paul laughed. "Her grandmother."

"Charlie Goodnight was a big rancher around the end of the century," Carroll said. "He trailed a lot of cattle up from Texas. Trouble was, a lot of his expensive bulls weren't making out so well. Their testicles—"

"Balls," said Paul.

"—kept dragging on the ground," she continued. "The bulls got torn up and infected. So Charlie Goodnight started getting his bulls ready for the overland trip with some amateur surgery. He'd cut into the scrotum and shove the balls up into the bull. Then he'd stitch up the sack and there'd be no problem with high-centering. That's called goodnight-ing."

"See," said Paul. "There are ways to beat the land."

Carroll said, "You do what you've got to. That's a quote from my father. Good pioneer stock."

"But not to me." Paul pulled her close and kissed her.

"Maybe we ought to explore the mountain a little," said Ginger to Steve. "You want to come with me?" She stared at Steve who was gawking at the sky as the moonlight suddenly vanished like a light switching off.

"Oh my God."

"What's wrong?" she said to the shrouded figure.

"I don't know—I mean, nothing, I guess." The moon appeared again. "Was that a cloud?"

"I don't see a cloud," said Paul, gesturing at the broad belt of stars. "The night's clear."

"Maybe you saw a UFO," said Carroll, her voice light.

"You okay?" Ginger touched his face. "Jesus, you're shivering." She held him tightly.

Steve's words were almost too low to hear. "It swam across the moon."

"What did?"

"I'm cold too," said Carroll. "Let's go back down." Nobody argued. Ginger remembered to put the metal cans into a paper sack and tied it to her belt with a hair-ribbon. Steve didn't say anything more for a while, but the others all could hear his teeth chatter. When they were halfway down, the moon finally set beyond the valley rim. Farther on, Paul stepped on a loose patch of shale, slipped, cursed, began to slide beyond the lip of the sheer rock face. Carroll grabbed his arm and pulled him back.

"Thanks, Irene." His voice shook slightly, belying the tone of the words.

"Funny," she said.

"I don't get it," said Ginger.

Paul whistled a few bars of the song.

"Good night," said Carroll. "You do what you've got to."

"And I'm grateful for that." Paul took a deep breath. "Let's get down to the car."

When they were on the winding road and driving back

toward Fremont, Ginger said, "What did you see up there, Steve?"

"Nothing. I guess I just remembered a dream."

"Some dream." She touched his shoulder. "You're still cold."

Carroll said, "So am I."

Paul took his right hand off the wheel to cover her hand. "We all are."

"I feel all right." Ginger sounded puzzled.

All the way into town, Steve felt he had drowned.

* * *

The Amble Inn in Thermopolis was built in the shadow of Round Top Mountain. On the slope above the Inn, huge letters formed from whitewashed stones proclaimed: WORLD'S LARGEST MINERAL HOT SPRING. Whether at night or noon, the inscription invariably reminded Steve of the Hollywood Sign. Early in his return from California, he realized the futility of jumping off the second letter "O". The stones were laid flush with the steep pitch of the ground. Would-be-suicides could only roll down the hill until they collided with the log side of the Inn.

On Friday and Saturday nights, the parking lot of the Amble Inn was filled almost exclusively with four-wheel-drive vehicles and conventional pickups. Most of them had black-enameled gun racks up in the rear window behind the seat. Steve's Chevy had a rack, but that was because he had bought the truck used. He had considered buying a toy rifle, one that shot caps or rubber darts, at a Penney's Christmas catalog sale. But like so many other projects, he never seemed to get around to it.

Tonight was the first Saturday night in June and Steve had money in his pocket from the paycheck he had cashed at Safeway. He had no reason to celebrate; but then he had no reason not to celebrate. So a little after nine he went to the Amble Inn to drink tequila hookers and listen to the music.

The Inn was uncharacteristically crowded for so early in the evening, but Steve secured a small table close to the dance floor when a guy threw up and his girl had to take him

home. Dancing couples covered the floor though the head-
line act. The band, Mountain Flyer, wouldn't be on until
eleven. The warmup group was a Montana band called the
Great Falls Dead. They had more enthusiasm than talent, but
they had the crowd dancing.

Steve threw down the shots, sucked limes, licked the salt,
intermittently tapped his hand on the table to the music, and
felt vaguely melancholy. Smoke drifted around him, almost
as thick as the special-effects fog in a bad horror movie. The
Inn's dance floor was in a dim, domed room lined with rough
pine.

He suddenly stared, puzzled by a flash of near-
recognition. He had been watching one dancer in particular,
a tall woman with curly raven hair, who had danced with a
succession of cowboys. When he looked at her face, he
thought he saw someone familiar. When he looked at her
body, he wondered whether she wore underwear beneath the
wide-weave red knit dress.

The Great Falls Dead launched into "Good-hearted Woman" and the floor was instantly filled with dancers. Across
the room, someone squealed, "Willieee!" This time the
woman in red danced very close to Steve's table. Her high
cheekbones looked hauntingly familiar. Her hair, he
thought. If it were longer—She met his eyes and smiled at
him.

The set ended, her partner drifted off toward the bar, but
she remained standing beside his table. "Carroll?" he said.
"*Carroll*?"

She stood there smiling, with right hand on hip. "I wondered when you'd figure it out."

Steve shoved his chair back and got up from the table. She
moved very easily into his arms for a hug. "It's been a long
time."

"It has."

"Fourteen years? Fifteen?"

"Something like that."

He asked her to sit at his table, and she did. She sipped a
Campari-and-tonic as they talked. He switched to beer. The

years unreeled. The Great Falls Dead pounded out a medley of country standards behind them.

". . . I never should have married, Steve. I was wrong for Paul. He was wrong for me."

". . . *thought* about getting married. I met a lot of women in Hollywood, but nothing ever seemed . . ."

". . . all the wrong reasons . . ."

". . . did end up in a few made-for-TV movies. Bad stuff. I was always cast as the assistant manager in a holdup scene, or got killed by the werewolf right near the beginning. I think there's something like ninety percent of all actors who are unemployed at any given moment, so I said . . ."

"You really came back here? How long ago?"

". . . to hell with it . . ."

"How long ago?"

". . . and sort of slunk back to Wyoming. I don't know. Several years ago. How long were you married, anyway?"

". . . a year more or less. What do you do here?"

". . . beer's getting warm. Think I'll get a pitcher . . ."

"What do you do here?"

". . . better cold. Not much. I get along. You . . ."

". . . lived in Taos for a time. Then Santa Fe. Bummed around the Southwest a lot. A friend got me into photography. Then I was sick for a while and that's when I tried painting . . ."

". . . landscapes of the Tetons to sell to tourists?"

"Hardly. A lot of landscapes, but trailer camps and oil fields and perspective vistas of I-80 across the Red Desert . . ."

"I tried taking pictures once . . . kept forgetting to load the camera."

". . . and then I ended up half-owner of a gallery called Good Stuff. My partner throws pots."

". . . must be dangerous . . ."

". . . located on Main Street in Lander . . ."

". . . going through. Think maybe I've seen it . . ."

"What do you do here?"

The comparative silence seemed to echo as the band ended

its set. "Very little," said Steve. "I worked a while as a hand on the Two-bar. Spent some time being a roughneck in the fields up around Buffalo. I've got a pickup—do some short-hauling for local businessmen who don't want to hire a trucker. I ran a little pot. Basically I do whatever I can find. You know."

Carroll said, "Yes, I do know." The silence lengthened between them. Finally she said, "Why did you come back here? Was it because—"

". . . because I'd failed?" Steve said, answering her hesitation. He looked at her steadily. "I thought about that a long time. I decided that I could fail anywhere, so I came back here." He shrugged. "I love it. I love the space."

"A lot of us have come back," Carroll said. "Ginger and Paul are here."

Steve was startled. He looked at the tables around them.

"Not tonight," said Carroll. "We'll see them tomorrow. They want to see you."

"Are you and Paul back—" he started to say.

She held up her palm. "Hardly. We're not exactly on the same wavelength. That's one thing that hasn't changed. He ended up being the sort of thing you thought you'd become."

Steve didn't remember what that was.

"Paul went to the School of Mines in Colorado. Now he's the chief exploratory geologist for Enerco."

"Not bad," said Steve.

"Not good," said Carroll. "He spent a decade in South America and the Middle East. Now he's come back home. He wants to gut the state like a fish."

"Coal?"

"And oil. And uranium. And gas. Enerco's got its thumb in a lot of holes." Her voice had lowered, sounded angry. "Anyway, we *are* having a reunion tomorrow, of sorts. And Ginger will be there."

Steve poured out the last of the beer. "I thought for sure she'd be in California."

"Never made it," said Carroll. "Scholarships fell through. Parents said they wouldn't support her if she went back to the west coast—you know how 105% converted immigrants are. So Ginger went to school in Laramie and ended up with a degree in elementary education. She did marry a grad student in journalism. After the divorce five or six years later, she let him keep the kid.''

Steve said, ''So Ginger never got to be an ace reporter.''

''Oh, she did. Now she's the best writer the *Salt Creek Gazette's* got. Ginger's the darling of the environmental groups and the bane of the energy corporations.''

''I'll be damned,'' he said. He accidentally knocked his glass off the table with his forearm. Reaching to retrieve the glass, he knocked over the empty pitcher.

''I think you're tired,'' Carroll said.

''I think you're right.''

''You ought to go home and sack out.'' He nodded. ''I don't want to drive all the way back to Lander tonight,'' Carroll said. ''Have you got room for me?''

When they reached the small house Steve rented off Highway 170, Carroll grimaced at the heaps of dirty clothes making soft moraines in the living room. ''I'll clear off the couch,'' she said. ''I've got a sleeping bag in my car.''

Steve hesitated a long several seconds and lightly touched her shoulders. ''You don't have to sleep on the couch unless you want to. All those years ago . . . You know, all through high school I had a crush on you? I was too shy to say anything.''

She smiled and allowed his hands to remain. ''I thought you were pretty nice too. A little shy, but cute. Definitely an underachiever.''

They remained standing, faces a few inches apart, for a while longer. ''Well?'' he said.

''It's been a lot of years,'' Carroll said. ''I'll sleep on the couch.''

Steve said disappointedly, ''Not even out of charity?''

''Especially not for charity.'' She smiled. ''But don't discount the future.'' She kissed him gently on the lips.

Steve slept soundly that night. He dreamed of sliding endlessly through a warm, fluid current. It was not a nightmare. Not even when he realized he had fins rather than hands and feet.

* * *

Morning brought rain.

When he awoke, the first thing Steve heard was the drumming of steady drizzle on the roof. The daylight outside the window was filtered gray by the sheets of water running down the pane. Steve leaned off the bed, picked up his watch from the floor, but it had stopped. He heard the sounds of someone moving in the living room and called, "Carroll? You up?"

Her voice was a soft contralto. "I am."

"What time is it?"

"Just after eight."

Steve started to get out of bed, but groaned and clasped the crown of his head with both hands. Carroll stood framed in the doorway and looked sympathetic. "What time's the reunion?" he said.

"When we get there. I called Paul a little earlier. He's tied up with some sort of meeting in Casper until late afternoon. He wants us to meet him in Shoshoni."

"What about Ginger?"

They both heard the knock on the front door. Carroll turned her head away from the bedroom, then looked back at Steve. "Right on cue," she said. "Ginger didn't want to wait until tonight." She started for the door, said back over her shoulder, "You might want to put on some clothes."

Steve pulled on his least filthy jeans and a sweatshirt labeled AMAX TOWN-LEAGUE VOLLEYBALL across the chest. He heard the front door open and close, and words murmured in his living room. When he exited the bedroom he found Carroll talking on the couch with a short blonde stranger who only slightly resembled the long-ago image he'd packed in his mind. Her hair was long and tied in a braid. Her gaze was direct and more inquisitive than he remembered.

She looked up at him and said, "I like the mustache. You look a hell of a lot better now than you ever did then."

"Except for the mustache," Steve said, "I could say the same."

The two women seemed amazed when Steve negotiated the disaster area that was the kitchen and extracted eggs and Chinese vegetables from the refrigerator. He served the huge omelet with toast and freshly brewed coffee in the living room. They all balanced plates on laps.

"Do you ever read the Gazoo?" said Ginger.

"Gazoo?"

"The *Salt Creek Gazette*," said Carroll.

Steve said, "I don't read any papers."

"I just finished a piece on Paul's company," said Ginger.

"Enerco?" Steve refilled all their cups.

Ginger shook her head. "A wholly owned subsidiary called Native American Resources. Pretty clever, huh?" Steve looked blank. "Not a poor damned Indian in the whole operation. The name's strictly sham while the company's been picking up an incredible number of mineral leases on the reservation. Paul's been concentrating on an enormous new coal field his teams have mapped out. It makes up a substantial proportion of the reservation's best lands."

"Including some sacred sites," said Carroll.

"Nearly a million acres," said Ginger. "That's more than a thousand square miles."

"The land's never the same," said Carroll, "no matter how much goes into reclamation, no matter how tight the EPA says they are."

Steve looked from one to the other. "I may not read the papers," he said, "but no one's holding a gun to anyone else's head."

"Might as well be," said Ginger. "If the Native American Resources deal goes through, the mineral royalty payments to the tribes'll go up precipitously."

Steve spread his palms. "Isn't that good?"

Ginger shook her head vehemently. "It's economic blackmail to keep the tribes from developing their own resources at their own pace."

"Slogans," said Steve. "The country needs the energy. If

the tribes don't have the investment capital—''

''They *would* if they weren't bought off with individual royalty payments.''

''The tribes have a choice—''

''—with the prospect of immediate gain dangled in front of them by NAR.''

''I can tell it's Sunday,'' said Steve, ''even if I haven't been inside a church door in fifteen years. I'm being preached at.''

''If you'd get off your ass and think,'' said Ginger, ''nobody'd have to lecture you.''

Steve grinned. ''I don't think with my ass.''

''Look,'' said Carroll. ''It's stopped raining.''

Ginger glared at Steve. He took advantage of Carroll's diversion and said, ''Anyone for a walk?''

The air outside was cool and rain-washed. It soothed tempers. The trio walked through the fresh morning along the cottonwood-lined creek. Meadowlarks sang. The rain front had moved far to the east; the rest of the sky was bright blue.

''Hell of a country, isn't it?'' said Steve.

''Not for much longer if—'' Ginger began.

''Gin,'' Carroll said warningly.

They strolled for another hour, angling south where they could see the hills as soft as blanket folds. The tree-lined draws snaked like green veins down the hillsides. The earth, Steve thought, seemed gathered, somehow expectant.

''How's Danny?'' Carrol said to Ginger.

''He's terrific. Kid wants to become an astronaut.'' A grin split her face. ''Bob's letting me have him for August.''

''Look at that,'' said Steve, pointing.

The women looked. ''I don't see anything,'' said Ginger.

''Southeast,'' Steve said. ''Right above the head of the canyon.''

''There—I'm not sure.'' Carroll shaded her eyes. ''I thought I saw something, but it was just a shadow.''

''Nothing there,'' said Ginger.

''Are you both blind?'' said Steve, astonished. ''There was something in the air. It was dark and cigar-shaped. It was there when I pointed.''

"Sorry," said Ginger, "didn't see a thing."

"Well, it *was* there," Steve said, disgruntled.

Carroll continued to stare off toward the pass. "I saw it too, but just for a second. I didn't see where it went."

"Damnedest thing. I don't think it was a plane. It just sort of cruised along, and then it was gone."

"All I saw was something blurry," Carroll said. "Maybe it was a UFO."

"Oh, you guys," Ginger said with an air of dawning comprehension. "Just like prom night, right? Just a joke."

Steve slowly shook his head. "I really saw something then, and I saw this now. This time Carroll saw it too." She nodded in agreement. He tasted salt.

The wind started to rise from the north, kicking up early spring weeds that had already died and begun to dry.

"I'm getting cold," said Ginger. "Let's go back to the house."

"Steve," said Carroll, "you're shaking."

They hurried him back across the land.

PHOSPHORIC FORMATION
Permian
225-270 MILLION YEARS

They rested for a while at the house; drank coffee and talked of the past, of what had happened and what had not. Then Carroll suggested they leave for the reunion. After a small confusion, Ginger rolled up the windows and locked her Saab and Carroll locked her Pinto.

"I hate having to do this," said Carroll.

"There's no choice any more," Steve said. "Too many people around now who don't know the rules."

The three of them got into Steve's pickup. In fifteen minutes they had traversed the doglegs of U.S. 20 through Thermopolis and crossed the Big Horn River. They passed the massive mobile home park with its trailers and RV's sprawling in a carapaced glitter.

The flood of hot June sunshine washed over them as they

passed between the twin bluffs, red with iron, and descended into the miles and years of canyon.

TENSLEEP FORMATION
PENNSYLVANIAN
270-310 MILLION YEARS

On both sides of the canyon, the rock layers lay stacked like sections from a giant meat slicer. In the pickup cab, the passengers had been listening to the news on KTWO. As the canyon deepened, the reception faded until only a trickle of static came from the speaker. Carroll clicked the radio off.

"They're screwed," said Ginger.

"Not necessarily." Carroll, riding shotgun, stared out the window at the slopes of flowers the same color as the bluffs. "The BIA's still got hearings. There'll be another tribal vote."

Ginger said again, "They're screwed. Money doesn't just talk—it makes obscene phone calls, you know? Paul's got this one bagged. You know Paul—I know him just about as well. Son of a bitch."

"Sorry there's no music," said Steve. "Tape player busted a while back and I've never fixed it."

They ignored him. "Damn it," said Ginger. "It took almost fifteen years, but I've learned to love this country."

"I know that," said Carroll.

No one said anything for a while. Steve glanced to his right and saw tears running down Ginger's cheeks. She glared back at him defiantly. "There's Kleenexes in the glove box," he said.

MADISON FORMATION
MISSISSIPPIAN
310-350 MILLION YEARS

The slopes of the canyon became more heavily forested. The walls were all shades of green, deeper green where the runoff had found channels. Steve felt time collect in the great gash in the earth, press inward.

"I don't feel so hot," said Ginger.

"Want to stop for a minute?"

She nodded and put her hand over her mouth.

Steve pulled the pickup over across both lanes. The Chevy skidded slightly as it stopped on the graveled turnout. Steve turned off the key and in the sudden silence they heard only the light wind and the tickings as the Chevy's engine cooled.

"Excuse me," said Ginger. They all got out of the cab. Ginger quickly moved through the Canadian thistle and the currant bushes and into the trees beyond. Steve and Carroll heard her throwing up.

"She had an affair with Paul," Carroll said casually. "Not too long ago. He's an extremely attractive man." Steve said nothing. "Ginger ended it. She still feels the tension." Carroll strolled over to the side of the thistle patch and hunkered down. "Look at this."

Steve realized how complex the ground cover was. Like the rock cliffs, it was layered. At first he saw among the sunflowers and dead dandelions only the wild sweetpeas with their blue blossoms like spades with the edges curled inward.

"Look closer," said Carroll.

Steve saw the hundreds of tiny purple moths swooping and swarming only inches from the earth. The creatures were the same color as the low purple blooms he couldn't identify. Intermixed were white bell-shaped blossoms with leaves that looked like primeval ferns.

"It's like going back in time," said Carroll. "It's a whole nearly-invisible world we never see."

The shadow crossed them with an almost subliminal flash, but they both looked up. Between them and the sun had been the wings of a large bird. It circled in a tight orbit, banking steeply when it approached the canyon wall. The creature's belly was dirty white, muting to an almost-black on its back. It seemed to Steve that the bird's eye was fixed on them. The eye was a dull black, like unpolished obsidian.

"That's one I've never seen," said Carroll. "What is it?"

"I don't know. The wingspread's got to be close to ten feet. The markings are strange. Maybe it's a hawk? An eagle?"

The bird's beak was heavy and blunt, curved slightly. As it circled, wings barely flexing to ride the thermals, the bird was eerily silent, pelagic, fish-like.

"What's it doing?" said Carroll.

"Watching us?" said Steve. He jumped as a hand touched his shoulder.

"Sorry," said Ginger. "I feel better now." She tilted her head back at the great circling bird. "I have a feeling our friend wants us to leave."

They left. The highway wound around a massive curtain of stone in which red splashed down through the strata like dinosaur blood. Around the curve, Steve swerved to miss a deer dead on the pavement—half a deer, rather. The animal's body had been truncated cleanly just in front of its haunches.

"Jesus," said Ginger. "What did that?"

"Must have been a truck," said Steve. "An eighteen-wheeler can really tear things up when it's barrelling."

Carroll looked back toward the carcass and the sky beyond. "Maybe that's what our friend was protecting."

GROS VENTRE FORMATION
CAMBRIAN
500-600 MILLION YEARS

"You know, this was all under water once," said Steve. He was answered only with silence. "Just about all of Wyoming was covered with an ancient sea. That accounts for a lot of the coal." No one said anything. "I think it was called the Sundance Sea. You know, like in the Sundance Kid. Some Exxon geologist told me that in a bar."

He turned and looked at the two women. And stared. And turned back to the road blindly. And then stared at them again. It seemed to Steve that he was looking at a double exposure, or a triple exposure, or—he couldn't count all the overlays. He started to say something, but could not. He existed in a silence that was also stasis, the death of all motion. He could only see.

Carroll and Ginger faced straight ahead. They looked as

they had earlier in the afternoon. They also looked as they
had fifteen years before. Steve saw them *in process*, lines
blurred. And Steve saw skin merge with feathers, and then
scales. He saw gill openings appear, vanish, reappear on
textured necks.

And then both of them turned to look at him. Their heads
swiveled slowly, smoothly. Four reptilian eyes watched him,
unblinking and incurious.

Steve wanted to look away.

The Chevy's tires whined on the level blacktop. The sign
read:

SPEED ZONE AHEAD
35 MPH

"Are you awake?" said Ginger.

Steve shook his head to clear it. "Sure," he said. "You
know that reverie you sometimes get into when you're driving? When you can drive miles without consciously thinking
about it, and then suddenly you realize what's happened?"

Ginger nodded.

"That's what happened."

The highway passed between modest frame houses, gas
stations, motels. They entered Shoshoni.

There was a brand new WELCOME TO SHOSHONI
sign, as yet without bullet holes. The population figure had
again been revised upward. "Want to bet on when they break
another thousand?" said Carroll.

Ginger shook her head silently.

Steve pulled up to the stop sign. "Which way?"

Carroll said, "Go left."

"I think I've got it." Steve saw the half-ton truck with the
Enerco decal and NATIVE AMERICAN RESOURCES DI-
VISION labeled below that on the door. It was parked in
front of the Yellowstone Drugstore. "Home of the world's
greatest shakes and malts," said Steve. "Let's go."

The interior of the Yellowstone had always reminded him

of nothing so much as an old-fashioned pharmacy blended with the interior of the cafe in *Bad Day at Black Rock*. They found Paul at a table near the fountain counter in the back. He was nursing a chocolate malted.

He looked up, smiled, said, "I've gained four pounds this afternoon. If you'd been any later, I'd probably have become diabetic."

Paul looked far older than Steve had expected. Ginger and Carroll both appeared older than they had been a decade and a half before, but Paul seemed to have aged thirty years in fifteen. The star quarterback's physique had gone a bit to pot. His face was creased with lines emphasized by the leathery curing of skin that has been exposed years to wind and hot sun. Paul's hair, black as coal, was streaked with *firn*-lines of glacial white. His eyes, Steve thought, looked tremendously old.

He greeted Steve with a warm hand-clasp. Carroll received a gentle hug and a kiss on the cheek. Ginger got a warm smile and a hello. The four of them sat down and the fountain-man came over. "Chocolate all around?" Paul said.

"Vanilla shake," said Ginger.

Steve sensed a tension at the table that seemed to go beyond dissolved marriages and terminated affairs. He wasn't sure what to say after all the years, but Paul saved him the trouble. Smiling and softspoken, Paul gently interrogated him.

So what have you been doing with yourself?

Really?

How did that work out?

That's too bad; then what?

What about afterward?

And you came back?

How about since?

What do you do now?

Paul sat back in the scrolled-wire ice cream parlor chair, still smiling, playing with the plastic straw. He tied knots in the straw and then untied them.

"Do you know," said Paul, "that this whole complicated reunion of the four of us is not a matter of chance?"

Steve studied the other man. Paul's smile faded to impassivity. "I'm not that paranoid," Steve said. "It didn't occur to me."

"It's a setup."

Steve considered that silently.

"It didn't take place until after I had tossed the yarrow stalks a considerable number of times," said Paul. His voice was wry. "I don't know what the official company policy on such irrational behavior is, but it all seemed right under extraordinary circumstances. I told Carroll where she could likely find you and left the means of contact up to her."

The two women waited and watched silently. Carroll's expression was, Steve thought, one of concern. Ginger looked apprehensive. "So what is it?" he said. "What kind of game am I in?"

"It's no game," said Carroll quickly. "We need you."

"You know what I thought ever since I met you in Miss Gorman's class?" said Paul. "You're not a loser. You've just needed some—direction."

Steve said impatiently, "Come on."

"It's true." Paul set down the straw. "Why we need you is because you seem to see things most others can't see."

Time's predator hunts.

Years scatter before her like a school of minnows surprised. The rush of her passage causes eons to eddy. Wind sweeps down the canyon with the roar of combers breaking on the sand. The moon, full and newly risen, exerts its tidal force.

Moonlight flashes on the slash of teeth.

She drives for the surface not out of rational decision. All blunt power embodied in smooth motion, she simply is what she is.

Steve sat without speaking. Finally he said vaguely, "Things."

"That's right. You see things. It's an ability."

"I don't know . . ."

"We think *we* do. We all remember that night after prom. And there were other times, back in school. None of us has seen you since we all played scatter-geese, but I've had the resources, through the corporation, to do some checking. The issue didn't come up until recently. In the last month, I've read your school records, Steve. I've read your psychiatric history."

"That must have taken some trouble," said Steve. "Should I feel flattered?"

"Tell him," said Ginger. "Tell him what this is all about."

"Yeah," said Steve. "Tell me."

For the first time in the conversation, Paul hesitated. "Okay," he finally said. "We're hunting a ghost on the Wind River."

"Say again?"

"That's perhaps poor terminology." Paul looked uncomfortable. "But what we're looking for is a presence, some sort of extranatural phenomenon."

" 'Ghost' is a perfectly good word," said Carroll.

"Better start from the beginning," said Steve.

When Paul didn't answer immediately, Carroll said, "I know you don't read the papers. Ever listen to the radio?"

Steve shook his head. "Not much."

"About a month ago, an Enerco mineral survey party on the Wind River got the living daylights scared out of them."

"Leave out what they saw," said Paul. "I'd like to include a control factor."

"It wasn't just the Enerco people. Others have seen it, both Indians and Anglos. The consistency of the witnesses has been remarkable. If you haven't heard about this at the bars, Steve, you must have been asleep."

"I haven't been all that social for a while," said Steve. "I did hear that someone's trying to scare the oil and coal people off the reservation."

"Not someone," said Paul. "Some *thing*. I'm convinced of that now."

"A ghost," said Steve.

"A presence."

"There're rumors," said Carroll, "that the tribes have revived the Ghost Dance—"

"Just a few extremists," said Paul.

"—to conjure back an avenger from the past who will drive every white out of the county."

Steve knew of the Ghost Dance, had read of the Paiute mystic Wovoka who, in 1888, had claimed that in a vision the spirits had promised the return of the buffalo and the restoration to the Indians of their ancestral lands. The Plains tribes had danced assiduously the Ghost Dance to ensure this. Then in 1890 the U.S. government suppressed the final Sioux uprising and, except for a few scattered incidents, that was that. Discredited, Wovoka survived to die in the midst of the Great Depression.

"I have it on good authority," said Paul, "that the Ghost Dance was revived *after* the presence terrified the survey crew."

"That really doesn't matter," Carroll said. "Remember prom night? I've checked the newspaper morgues in Fremont and Lander and Riverton. There've been strange sightings for more than a century."

"That was then," said Paul. "The problem now is that the tribes are infinitely more restive, and my people are actually getting frightened to go out into the field." His voice took on a bemused tone. "Arab terrorists couldn't do it, civil wars didn't bother them, but a damned ghost is scaring the wits out of them—literally."

"Too bad," said Ginger. She did not sound regretful.

Steve looked at the three gathered around the table. He knew he did not understand all the details and nuances of the love and hate and trust and broken affections. "I can understand Paul's concern," he said. "But why the rest of you?"

The women exchanged glances. "One way or another," said Carroll, "we're all tied together. I think it includes you, Steve."

"Maybe," said Ginger soberly. "Maybe not. She's an artist. I'm a journalist. We've all got our reasons for wanting to know more about what's up there."

"In the past few years," said Carroll, "I've caught a

tremendous amount of Wyoming in my paintings. Now I want to capture this too.''

Conversation languished. The soda fountain-man looked as though he were unsure whether to solicit a new round of malteds.

"What now?" Steve said.

"If you'll agree," said Paul, "we're going to go back up into the Wind River Canyon to search.''

"So what am I? Some sort of damned occult Geiger counter?''

Ginger said, "It's a nicer phrase than calling yourself bait.''

"Jesus," Steve said. "That doesn't reassure me much." He looked from one to the next. "Control factor or not, give me some clue to what we're going to look for.''

Everyone looked at Paul. Eventually he shrugged and said, "You know the Highway Department signs in the canyon? The geological time chart you travel when you're driving U.S. 20?''

Steve nodded.

"We're looking for a relic of the ancient, inland sea."

After the sun sank in blood in the west, they drove north and watched dusk unfold into the splendor of the night sky.

"I'll always marvel at that," said Paul. "Do you know, you can see three times as many stars in the sky here as you can from any city?''

"It scares the tourists sometimes," said Carroll.

Ginger said, "It won't after a few more of those coal-fired generating plants are built.''

Paul chuckled humorlessly. "I thought they were preferable to your nemesis, the nukes.''

Ginger was sitting with Steve in the back seat of the Enerco truck. Her words were controlled and even. "There are alternatives to both those.''

"Try supplying power to the rest of the country with them before the next century," Paul said. He braked suddenly as a jackrabbit darted into the bright cones of light. The rabbit made it across the road.

"Nobody actually *needs* air conditioners," said Ginger.

"I won't argue that point," Paul said. "You'll just have to argue with the reality of all the people who think they do."

Ginger lapsed into silence. Carroll said, "I suppose you should be congratulated for the tribal council vote today. We heard about it on the news."

"It's not binding," said Paul. "When it finally goes through, we hope it will whittle the fifty percent jobless rate on the reservation."

"It sure as hell won't!" Ginger burst out. "Higher mineral royalties mean more incentive not to have a career."

Paul laughed. "Are you blaming me for being the chicken, or the egg?"

No one answered him.

"I'm not a monster," he said.

"I don't think you are," said Steve.

"I know it puts me in a logical trap, but I think I'm doing the right thing."

"All right," said Ginger. "I won't take any easy shots. At least, I'll try."

From the back seat, Steve looked around his uneasy allies and hoped to hell that someone had brought aspirin. Carroll had aspirin in her handbag and Steve washed it down with beer from Paul's cooler.

GRANITE
PRE-CAMBRIAN
600+ MILLION YEARS

The moon had risen by now, a full, icy disc. The highway curved around a formation that looked like a vast, layered birthday cake. Cedar provided spectral candles.

"I've never believed in ghosts," said Steve. He caught the flicker of Paul's eyes in the rearview mirror and knew the geologist was looking at him.

"There are ghosts," said Paul, "and there are ghosts. In spectroscopy, ghosts are false readings. In television, ghost images—"

"What about the kind that haunt houses?"

"In television," Paul continued, "a ghost is a reflected electronic image arriving at the antenna some interval after the desired wave."

"And are they into groans and chains?"

"Some people are better antennas than others, Steve." Steve fell silent.

"There is a theory," said Paul, "that molecular structures, no matter how altered by process, still retain some sort of 'memory' of their original form."

"Ghosts."

"If you like." He stared ahead at the highway and said, as if musing, "When an ancient organism becomes fossilized, even the DNA patterns that determine its structure are preserved in the stone."

GALLATIN FORMATION
CAMBRIAN
500-600 MILLION YEARS

Paul shifted into a lower gear as the half-ton began to climb one of the long, gradual grades. Streaming black smoke and bellowing like a great saurian lumbering into extinction, an eighteen-wheel semi with oil field gear on its back passed them, forcing Paul part of the way onto the right shoulder. Trailing a dopplered call from its airhorn, the rig disappeared into the first of three short highway tunnels quarried out of the rock.

"One of yours?" said Ginger.

"Nope."

"Maybe he'll crash and burn."

"I'm sure he's just trying to make a living," said Paul mildly.

"Raping the land's a living?" said Ginger. "Cannibalizing the past is a living?"

"Shut up, Gin." Quietly, Carroll said, "Wyoming didn't do anything to your family, Paul. Whatever was done, people did it."

"The land gets into the people," said Paul.

"That isn't the only thing that defines them."

"This always has been a fruitless argument," said Paul. "It's a dead past."

"If the past is dead," Steve said, "then why are we driving up this cockamamie canyon?"

AMSDEN FORMATION
PENNSYLVANIAN
270-310 MILLION YEARS

Boysen Reservoir spread to their left, rippled surface glittering in the moonlight. The road hugged the eastern edge. Once the crimson tail-lights of the oil field truck had disappeared in the distance, they encountered no other vehicle.

"Are we just going to drive up and down Twenty all night?" said Steve. "Who brought the plan?" He did not feel flippant, but he had to say something. He felt the burden of time.

"We'll go where the survey crew saw the presence," Paul said. "It's just a few more miles."

"And then?"

"Then we walk. It should be at least as interesting as our hike prom night."

Steve sensed that a lot of things were almost said by each of them at that point.

I didn't know then . . .

Nor do I know for sure yet.

I'm seeking . . .

What?

Time's flowed. I want to know where now, finally, to direct it.

"Who would have thought . . ." said Ginger.

Whatever was thought, nothing more was said.

The headlights picked out the reflective green-and-white Highway Department sign. "We're there," said Paul. "Somewhere on the right there ought to be a dirt access road."

SHARKTOOTH FORMATION
CRETACEOUS
100 MILLION YEARS

"Are we going to use a net?" said Steve. "Tranquilizer darts? What?"

"I don't think we can catch a ghost in a net," said Carroll. "You catch a ghost in your soul."

A small smile curved Paul's lips. "Think of this as the Old West. We're only a scouting party. Once we observe whatever's up here, we'll figure out how to get rid of it."

"That won't be possible," said Carroll.

"Why do you say that?"

"I don't know," she said. "I just feel it."

"Woman's intuition?" He said it lightly.

"*My* intuition."

"Anything's possible," said Paul.

"If we really thought you could destroy it," said Ginger, "I doubt either of us would be up here with you."

Paul had stopped the truck to lock the front hubs into four-wheel drive. Now the vehicle clanked and lurched over rocks and across potholes eroded by the spring rain. The road twisted tortuously around series of barely-graded switchbacks. Already they had climbed hundreds of feet above the canyon floor. They could see no lights anywhere below.

"Very scenic," said Steve. If he had wanted to, he could have reached out the right passenger's side window and touched the porous rock. Pine branches whispered along the paint on the left side.

"Thanks to Native American Resources," said Ginger, "this is the sort of country that'll go."

"For Christ's sake," said Paul, finally sounding angry. "I'm *not* the anti-Christ."

"I know that." Ginger's voice softened. "I've loved you, remember? Probably I still do. Is there no way?"

The geologist didn't answer.

"Paul?"

"We're just about there," he said. The grade moderated and he shifted to a higher gear.

"Paul—" Steve wasn't sure whether he actually said the word or not. He closed his eyes and saw glowing fires, opened them again and wasn't sure what he saw. He felt the past, vast and primeval, rush over him like a tide. It filled his nose and mouth, his lungs, his brain. It—

"Oh my God!"

Someone screamed.

"Let go!"

The headlight beams twitched crazily as the truck skidded toward the edge of a sheer dark drop. Both Paul and Carroll wrestled for the wheel. For an instant, Steve wondered whether both of them or, indeed, either of them were trying to turn the truck back from the dark.

Then he saw the great, bulky, streamlined form coasting over the slope toward them. He had the impression of smooth power, immense and inexorable. The dead stare from flat black eyes, each one inches across, fixed them like insects in amber.

"Paul!" Steve heard his own voice. He heard the word echo and then it was swallowed up by the crashing waves. He felt unreasoning terror, but more than that, he felt—awe. What he beheld was juxtaposed on this western canyon, but yet it was not out of place. *Genius loci,* guardian, the words hissed like the surf.

It swam toward them, impossibly gliding on powerful gray-black fins.

Brakes screamed. A tire blew out like a gunshot.

Steve watched its jaws open in front of the windshield; the snout pulling up and back, the lower jaw thrusting forward. The maw could have taken in a heifer. The teeth glared white in reflected light, white with serrated, razor edges. Its teeth were as large as shovel blades.

"Paul!"

The Enerco truck fish-tailed a final time; then toppled sideways into the dark. It fell, caromed off something massive and unseen, and began to roll.

Steve had time for one thought. *Is it going to hurt?*

When the truck came to rest, it was upright. Steve groped toward the window and felt rough bark rather than glass. They were wedged against a pine.

The silence astonished him. That there was no fire astonished him. That he was alive— "Carroll?" he said. "Ginger? Paul?" For a moment, no one spoke.

"I'm here," said Carroll, muffled, from the front of the truck. "Paul's on top of me. Or somebody is. I can't tell."

"Oh God, I hurt," said Ginger from beside Steve. "My shoulder hurts."

"Can you move your arm?" said Steve.

"A little, but it hurts."

"Okay." Steve leaned forward across the front seat. He didn't feel anything like grating, broken bone-ends in himself. His fingers touched flesh. Some of it was sticky with fluid. Gently he pulled whom he assumed was Paul from Carroll beneath. She moaned and struggled upright.

"There should be a flashlight in the glove box," he said.

The darkness was almost complete. Steve could see only vague shapes inside the truck. When Carroll switched on the flashlight, they realized the truck was buried in thick, resilient brush. Carroll and Ginger stared back at him. Ginger looked as if she might be in shock. Paul slumped on the front seat. The angle of his neck was all wrong.

His eyes opened and he tried to focus. Then he said something. They couldn't understand him. Paul tried again. They made out, "Goodnight, Irene." Then he said, "Do what you have . . ." His eyes remained open, but all the life went out of them.

Steve and the women stared at one another as though they were accomplices. The moment crystallized and shattered. He braced himself as best he could and kicked with both feet at the rear door. The brush allowed the door to swing open one foot, then another. Carroll had her door open at almost the same time. It took another few minutes to get Ginger out. They left Paul in the truck.

They huddled on a naturally terraced ledge about halfway

between the summit and the canyon floor. There was a roar
and bright lights for a few minutes when a Burlington Northern freight came down the tracks on the other side of the
river. It would have done no good to shout and wave their
arms, so they didn't.

No one seemed to have broken any bones. Ginger's shoulder was apparently separated. Carroll had a nosebleed.
Steve's head felt as though he'd been walloped with a two-
by-four.

"It's not cold," he said. "If we have to, we can stay in the
truck. No way we're going to get down at night. In the
morning we can signal people on the road."

Ginger started to cry and they both held her. "I saw
something," she said. "I couldn't tell—what was it?"

Steve hesitated. He had a hard time separating his dreams
from Paul's theories. The two did not now seem mutually
exclusive. He still heard the echoing thunder of ancient gulfs.
"I'm guessing it's something that lived here a hundred million years ago," he finally said. "It lived in the inland sea
and died here. The sea left, but it never did."

"A native . . ." Ginger said and trailed off. Steve
touched her forehead; it felt feverish. "I finally saw," she
said. "Now I'm a part of it." In a smaller voice, "Paul."
Starting awake like a child from a nightmare, "Paul?"

"He's—all right now," said Carroll, her even tone plainly
forced.

"No, he's not," said Ginger. "He's not." She was silent
for a time. "He's dead." Tears streamed down her face. "It
won't really stop the coal leases, will it?"

"Probably not."

"Politics," Ginger said wanly. "Politics and death. What
the hell difference does any of it make now?"

No one answered her.

Steve turned toward the truck in the brush. He suddenly
remembered from his childhood how he had hoped everyone
he knew, everyone he loved, would live forever. He hadn't
wanted change. He hadn't wanted to recognize time. He
remembered the split-second image of Paul and Carroll

struggling to control the wheel. "The land," he said, feeling the sorrow. "It doesn't forgive."

"That's not true." Carroll slowly shook her head. "The land just *is*. The land doesn't care."

"I care," said Steve.

Amazingly, Ginger started to go to sleep. They laid her down gently on the precipice, covered her with Steve's jacket, and cradled her head, stroking her hair. "Look," she said. "Look." As the moon illuminated the glowing sea.

Far below them, a fin broke the dark surface of the forest.

Probers of the past have been making contact with cave men for almost as long as writers have had those too-convenient Time Machines at their disposal. And scientists of the ruthless, not to say mad, variety have frequently been part of the exploration team. But progress in the real sciences provides the tools of fictional stitchery with which to reshape our modern, only decades-ancient myths.

FOREFATHER FIGURE

Charles Sheffield

"Who are you?"

The words rang around the tiled walls. The naked figure on the table did not move. His chest rose and fell steadily, lifting with it the tangle of catheters and electrodes that covered the rib cage.

"Still no change." The woman who crouched over the oscilloscope made a tiny adjustment to the controls with her left hand. She was nervous, her eyes flicking to the screen, to the table, and to the man who stood by her side. "He's still in a sleep rhythm. Heart and blood pressure stable."

The man nodded. "Keep watching. Increase the level of stimulation. I think he's coming up, but it will take a while."

He turned back to the recumbent figure.

"Who are you? What is your name? Tell me, who are you?"

As the questions went on, the only sound in the big room, the woman ran her tongue over her lips, seemingly ready to respond herself to the insistent queries. She was big-boned and tall, her nervous manner an odd contrast to her round and impassive-looking face.

"Here he comes," she said abruptly.

There was a stir of movement from the body's left arm. It

rose a couple of inches from the table, twitching the powerful sinews of the wrist and hand.

"Reduce the feedback." The man leaned over the table, peering down at the fluttering eyelids. *"Who are you?"*

There was a sigh, a grunt, the experimental run of air over the vocal chords. "Ah—Ah'm—Bayle." The voice was thick and choking, a mouthing through an unfamiliar throat and lips. "I'm Bayle. I'm Bayle Richards." The eyes opened suddenly, an unfocussed and startling blue.

"Got it. By God, I've got it." John Cramer flashed a fierce look of triumph at the woman and straightened up from the table. "I wondered if we ever would." He laughed. "We don't need the stimulants now. Turn to a sedative—he'll need sleep in a few minutes. Let's see how well it took, then we'll end it for today."

He leaned again over the table. "Bayle Richards. Do you remember me? I'm John Cramer. Remember? John Cramer?"

The blue eyes rolled slowly, struggling to find a focus. After a few seconds they fixed on Cramer's face.

"John Cramer. Uh, I think so. Don't know what happened. John Cramer." He moved his arm and made a weak effort to sit up. "Think I remember. Not sure."

The eyes focussed more sharply, filled with alarm. "What happened to me? What's wrong with me?"

"Not a thing." Cramer was smiling broadly, nodding to the woman. "Bayle, you're going to be better than you ever were in all your life. You'll feel dizzy for a while. Do you have any pain?"

"My mouth, and my chest . . . stiff. What you do to me? Was I in an accident?"

"No. Bayle, you're fine. Don't you remember? This was mostly your idea."

The woman turned her head quickly at that. "John. That's not what he—"

"Shut up, Lana." He waved her to silence with an abrupt chop of his hand and returned his attention to the man. "Bayle, I'll tell you all about this later. Now you ought to get some rest. Just lie there quietly, and we'll get this plumbing off you.''

As the sedatives began to take effect, Bayle Richard's eyes closed again. Cramer began to strip the electrodes and the monitoring sensors off the naked body, his fingers working rapidly and accurately.

''John.'' The woman stood up from the control console and moved to the table. ''Don't you think you ought to slow down? I thought we were going to watch the monitors for a couple of hours, see if it was all normal. Suppose we get a new problem?''

''No chance of it.'' Cramer's voice was exultant. ''Lana, don't try and tell my my business. This is a *success*, I feel it in my bones. Did you see any sign of instability on those monitors? Let's get him in full control, then we can start the second transfer.'' He laughed again. ''We'll pull in those memories as soon as we can hook him up. Twenty-two thousand years, the carbon dating says. He'll tell a story, once we get him started.''

His gaze moved over the figure on the table, revelling in the firm, unblemished skin and the smooth muscles. ''Look at that body. Bayle, you never had it so good! Wait until he sees himself in a mirror.''

Lana Cramer was automatically beginning to strip off the sensors and uncouple the I-V's. Her placid face was still troubled.

''John, do you think you're being fair to him? We still haven't explained what caused the trouble in the primary transfer—suppose that produces a complication when we try and connect with the memories?''

Cramer continued his systematic treatment of Bayle Richards, his manner confident and casual. He did not look up at her.

''Don't you worry about that, Lana. Thinking isn't your department. A week from now, we'll know more about Cro-Magnon man than anyone has ever known. Bayle Richards should have known the risks when he got into this. If he didn't, the more fool he is.''

The image flashed up on the big screen, an accurate color reproduction. Cramer adjusted the focus.

"There, Bayle. That used to be you. Now you can see what a good trade you made."

Bayle Richards fidgeted as he examined the screen. He was dressed now in a grey suit that hung elegantly on his tall, thin frame, but somehow his air of discomfort extended beyond the clothing to the body itself. He moved as though the limbs themselves were a poor fit. He kept looking down at his hands, examining the smooth muscles in the palm and along the base of his thumbs. When he looked at the screen, his eyes were afraid.

"Was that really me? Why don't I have a clearer memory of it? It seems like something I dreamed."

"That was you, all right." Cramer looked at the screen with great satisfaction. The figure shown there was small and thin, with a sideways curve to the spine and a big head that sat crooked on the thin shoulders. Big brown eyes swam myopically out of the screen through thick-lensed glasses.

"You lived in that for twenty-six years, Bayle. You never had a good job, never had a woman. When we've finished and you leave here, you'll have both—but we've got to run a few experiments before that happens."

"Experiments?" The expression of fear mirrored the world-view of the old Bayle Richards. It did not match the tall, poised body, with its clear eyes and regular features. "Dr. Cramer, I don't remember things right. Did I agree to some experiments?"

"You did. As a matter of fact, I could say that body is on loan to you—it won't be yours until we complete the experiments. I'll show you the contract that you signed, if you want it. Don't worry. We're not going to do anything bad to you, just explore some old memories."

"I don't seem to *have* memories, not real ones. I have little incidents in my head, but I can't put them together." Bayle Richards looked again at his hands.

"John." She had been sitting quietly, watching the two men. Now Lana Cramer leaned forward and placed her hand on her husband's arm. "John, do we have to do this now? I was wondering, wouldn't it be better to let Bayle take a couple of weeks to get comfortable first? Pierre will still be waiting, even if we took a month before we began."

The flash of irritation in John Cramer's eyes came and went so quickly that it was hard to catch. After a moment he patted Lana's hand reassuringly, but he did not look at her.

"Now then, dear, you know I can't do that." His tone was mildly reproving. "I told the Paris Institute that Pierre would be back there in thirty days. We have to begin work now, as soon as the equipment is set up. Bayle and I agreed to all this long ago."

"But he doesn't remember it."

John Cramer shrugged. He was of middle height, broad and well-built, with a heavy chin and thick, barred eyebrows.

"We have it all in writing—on videotape, too. You know we always wondered if all the memories would carry over, that's why we took such complete records."

"And I remember it," said Bayle Richards suddenly. "You showed me what I would look like, and I signed the paper. I can *see* it, see my hand doing it." He shuddered. "I was in pain all the time, from my back and my arm. God, no wonder I signed. I'd have signed anything."

"Maybe." Cramer's voice was soft but insistent. "Maybe you would have signed anything, I can't tell. But you *did* sign, and I approved this work because of that. Now we have to carry through on it, and do what you agreed to do. It's not anything that will harm you, Bayle—even Lana will agree with me there. But we have to get started soon, or we won't be finished in a month."

"But I must know some other things." Richards' voice showed that he had lost any real argument. "I haven't been told what you were doing, and I don't remember it. You said my memory will come back in patches, but when?"

John Cramer shrugged and stood up. "I can't say. We have no history on that. I don't see a problem, though, we can tell you anything you need to know. Or Lana can, I should say. I have to go now and get the equipment ready. We have approval to begin work tomorrow, and I don't want to lose time at the beginning.''

"John!" Lana Cramer's voice halted him at the door. "I don't know some of the technical details myself. You're the only one who has the full picture.''

Cramer shrugged. "I can't see why you'd want that much detail. If you do, call out some of the files onto the screen. I have a record of everything, and the index is set up to be used by anybody. I'll be back in a few hours.''

After he was gone, Lana Cramer smiled uncertainly at Bayle Richards. "I'm sorry. That's just John, he never has enough time for anything, especially explanations. I'll do my best. What is it you want to know first?''

"Who am I?"

"What?'' She was confused, suddenly carried back to the previous day, with Cramer's insistent "Who are you?" ringing through the operating theater.

"I want to know who I am.'' Richards leaned forward, stunning her with those startling, clear eyes. "I'm Bayle Richards, sure. But this isn't my body, my body was a wreck. I want to know who I am now. Where's the original owner?''

"You don't remember *that*? It was the last thing you talked about with John before we began.''

"I'm telling you, I don't remember it. I remember a bit about cloning, how it's done, but I don't remember anything about this body. Did I meet the owner?''

Lana paused. Maybe the personality was Bayle's, but he seemed to be picking up something from the physiology and glandular balance of his new body. The old Bayle had never been so insistent on answers. She looked at him again, seeing the fit of mind and body for the first time.

"I think it would be best if I show you. It may be a shock whatever we do. Come on.''

She stood up and led the way out of the room. Moving along the corridor behind her, Bayle Richards seemed to be still experimenting with movement, feeling the flex of muscles in his long legs. She was a big woman, but he was half a head taller. It was a new experience. He could remember the old Bayle Richards, peering *up* at everyone. That sudden memory was so painful that he paused and stretched upwards, savoring the new look of the world.

Lana Cramer had stopped at a door near the end of the corridor and was working the combination, shielding it with her body. Watching her bent over, Richards felt another unfamiliar sensation, a surge of lust more powerful than the old body had ever known. He remembered Cramer's words, "never had a woman". Part of the reason for that was a lack of desire. The old body was too racked by pain and physical malfunction to support a strong sexual urge.

He moved forward as Lana swung open the heavy door. A gust of cold air met them as they entered the long, high-ceilinged room. The white tile walls gave off a breath of formaldehyde and methyl alcohol. The whole far wall was a bank of massive drawers, a couple of feet wide and high. Each of them bore its own neatly typed label.

Bayle Richards shivered with sudden recognition, as Lana turned to him.

"You remember what this is, Bayle?"

"Yes. Now I do. It's a morgue. You made me a clone from a dead man's body, right?"

"Sort of." Lana Cramer moved forward to one of the drawers and placed her finger on the button that would open it. "You don't remember it all yet? Bayle, I was hoping this would trigger it for you. You're a clone from a dead man all right."

"I don't mind that." He seemed relieved. No chance now that he would meet himself in a hospital corridor, or out on the street. "Show me the body, that won't worry me."

"It might." Lana remained with her finger on the button but she did not press it. "Bayle, I want to tell you before I show you, because this may be a shock. You heard John say that we had promised to get Pierre back to the Paris Institute in thirty days? Well, you are Pierre. And Pierre is the body inside here."

"Well? What difference does the nationality make?"

"It's not the nationality that matters, Bayle. John borrowed Pierre from Paris, and over there he's known as 'Vieux Pierre'—old Pierre. He comes from a sort of peaty salt march near the Dordogne River, just east of Bordeaux."

She pressed the button, and the drawer began to slowly slide open with a low hum of an electric motor.

"Pierre died fighting in the marsh, and fell over into a deep part. They found him when they were draining the marsh two years ago. For some reason, the chemical balance there in the marsh preserves animal tissue perfectly. When they got him out, Old Pierre had been lying there for twenty-two thousand years."

The body was a dark, uniform brown, wrinkled deeply all over like a dried fruit. Bayle had managed one long look before he moved back, nauseated, to lean against the wall. There was nothing horrifying in the appearance of the body itself. It was hard to think of it as human tissue. The shrunken skin suggested a model of painted papier mâché, a child's attempt to shape the human form with paste and paper. Bayle Richards's nausea came from a deeper cause, a sudden feeling that he had lurched back through time to the salt marsh where Pierre had met his violent end. A gaping hole in the throat—from man or beast?—told how he had died. Violently, and quickly.

"But how did Dr. Cramer do it?" he asked, looking across the table at Lana and again feeling the comfort of the long, straight spine and well-set head and neck. "I've heard of clones, but how could he clone from a dead man? He would need complete cells to do it—how could he get those from Pierre?"

"He didn't." Lana had seen how shaken he was by the sight of the mummified body. She had taken him back to their rooms in the hospital and given him coffee and brandy—tiny amounts of both. The stimulants were completely new to that body, and there would be no built-in tolerance for them. She felt guilty about how she had handled the situation. There had been no need to *show* Bayle Richards, she ought to have been able to do it all with more indirect explanations. He had taken the shock probably as well as anyone could, but there was still a look of perplexity in his eyes.

"John knew he couldn't do a direct cloning," she went on. "He transplanted the nucleic structures from a diploid cell in Pierre's arm to a denucleated ovum from a host female." She blushed a little as she spoke. "We did forced growth of that to maturity in the vitro-labs in the hospital basement. The chromosome transfer was tedious, but we've done it before with no problems."

"Your ovum?" Bayle had caught her look when she spoke of it.

"Yes. But it could have been anybody—none of my DNA got through to the final cell. You are all Pierre."

"Except for my mind. I have no memories of Pierre."

"Of course not. They are all carried in Pierre's brain, not in his DNA. That was John's next step. He had to do the memory transfer from you, the old Bayle, to the cloned body. That was the hard piece. He had built the scanning instrument to read out from you, and read into the new body, but he had problems with it."

Richards was sipping tentatively at the brandy, his nose wrinkling up in surprise. "If I didn't *know* I could drink this, my body would insist it was poison. Twenty-two thousand years, you say." He shook his head. "Lana, if I'm a cave man—I still have trouble accepting the idea at all—why don't I *look* like a cave man? The pictures I've seen looked more like my old body, all hunched over the chinless. I'm nothing like that."

"You're probably remembering pictures people drew of Neanderthal man. But you're Cro-Magnon. From all we can tell, he had a better body and a bigger brain than people do now." She looked him up and down as he lounged back in the armchair. It was as if she were doing what he had been doing himself for the past twenty-four hours, taking an inventory of a new property that had been around for a while but had not been previously appreciated. It was impossible to relate the strong, handsome man in front of her with the old Bayle Richards. She could feel his interest in her. With

Bayle, she had never been aware of any questions of sexual attitudes. The man sitting opposite her made such a thought unavoidable.

Lana forced herself to continue, to ignore the sudden sexual tension in the room. "Cro-Magnon man is probably what we all descended from, but we don't know much about him. When you feel like it, I'll show you some of the cave paintings that he did. After all''—she smiled, trying to change the mood—"you're a lot closer to him than most of us now."

"Yes. But you haven't told me *why*."

"I will. But there's one other thing I have to tell you first." She hesitated, knowing that she was going to do something that would enrage John Cramer if he found out about it. Usually she did anything she could to avoid his disapproval, but this was literally a life-and-death issue for Bayle Richards.

"You signed an agreement with John to let him transfer your memories to Pierre's cloned body. You agreed when you signed that he would not be held responsible for any failure, no matter what happened."

"But nothing did happen, did it?" Richards was looking slightly dizzy. Even the small amount of alcohol—less than half an ounce—was producing an effect on him. "I mean, I'm sitting here, in Pierre's body, and I feel fine."

"You look fine. I don't want you to ever tell John that I said this to you—promise me that—but something *did* happen. No one has ever done a successful transfer of memories to a stranger's cloned body before. John is the expert in it, and he had troubles. Everything went smoothly for the first few hours, and we were scanning memories out of your old body and into the one you have now. A couple of hours before we were finished, things went wrong."

"What do you mean, things went wrong? I'm here, and I'm in good shape."

"You seem to be. But before all the memories were transferred, the old body died. We don't know why. Bayle Richards just stopped breathing, and we couldn't start him again."

Lana leaned forward, her calm face full of unusual urgency. "Bayle, you may not think you care about this one way or the other, but your old body doesn't exist now. John won't admit it, but there are things about the consciousness transfer process that no one understands yet."

"So why should I care about that?" Richards was gradually moving to the acceptance of his new status. Cramer had completed the transfer, and the loss of the old body was perhaps a good thing. It was no pleasure to be reminded of that crippled, tormented past.

"So what?" he repeated. "I'm here, aren't I?"

"You're here, Bayle, but you don't understand." She leaned forward, took his hands in hers, then quickly released them. She dare not give the wrong signals to the new Bayle Richards. "You signed an agreement that if you occupied this new body, old Pierre's clone, you would help John in his experiments with it. Don't you know what he wants to do next? He didn't pick out this old body, and perform all that work on it, for nothing."

She was looking nervously around her, afraid suddenly that John Cramer would appear while she was speaking. "Bayle, John wants to try and do some memory transfer from old Pierre to *you*, to this body. He failed when he tried to do transfers to another subject, but he thinks that it would be possible with a cloned body form of Old Pierre when it wouldn't work with a stranger. Now do you see why I'm worried? John is going to insist on it, but there are still things about the process that we *know* we don't understand. If we *did* understand, why would the old Bayle Richards have died in the last transfer?"

The French countryside was flat and baked under the hot August sun. In the west the land fell slowly away towards the river. The focus moved in, shrinking the broad landscape view to a narrower scene of moss and isolated clumps of grey-green sedge. That dreary prospect seemed far removed in time and space from the Bordeaux land of vines and lush fruit.

John Cramer paused as he was about to move the scene to

closer focus. He looked up in annoyance as the door was opened and light flooded into the darkened room.

"Keep that door shut!" He squinted up, eyes unable to handle the brighter light. "Lana, what the hell are you doing. You know I'm not to be interrupted when I'm working here."

"John." She closed the door and sat down next to him. "I have to talk to you."

"Not now. I'm micro-viewing some of the French material for tomorrow. We have to have it ready so I can navigate with Pierre."

"That's what I have to talk to you about, John. You have to give up the experiment. Last night I did as you asked with Bayle, and we went over a lot of things that he should remember from before the transfer."

John Cramer signed and switched off the micro-viewer with a gesture of irritation. "Lana, what's got into you? There's no way I'm going to stop the experiments now— we're almost halfway there."

She was sitting so close that he could sense her nervous hand movements. "We're not halfway, John. That's why we have to stop. Look, you think that you transferred most of Bayle's memories, so you still think he's the old Bayle. He isn't. For one thing, he has less memories than we realized—when we looked in detail at what he recalls of his old life, it's mostly blanks and vague emotional recall."

"Of course it is." John Cramer felt a sudden impulse to violence. A week ago, she would never have dared to press him with this kind of intrusion. His working hours were sacred. "Look, Lana, I'll say one more thing, then I want you out of here so I can get my materials prepared. Bayle Richards is in a new body—one that I still own. The less he remembers of the old body, the better the chance that we can induce memories from Pierre into the new one. He doesn't recall much of the old Bayle *because he doesn't want to.* Can't you see it, the last thing he needs cluttering up his head is the knowledge of what a disaster he used to be? I don't think the experiment went wrong—I think he suppresses the old Bayle's memories, rejects them from his mind."

There was a silence next to him, but he sensed that it was not the silence of acceptance. She was refusing to argue, waiting him out. He felt a rising fury at Richards, at the other man's attitudes. Just as Bayle Richards had been replaced by a new Bayle, the same process seemed to be turning the familiar and pliable Lana to a more obstinate and annoying form.

"Well?" he said after a few more seconds. "Do you agree with me, or don't you? I've got work to do."

She recoiled at the intensity in his voice.

"I'm sorry," she said at last. "Maybe you're right, he can't bear to think of what he used to be."

"Do you wonder?"

"No. I can't bear to think of it, either. John, I'll go now, but tell me one thing. What will you do if he refuses to work with you on the next set of transfer experiments?"

There was a creak from his chair as Cramer jerked forward on it. "Refuses? Now, when we're so committed, and he signed the papers to agree to it? You ought to know the answer to that, Lana. I don't let *anybody* cross me like that, ever. He won't keep that new body of his for a day. I'll trash him, that's what I'll do."

"But his old body died. Anyway, you couldn't condemn him to live in that again—you've seen how he is now."

"Wait and see what I'd do, Lana. I've seen you getting closer to Richards in the past couple of days. Do that all you like, help him get adjusted to that new body. But remember, *I own that cloned body*. Legally, it's no more than a piece of experimental tissue I assembled in the labs. I'll get cooperation from Richards, or I'll recycle the tissue."

She stood up abruptly. "That's murder, John."

He laughed, a snarl of bitter amusement in the darkness. "Go and learn the law, Lana. Until I sign off on it, that body has no independent status. It's what I make it, that's all. If I have to, I'll start again with another subject. Now, get the hell out of here. Go and tell all that to Richards. I have work to do. If you're so fond of him, you'd better explain what he has to do if he wants to keep that handsome new body."

She made a noise between a sigh and a groan, blundering

in the darkness towards the door. Before she reached it he had turned the micro-viewer back on and was adjusting its focus to the French scene. His expression in the darkness was of grim satisfaction. He knew Lana. Now and again, it was necessary to show her who was in control.

"Do I need to run over it again, or do you have everything clear?"

John Cramer's voice was dispassionate but not unfriendly. Now that the experiment was beginning, he had no room for emotions.

"I know what to do." Bayle Richards was lying flat on the bed, a sheet draped over his naked body. A set of electrodes rose from his shaven skull to the computer monitor that hung suspended above him like a silver bee-hive. A second tangle of wires led to the sealed coffin on the table.

"Let's get on with it," he said. "I assume Old Pierre knows what he's doing?"

His voice, unlike Cramer's, was bitter. He and Lana had spent many hours discussing the situation, but always they came to the same conclusion. John Cramer was in control, and all that he cared about was the continued experiments with Old Pierre.

"Do you think he's doing this because of—us?" Lana had asked.

"I don't think he cares what we do." Richards still felt uncomfortable, even though Cramer had made it clear during their discussions that he knew there was something between them. "He as good as told me that you would do whatever he told you to do. I don't think he worries about your body—he wants possession of your mind."

She had clung to him, but neither of them had faced the real question. Did John Cramer control her? Bayle Richards thought so, but Lana would have denied it.

There was one sustaining thought that lessened Bayle's concerns: no matter what John Cramer's views might be of Lana, or what he might know of the affair, nothing would be allowed to stand in the way of the experiments—and Bayle was central to those. Attempts to transfer memories from Old

Pierre through random volunteers had all been dismal failures.

Cramer was peering at the array of dials on the outside of the coffin, then adjusting the settings of the controls that ran inside it.

"I think we've reached the best possible temperature in the casket. It's warm enough to stimulate the right brain areas, and it's cool enough to let us keep going without setting up interference reactions in the body. Bayle, just let your mind run where it wants to. If you begin to get visual or auditory images, just talk into the microphone. I've put that there as a stimulus—we'll pick you up anyway, if you begin to subvocalize."

He turned to Lana, who was again at her position as anesthetist and monitor of signal transfer.

"All right. Run a low level sedation rhythm. I think we'll get better response if Bayle's activity level is down from normal. He has to be conscious enough to comment, but not to do too much thinking. Can you find that setting?"

Lana nodded. Her wide mouth was firmed to a worried line. Bayle had not only refused to fight against John Cramer's intent—he had displayed a surprising interest in the project himself.

"You don't understand, Lana," he had said. "I want to know all I can about Pierre. It sounds stupid, but he's closer to me than any of the rest of you."

That remark had wounded her. She had done all she knew to draw him closer, to make him feel that the future would belong to the two of them. Bayle had taken what she offered, but little more than physical attention had been given in return. How much of that was simple physical need? John was unreachable, locked into his world of charts and plans. She sometimes suspected that he had *planned* her affair with Bayle, to give him more control over both of them.

Her attention was suddenly drawn back to the controls in front of her.

"Something's coming through," she said. "I'm getting primary brain rhythm from Pierre."

Cramer grunted. "Predicted. We got that far with the last

subject, it's not an information-carrying signal. Watch for that mixture of alpha and beta waves that you saw when we were doing the Richards transfer to Pierre. That's when a real signal will be getting through.''

"I'm getting that too."

"What!" Cramer was over by her side instantly, watching the monitors intently. "Damn it, you're right. We never had *that* with the others, not even when we tried for hours." He was as excited as a small child with a new toy. "Keep the signal to Bayle as constant as you can, let him start to soak up the flow. After he's had five minutes, we'll cut off the inputs from Pierre and see what we've got. I don't think we can expect—"

"Sun. Bright sun." The murmured words from the figure on the table cut Cramer off in mid-sentence. He swung around, moved quietly to Bayle Richards' side.

"Keep it going, Lana. Don't cut back on the transfer."

"Some of us." Richards paused, as though somehow looking around him, although the form on the table did not move. "Five of us, walking towards the sun. Feels like soft mud under our feet. Skin itches, itches a lot. Something bad there."

Cramer saw that Lana was looking at him, her expression worried. "Parasites. Pierre wouldn't notice them, he was used to fleas and lice. Bayle's too sensitive to feel comfortable in the Stone Age. Keep the signal going."

She looked unhappy, then nodded. "Data rate is up again. Want me to back it off?"

"No. Let's get all the sensory signals we can. I'm tuned in to pick up mainly visuals from Pierre, but I'm going to increase band width and see if we can get audio and tactile— looks as though Bayle has been picking up some of them anyway, he's aware of the skin sensations coming through from Pierre."

He went to the casket and began to reset the probe levels. After a few moments Bayle Richards began to grunt.

"Hungry. Following scent. Horns went this way, two days ago, must keep following until we can surround them at night. Don't like smell. Danger somewhere near us, not our people.''

He was sniffing the air, turning his head from side to side. Somehow his features seemed to have become more primitive, full of a suggestion of animal awareness. After a few seconds his eyelids flicked open, then closed again.

''Won't find today,'' he said at last. ''Dark coming, country here strange, can't keep going now. Look for safe place, see if can find water and bad food. Hungry. Hungry.''

His voice was trailing off, the words losing clarity.

''All right.'' Cramer turned back from the casket. ''We could keep going and pick up another signal, but there's enough there for me to analyze. I'm cutting off Pierre's inputs. Bring him round, I want to try him with a few visual comparisons.''

Ten minutes later, and the electrodes had been removed. Bayle Richards had sunk into a deep natural sleep.

''Do you want me to give him a stimulant?'' Lana Cramer seemed relieved, as much as her husband was exhilarated.

''No.'' He laughed. ''Let him sleep a while, he has some information processing to do. Then we'll talk to him about what he saw—couldn't get that out while we were working there, but I'll bet he kept most of those visual images that came across from Old Pierre. Just think of it, Lana. He's been looking at the earth today as it was twenty-two thousand years ago—he could tell you the colors of the butterflies, describe the actual weather.'' He took a deep breath. ''God, it's enough to make me want to have myself cloned into Pierre's body form. Do you realize what this means? We have a new way to explore the whole of history, right back to the earliest fossils of man. We can find out when language developed, when writing was invented, when we mastered fire—everything.''

He looked for a long moment at the body on the table, then turned to leave. ''Stay with him, Lana. Stay with him, but let me know as soon as he wakes. I want to hear every word.''

''John, what did he mean by 'bad food'?'' Her face was puzzled, while she watched tenderly over the unconscious

form of Bayle Richards. "Was that something to harm
them?"

He shook his head. "I don't know, but I don't think so. I
think that he was talking about grasses and berries—things
that they could eat if they had to, just to keep going, but
things that didn't really count. They were meat eaters, that's
what they wanted. Deer, and cattle, and wild boar—risky
business. That's why they had to hunt in groups. We'll know
soon enough. Watch him, Lana."

His words were unnecessary. Lana Cramer was crouched
over the body. Everything seemed to have gone well, but she
wanted to see him awaken, to hear him talk to her again
before she would be convinced.

"We were walking across some kind of—what's the
word?—scree? Loose shale and gravel. Funny thing is, I
have no idea at all what it *looked* like. Seems as though I've
blanked it out." Bayle Richards looked up at the ceiling,
squeezing his eyes hard shut with the effort of recollection.
"Same with the trees and the grasses," he said at last. "I
don't get much from them—just their smell, and a feeling
about some of them."

"What sort of feeling?" Cramer was listening intently, the
tape recorder by his side silently preserving every word.
"Colors?"

"No. Definitely not colors. A feeling for *uses*. That's not
right either. A feeling for some special function." He shook
his head in annoyance. "What's wrong with me? It's as
though there are big blank spots in my memory—but I can
see a lot of the surroundings when I close my eyes, and I can
hear the sound of the birds and the wind. Is it a bad transfer?"

"Bad?" Cramer laughed, excited and stimulated enough
to drop his usual role of the impassive scientist. "It's not bad,
it's more than I dared hope for. Bayle, you're doing fine.
You have three things working against total recall, and I was
afraid that any one of them might make the whole experiment
a failure. First, Lana probably told you that Pierre is perfectly
preserved, but that's not really possible. There was some

decay, there had to be. We were lucky to find as much as we have of preserved chemical memories. Then we had to transfer to you, and *that* has been a big success. You've been getting more sensation than we ever hoped you'd experience.''

''I've had sensation all right.'' Richards wriggled his shoulders. ''Old Pierre had cuts and scratches all over him. He didn't even register them, but they came across to me down below the conscious level. When I woke up I felt as though I had been cut and bitten and stung by every plant and insect in creation. He didn't notice any of it. But what's the other thing working against us?''

''Outlook.'' Cramer began to flick through the slides in the big projector. ''You are trying to see the world through his eyes, but his universe is totally different from the one we have in our heads. Ninety percent of the things that he thought were important are not in your data base at all. You will interpret what he saw, what he did—but the *reasons* he did them? That's something we'll never know. Here, do any of these look familiar to you?''

The slides that flashed onto the screen represented months of careful work in France. John and Lana Cramer had travelled over the whole region, recording characteristic land forms and geological features—anything that might have survived for over twenty thousand years. As image after image passed across the screen, Bayle Richards shook his head.

''Not a glimmer. Dr. Cramer, I guess you're right. Pierre didn't even *see* things like this.''

''Keep looking. They must have had some way of knowing where they were, and how to get back from the hunt.''

''I'll look, but I think you may be on the wrong track. The one thing that Pierre *always* seemed to be conscious of is the position of the sun. Could he be navigating by that?''

''Maybe. But what about cloudy days?'' Cramer shrugged. ''Let's keep looking. What about fire? Did you carry any with you?''

''Fire.'' Richards hunched his head forward. ''Yeah. That

brings up all sorts of images. But not on the hunt. There was
fire back where we came from—a long way back. Seems to
me we had been farther on this hunt than ever before. They
were worried about getting into enemy territory, some place
where there were other animals or people that would hurt
them. Pierre has a sort of built-in smell reaction, his test for
aliens. No fire on the hunt, though, and a feeling that we were
an *awful* long way from home. Many days. Maybe we were
doing more than just hunting.''

"Many days?'' Cramer turned to Lana, who had been
patiently taking notes of the conversation. "Maybe we spent
too much time in the west when we were over there. Do you
have anything fifty or a hundred miles to the east? I didn't
bother.''

"Skip to the end.'' She frowned, uneasy with the role of
decision maker. "You remember, when you went up to Paris
I stayed behind and did some sight-seeing. There may be a
few shots in there.''

Cramer began to flick rapidly through an assortment of
images, pastoral villages, inns, river valleys, and mountain
valleys.

"Hold it.'' Richards sat upright. "Back up a couple.
There. What's that one? I recognize it, and I've never been to
France in my life.''

"This one?'' Cramer froze on one slide.

"That's it. That's where we came from. We live in caves
along the side of one of those big ridges. I'm sure of it—I can
even remember which cave I lived in, one with a narrow part
that broadens out again into a second chamber.'' Richards
stood up. "Where is that?''

Lana Cramer was consulting her notes. "It's Auvergne, in
the hills of the *Massif Central,* a hundred miles east of the
Dordogne. We didn't cover that far over—I took that just as a
good view.''

"Damn good thing you did.'' Cramer slapped his
notebook against his knee. "That's frustrating. We didn't
expect that Pierre would have been so far away from his
home base when he got into trouble. I'll have to call Paris and

see if they can ship me a couple of hundred other slides of the eastern area. I want to pin down his travels as much as I can.''

"You want to end it for today?'' Richards was looking tired, but still stimulated by Pierre's memories. "I'd like to keep going for a while. When you showed that shot, I got a whole bunch of other thoughts. A woman, and a child. I think they may be Pierre's.''

"You and Lana can keep going for a while. I want to get these other images ordered, but I don't see any problem if you take notes of everything.'' Cramer stood up. "Tomorrow, we'll see if we can tap that same area, keep the hunt going and find out how it ends. Make sure you get enough sleep. I think we get better transfer if you are rested.''

He left abruptly, his mind already moving on to the next session of the experiment. Lana moved in and turned off the tape recorder. Her calm face had changed, become that of a tormented woman who cannot see any answer to a difficult problem.

"Bayle, I can't go on pretending. It sounds trite, but it's a fact.''

"You said you were going to talk to him. Did you change your mind about that?'' Bayle Richards did not sound particularly interested in her answer. His eyes were far away, still back in the mesh of alien memories.

"Bayle, I can't face John.'' Lana sensed the separation but misunderstood the reason for it. "You know he can beat me down, he always could. Can you do it? If I try and talk to him now, he'll ignore me unless he thinks that *you* can affect his precious experiments by refusing to cooperate with him.''

"He can force me to.''

"No. He can force you to *pretend* to work with him, but he knows that he's at your mercy when it comes to the memories you say you have or don't have. That's your edge, Bayle.''

He looked at her uneasily. "What are you suggesting, Lana? What should I tell him?''

"Make the bargain with him. You'll work with him to the end of the experiments with old Pierre. But set your price for that.''

''And my price?'' His voice was too cold, she did not think she was persuading him.

''Your price is your freedom.'' Her voice dropped. ''And mine. I could never win it from him without you helping. He's too strong for me.''

He shrugged. ''What makes you sure there will be an end to the experiments? Suppose that he wants to go on with them forever?''

''No. Not this experiment. You heard what John said, he thinks he has a key that will unlock all human history. There are another twenty preserved bodies scattered in Institutes around the world. If he wants to explore the past with them, he'll need to have other clones developed, give them consciousness from other Bayle Richardses. When he does that, we'll be free. He won't care where you go when this experiment is over.''

He was quiet for a long time, so long that she thought he was not going to give any reply at all. His face was unreadable in the dim light.

''All right,'' he said at last. ''We need to know how long this is likely to go on, whatever happens after it. He has access to those other preserved bodies?''

''He already made the arrangements. I helped him do it. Bayle''—she moved close to him, touching his head gently as though she was afraid that he would suddenly disappear into the shadows of the room—''when will you do it, Bayle?''

''Tomorrow. Before the experiment. Don't worry, I'll do it. I don't want to stay in this place forever, when I could be out there in the world starting everything over with a decent body.''

''Both of us.''

He was silent again. Finally he shrugged. ''I guess so. If John Cramer agrees. You're his wife. You ought to know him well, but if he says no, what do I do then?''

She put her arms round him. ''He won't say no.'' The words were more like a prayer than a statement. ''He won't say no to you.''

The images that John Cramer had requested from Paris had been scanned and transmitted overnight. Lana Cramer, hurrying back with them from the communications office of the hospital, found the lab already a scene of great activity when she arrived there. John Cramer was supervising the installation of a ceiling projector directly above the table where Bayle Richards would again lie during the information transfer from Old Pierre.

"Over there, then get to the anesthetist station." Cramer's manner to her was cold and brusque. She placed the images on the side table, near the projector, and looked across to where Bayle was already connected to the multiple electrodes that would carry the signal for memory transfer. He was staring across at her.

"Did you talk?" she mouthed to him. Her husband was bending over the casket that contained Pierre's body, but she dare not go across to Bayle.

He nodded, and she gave him an exaggerated questioning look and a shrug of interrogation. He turned his thumb up, then down, and returned her shrug. John had listened, but he hadn't given any definite answer at all. She knew that reaction, the steady nodding of his head, then the sudden turn away or the switch of subject.

"Ask him again later?" She mouthed her question, not sure how well Bayle was getting her meaning.

He nodded, then lay back on the table. She would have to wait until this session was over for details—there was no chance that they would be coming from John, and his stony look made her fear the worst.

"Sedation patterns again, same as yesterday," he ordered, abruptly standing up from his position by the casket. "We're set up today so that we can throw scenes for Bayle's inspection while the experiments are still going on. We'll have to bring him in and out of contact with Pierre while that's being done, but I believe we have that degree of control now. Tell me when you are getting first signal transfer."

Lana forced her attention to the control console and watched the pattern of brain waves that was crawling across the oscilloscope. It was establishing itself even quicker than last time, the resonances building between Bayle's brain and Old Pierre's.

"It ought to get easier and easier," Cramer had told her when she expressed surprise at the ease of contact. "Don't forget their brains are structurally *identical*. It's not like trying to establish contact between two dissimilar objects. When these experiments are over, we ought to have sucked out most of Pierre's useful memories. It ought to be a bigger challenge when we leave the Cro-Magnons and try it with *Neanderthalensis* and *Habilis*. I've located well-preserved specimens of both of them."

Put that way, all the complex experiments that had led to Bayle's links with Old Pierre sounded easy and natural. Lana comforted herself with that thought as the transfer signal strength grew on the screen.

"Don't like smell." The words came suddenly from the figure on the table. "Bad smell. Like the others." Bayle Richards' hand moved convulsively, grasping at something by his side. "Will have to fight again, beat the others to the horns."

"He's still on the trail," said Cramer softly. "I've edited the images that came in from Paris. Keep the transfer rate high until I tell you, then push it right down. I want him to look at one of the images."

Lana nodded. Cramer seemed to be the same as yesterday, but she knew from long experience that her own ability to read his emotions was negligible. At least the experiment was going well, that suggested he would be in a good mood later.

"Others ahead," said the figure on the table. Was it Bayle Richards at the moment, or was he no more than a vessel for Old Pierre's memories? "Must fight the others, can't go back without food. Cold, need food."

"Northern France still glaciated." Cramer sounded pleased. "I couldn't understand yesterday, when he said it was hot. Makes more sense for him to feel cold today."

"See many ahead of us. They are not the people, they are

others. We get ready, move towards them. Bad place to fight ahead, not covered.''

''Now.'' Cramer gestured across to Lana. ''Cut the transfer for the moment, I want to try and get a fix on where he is.''

As the signal switched from mildly sedating to stimulating, Cramer flashed a scene onto the ceiling above Richard's unconscious form.

''Bayle.'' The eyes flickered open, then closed again. ''Bayle, look up there. Do you recognize that scene? Is it one that you've just looked at?''

The eyes flickered open again, stared up at the color image. Bayle Richards shuddered.

''That's it. That's where we are heading, where the others are. Danger, I think there's danger.''

''Shall I cut the connection?'' Lana sat with her hand poised over the switch that would inhibit all transfer from Pierre to Bayle.

''No.'' John Cramer's voice was full of some strange satisfaction. ''I know what's happening, it's all right. Put him back to full transfer, let's keep this going.''

''But what's the scene you showed him?'' Lana, poised over the dials, had a poor view of the ceiling display.

''I'll tell you later.'' He looked at her impatiently. ''Lana, get that signal back up *now*. We'll lose transfer, and that would ruin everything.''

Automatically she responded to the command in his voice and turned on the full signal again. Bayle Richards jerked spasmodically, strained his head around him.

''See them now, they see us. Go forward now, must win and follow the horns. We all go forward together.''

He had begun to pant, his deep chest filling to its maximum capacity beneath the covering sheet.

''John, what's happening?'' She could hear the deep grunt of effort coming from the man on the table. ''Shall I cut the signal?''

''No.'' John Cramer had moved to her side, leaning over the control panel. ''Keep it like that, maximum transfer rate.

I'll tell you when to change it.''

"But, John, what's he *doing*." She looked again at the groaning figure on the table. "He doesn't seem to be walking, and look at his arms moving. Do you know what's going on?''

Struck by a sudden thought, she pushed her chair away from the console and leaned far back, looking up at the scene on the ceiling projector. She screamed as soon as she saw the flat plain with its sparse cover of grass and sedges.

"John! That's the salt marsh where Old Pierre was found. If Bayle is there now, it means that he'll—''

She screamed again and threw herself at the control panel. John Cramer was there before her. As the figure on the table thrashed and gargled, the sounds coming from his throat suddenly agonized and blood-clogged, Cramer held the transfer rate switch open to full maximum. He was too strong for Lana to get near it, even though she struggled desperately. The sound from the table took on a new and more terrible urgency.

He came awake in one piece, his muscles flexing him upright at the same time as his eyes opened to the flat white light. Although he was lying up high, he instinctively rolled down to the floor, reaching up to his head to tear away the uncomfortable attachments to his bare scalp.

Naked, he crouched low and looked around him. He had been brought here without the comforting presence of stone axe and spear, without the cheering smells and sounds of the People. The smells that filled his nostrils now were alien and menacing. In front of him, two others struggled together, not seeming to see him at all or to detect his scent. Before they could attack, he had leapt forward to strike hard at the base of the neck, first the man, then the woman. To his surprise, they both crumpled unconscious to the level floor of the white cave.

He bent over and sniffed more closely at the man. Certainly alien, not of the People. With one efficient movement he snapped the neck, then bit the jugular vein to reach the blood. It had been many days since he remembered eating, but for some reason his hunger was satisfied almost at once. He dropped the man's body to the floor, surprised by the peculiar skins that seemed to cover it.

The woman's scent was different. She was not of the People, but it was good to mate outside the People. If he could find his way out of the strange cave, he would take the white-haired woman with her strange mixed smell back with him to the Home. But he wondered if he would find his way Home. If he had been ended in the marsh—his last memory was of the spear in his throat—then he must make a new life for himself here, in the After-Life. First he must possess the woman, to show that she belonged to him.

He knew how to be patient. Looking around the new cave, he squatted next to her on the floor and waited for her to wake. Already her eyelids were moving. It would not take long now.

*Rivka Jacobs is on the threshold of a writing career. This
is, if I am not too far wrong with my guesstimates of publish-
ing schedules in the field, her first professionally published
fiction. Another of the things that make me happy to have
done this book is that in the future I will be able to say I was
the first editor to buy her work.*

EXPERIMENTUM CRUCIS

Rivka Jacobs

The sky was silver at midday, the clouds sank to the Earth
forcing an unseemly sweat from the recent erected parapet
beneath the renovated Town Hall. The Church of St.
Nicholas reposed within sight of the prisoners. The basilica's
cupola and body glowered darkly, a Gothic corpse crying
condensing mist. The Mala Strana of Prague was silent.
Spectators shivered in bundled groups, more alert to the
numerous Habsburg soldiery than another execution. The
Vltava River, swollen with the thunder shower and human
refuse, could be heard hissing beyond the slick, mossy,
chilly square. The two prisoners were driven together,
neither ever having known the other, and halted a body's
width apart at the base of the steps. Atop the bloodstained
architecturally perfect breastwork a swordsman leaned on his
dull instrument. He wore an infantry uniform of Maximilian
of Bavaria, the conqueror of Prague. There was no drumroll,
no dramatic tension. Beside the executioner another occupation officer read the official orders while the subjects pas-
sively waited below, one in shirt sleeves, the other in monk's
habit.

"On this day the twenty-fourth day of November this year
of our Lord 1621, by the command of His Most Catholic
Majesty Holy Emperor Ferdinand, son of the House of
Habsburg, this man Matyas of Braunau and this man Vaclav
of Moravia are obliged to pay the supreme penalty for crimes

against humanity and God. They shall not be denied a confessor of the One True Church.''

A priest was already in intimate conversation with Vaclav. Matyas' sullen eyes glittered briefly as he ignored the ministrations next to him.

''As the man Matyas of Braunau has refused the last Sacrament,'' he lowered the parchment, spoke seemingly from his own conscience, ''so may he be consumed by the fires of Hell alongside all else who deny the True Faith.'' The officer's beard sparkled with wetness, moisture dangled and sprinkled from his chin as his jaw worked. He coughed laboriously—the darkness picked up the sound and tossed it to the surrounding marble, basalt and granite. He signaled the guards, stepped to the far side.

The prisoners ascended together at a steady, almost brisk pace. They were unfettered; their exposed skin bore the marks of previous inducement. Level once again, they were herded toward the center. One of the captors prodded Vaclav, separated him, pushed him and detained Matyas. An emaciated, bearded figure, his blue eyes like incandescent windows, Vaclav knelt facing the stretch of Prague. He did not pray. He appeared to be watching an unseen prompter.

The clean-shaven soldier roused, lifted the heavy nicked sword with assiduous nonchalance. He swung the blade to full arms' length above his head.

There was a muted thud and sharp rattle. Vaclav instinctively twisted to observe—the weapon lay broken beside its fallen wielder. The lithic surface seemed to shine more brightly. Deepened by underlying blemishes, it seemed to glisten an accentuation.

''Witchcraft,'' he muttered. He rose, one hand kneading a knee.

Vaclav blinked vacantly, unable to focus on the event. Matyas smiled faintly. The officer tucked the scrolled indictment into his belt, drew in breath with enough implication to reestablish the inexorable course of their respective roles. He motioned the guards to retrieve the Moravian while he himself kicked aside the shards of Imperial enforcement. Another round of hacking shook him, temporarily halting proceedings. The executioner stepped away; plague was still rampant within the Bohemian domain. Angered by his apparent show of weakness the officer barked a command across the plaza. Instantly a young foot soldier bounded to and up the steps. The crack of his stride echoed fortissimo to pianissimo in a web of noise.

The new sword was lighter, smaller, not meant for beheading. The Bavarian seemed content that this would force a more agonizing demise.

Matyas was shoved and continued of his own accord to assume Vaclav's place. His guard knocked his feet from under him with a grimy boot—he landed painfully.

Positions were resumed, order restored. A nod and again the weapon swept like a knife through the leaden air. The climactic arc, the point posed upright and high; its tip abruptly began to blur, take on a blue-purple then green aura. There were frightened gasps from the guards. Soldiers beneath shrank backward. The officer goggled, his mouth forming soundless prophylactic syllables while he crossed himself. Conversely, civilian witnesses straightened.

The dots of pair and triplet gatherings became illuminated with raised, wonder-filled faces.

Lastly, the executioner caught their reactions and gazed up. He yelped like a beaten dog—a ball of luminescence was rapidly expanded and draining down toward his hands. Above, the cloud bellies rolled, bellowed. Droplets began to spatter. He threw the weapon wide. It landed with a clatter at the foot of the parapet.

The priest was loudly intoning, the swordsman moaned. Static electricity pricked the rear of Matyas' neck as he rose without hindrance. A booming crash flattened all of them. The sour smell, a telltale of lightning, drifted in aftermath. Rain sprayed and lazily blew in billowing waves. Matyas and Vaclav, their chins touching the frigid stones, watched rivulets of clean water gush through mortar depressed crosshatching and fall to the distant plaza floor amid crystalline, life-giving splashes.

A House of the Jednota Bratrska, the Brethren, had been

converted with Austrian efficiency and irony into a stockade,
a chamber of torture and inquisition. Seizing the residence—
the bare walls, the tables—or burning the heretical books had
been a stroke of frustration as the Order's members whether
in Sweden, Moravia, Hungary or perishing as martyrs, could
not be so changed.

In the former library stinking with the excrement of countless shifts of prisoners and scattered with fetid straw, Matyas
of Braunau and Vaclav of Moravia lay chained across from
one another. Motionless, they stared into the twilight of the
remainder of November 24. Each searched the other's face,
each found only a reflected search. Night squeezed out the
meagre light; hollow winter returned along with nocturnal
insects. Continual flies droned. They listened as the tread of a
guard approached and passed along the hall beyond the iron
bolted, incongruously beautiful wood door.

"Do you understand it?" Matyas whispered first. His
hoarse voice seemed newborn, unneeded until that moment.
Receiving no reply, pausing for a sound of boots, he repeated, "Do you understand?"

Vaclav deeply sighed. "I wish I could. Suffice it that we
are both alive, albeit for only one more day."

"They were felled like saplings in a gale. They couldn't
call it heavenly intervention, that would have contradicted
their reason for existence."

"What do we call it?" Vaclav asked.

"We? I assume you are one of us?"

"Us? I am a Jesuit priest, you a disciple of the Utra-
quists."

There was a moment of nothingness, then, "That's impossible. Your Order is the right hand of the Imperial Dignity."

"I am a Moravian, a scholar, a friend of Charles of Zerotin
and Jan Komensky but also a priest loyal to the Pope in
Rome. . . ." Vaclav sighed. "I suppose to you that seems
highly improbable."

"You've met Comenius?"

"Yes. I wanted nothing more than peace for my people so
I supported the moderate Charles in the hope that an agreement could be reached which would forestall a punitive war.

For this my Jesuit brothers denounced me as a traitor. When your Count Schlick invaded Moravia and set the radicals in power, I was labeled a vassal of Rome and so imprisoned. After White Mountain, with Ferdinand's victory, I was again a traitor for having supported Charles. Neither fish nor fowl in this world gone mad.''

"But which side are you on?" Matyas insisted.

"The side of God."

"So we all say. I was one of the first sent to prison for helping erect a Protestant church in Braunau. I was released by the Defensores after the Defenestration. After White Mountain I was again condemned as a ringleader by Maximilian's tribunal.''

"So here we are. Both saved, as the case may be."

"If the tide of war changed tonight we could be free."

"No. We are already casualties. Dismissed, relegated to death. Except . . ." The tone was confused.

"Except . . ." Matyas' tone was a definite invitation.

"Miracles, a deus ex machina for two innocent victims?"

"But that depends on who calls whom guilty. To the Habsburgs I am not innocent."

"We must analyze. Let us use the Socratic method."

"Agreed. One: a miracle."

"Bilaterally not possible to explain."

"Well, the man slipped and you were spared. I, on the other hand, drew radiance . . ."

"A natural phenomenon. To those of us who study Italian sciences or ancient Greek accounts, a purely deductible possible side effect of inclement weather."

"In any case, what does it matter? I've been resigned to death." Matyas paused. "Tomorrow is the end."

Insulated by a platoon of priests which was ringed by soldiers, the duo was marched through the winding streets of Prague. Dawn was blotched with jagged, threatening cumulus nodules. The eastern horizon was an ugly yellow-gray. The party progressed in slow measure, reversing the route the Bohemian Assemblymen had taken three years earlier. That procession had culminated with the Imperial ministers being thrown from the windows of Prague Castle. The present advance aimed no farther than the Charles Bridge.

Suspecting demonic influence the company moved languidly, allowing benevolent power to thoroughly fence the prisoners.

Hands bound behind, gagged, Matyas and Vaclav stepped through the tower-gate simultaneously, and onto the historic ediface. The Vltava had grown more quiet, though it still gurgled in a feverish temper. The depths were ink. Froth and debris laced the twining currents, the lesser and lesser sub-currents. Swishing, sucking, slapping rose from the bridge pilings, from the heart of the structure itself.

Neither man averted his attention, each knowing that the foul picked heads of comrades flanked them in a grotesque double line.

The cortege halted. Their gaoler, the tenacious consumptive officer who had previously postponed this moment, had no speech to read. He directed leather straps be applied to the legs and feet of his charges. Words reverberated in his imagination—*Utere iure tuo, Caesar . . . kill them by sword, by wheel, by water, by rope and by fire.*

No last rites were offered and none were desired. Vaclav breathed the substance of his terrestrial habitation, drinking the draughts to lung capacity. Matyas closed his eyes, a mental picture of himself gulping water like a fish flirted with reality. The gag cut the corners of his mouth as he lost the dream and likewise filled his senses with massive inhalations.

The scene froze. An awesome silence descended. Puffs of frost played about the congregation. Tiny nervous whispers became magnified. Participants shivered uncontrollably. The officer self-confidently raised his blue-tipped fingers to break the spell. Shadow spread like black wings over the old city. A sunrise streak vainly shone through a pocket of sky, its beams at wide dispersion, fanning like a celestial nimbus. In a wink this last display vanished as a subzero gust coiled

and sprang, its force plugging the hole with more dirty cloud.
Cowls, vestments, cloaks, hair snaked and danced. Like
frenzied moths specks of white, initially a handful but rapidly
multiplying, circled and reeled about the heads. With stunning swiftness sheets of snow curtained them. The officer's
eyes burned in a hot rage; his shouts were lost to the roaring
wind. He pantomimed his soldiers to complete the drowning.
Three, their progress retarded to a dream stagger, seized
Matyas. The Bohemian's dark moon mien was beaming with
incredulity. His Moravian counterpart's fair almost delicate
face burst into awareness as lids flew up. Three more pawns
grasped him. The officer's mantle seemed a living creature as
it tugged him off balance, to the edge of the wall—he peered
into the blizzard and was granted enough clarity to perceive
that where the Vltava had been now a crust of translucence
had grown. That proximate to the bridge supports the river
had stopped in mid flow, its form preserved like Italian glass.
''Never!'' he screamed to the chaos that enshrouded them.
''Never!'' He lost track of his own questions; he swore
before God. With an extravagant gesture that bordered on
panic he set the execution in motion.

The Charles Bridge seemed lower, or the river higher. The
ice did not break. Enough snow had accumulated to cushion
their impact. They lay helplessly alive like newly delivered
infants. Bonds became brittle—Matyas snapped his legs
apart, rose to his knees. Without hesitation he crawled to
Vaclav's side. Before he could maneuver to facilitate a
mutual rescue, infantrymen were scrambling down both
slippery banks.

''He will have our lives. It has become a personal matter
for him,'' Matyas whispered.

Vaclav's shackles gave off a dreary jingle as he shifted
position. ''I believe I escaped without frostbite.''

There was a heavy exhalation, a semi-sigh. ''What rele-
vance do toes and fingers have to dead men.''

''This is thrice for me. They tried the wheel earlier. I
neither lied nor renounced. And I survived.''

"It was the same with me." He spoke loudly, noisily straightened.

They grew quiet as the monotonous trudge paused by the library door. It passed on.

Emotion pulsed within each of them, through canals of thought and soul long dried by torture and terror. They were like adolescents first tasting the possibilities of life.

"We must find a reason, we must not let ourselves sink into apathy. I do not think we resolved our first argument, but let us forgo miracles and continue our quest."

"Agreed. How about the opposite; which is no doubt what the Emperor's men are assuming; malefic interference of a devilish genesis."

Vaclav's corner was a vacuum. Finally, "It's the back side of the same coin. Who or what would intercede for both of us, did either of us contact demons or familiars to come to our aid? Surely I have spent my entire life crusading against such foolery. Do you suspect me of summoning Satan?"

"No. But the Devil would need no comprehensible premise and he wouldn't offer an explanation any more than our Lord needs or does."

"Have you read Proverbs? The only angel a man can become is the Angel of Death?"

"Thus men are the angels and devils—you are indeed a heretic. And I agree with you. Though our existence at the moment would appear to be proof of one or the other's metaphysical status."

"We have badly knocked both theories. A third is: natural phenomenon or natural coincidence."

"A fourth is: luck or chance."

"They would seem to be distant cousins."

"All right. Natural is self-evident. These were events, taken as isolated, well within mankind's experience on this Earth. We could belabor each incident and no doubt you would conduct a factual dissection. But coincidence makes me laugh. Why us? Why now?"

"Luck, however, fares no better for it implies a previous

possession or lack of the same. A prerequisite belief in or
dependence on Hecuba's hegemony. It also erases the responsibility of our tormentors for now we take upon ourselves the benign or malignant turn of our respective wheels.
We become unstuck, adrift in our mundane sphere with no
spiritual or temporal guide. Why should we exercise our
minds, why should we question? We will live or die as
chance dictates.''

"That is too blithe. *Nahoda* intrudes, it doesn't unsurp.
Any peasant will tell you that to be condemned to die and be
twice spared is *stastna nahoda*, a lucky chance.''

"What happened to the serf's faith in divinity? Or does he,
for such basic matters, return to an even older pantheon?''

"I accept *nahoda*.''

"I am not so practical. I will not dismiss an intelligent
purpose.''

"Our speculations have saved our dignity, these discussions my sanity. Alone, how could I have borne such fickle
happenstance?''

"If our inquisitor, in his warm bed with his Bohemian
prostitutes, does not cough his blood away this coldest of
mornings while we, though our clothes are rags and the hoar
frost paints the walls at our backs, are aflame with the honor
of being rational beings, if he lives another three hours we
surely shall not last another four.''

"Amen. May whichever god you prefer bless you.''

"Farewell, my friend.''

Ripples and wavelets, like those on a pond's surface during a blowing summer afternoon, skimmed the sooty crushed
snow which carpeted what had been the Brethren's vegetable
garden. On this morning the enclosure, with somber rec-
titude, sported a rudimentary gallows. Wood scaffolding, a
platform, two bracing beams, a single crossbar and five limp
nooses sent a distorted silhouette like an insect petrified by a
ray of brightness against the dead vine-veined western wall.

Weakened by hunger the two prisoners were supported,
not unkindly, by youthful troops of the Bavarian officer. No

other sentinels were stationed. Sun was visible, a pale blue sky domed unmarred. The arctic air settled, motionless, weighted with tearing cold. The soldiers exuded stream; young colts set loose, their new commissions reflected in virgin eyes. A war was nothing more than lazy days in refractory Bohemia, executing those adjudged guilty of heresy. These two, resembling the meanest beggars found on the streets of Munich or Augsburg, were to be hanged without delay.

A gap in the high palisade evidenced a missing gate which perhaps had been soldered of iron and thus confiscated, melted down for cannon by either the Defensores or Imperials. Materializing in gilded finery, the crater-cheeked commandant filled this space for a moment, stopping as if to reassure himself that physical law was corralled, the counter-reformation was securely anchored, his moving picture was painted according to his will. With satisfaction he viewed the stupor of impending calamity, that expression he had seen so often, returned to quench rekindlings of defiance. In Matyas' eyes while the last Sacrament was administered to Vaclav, in both of them when recaptured on the Vltava's ice and this morning, when roused—an annoying mental resistance had become evident. This was now dampened, forever, he promised himself.

He strode in a blend of military perfunctoriness and aristocratic ease toward the gallows. The Bohemian and Moravian had been brought to the first wooden step. The operation seemed to interminably ossify, the chimera of legality was a gorgon that flew over and preserved the actors in stone. The officer's anger again flared as he sensed this. Quickly, it was gone. He spoke earnestly, energetically and the hanging commenced.

The climb was difficult. Leg muscles were liquid after three foodless days. On the platform they were made to stand upon lumber blocks that would shortly be yanked away. A soldier ascended beside each, positioned and adjusted each mildewed, brown and tattered noose. In unison these hopped again to the platform and bound the prisoners' ankles.

Calm—the world, the garden, the officer and his men.
Matyas of Braunau and Vaclav of Moravia, hands tightly tied
at the small of their backs, waited.

A phlegm-cluttered cough punctured the bubble of
fatalism. The officer, via a spastic swipe of a hand, signaled
the deed be done. He bent, and spat red matter into the snow.
Hematic droplets remained on the fine beard hairs around his
mouth.

With a scrape and a knock as the blocks tumbled, and
instantly snaps and a double thump, he recoiled upright, the
rear of a gloved hand pressed to his lips. He stared, his flesh
losing its febrile points of color. His men, beside him and
those above, stood stunned, their arms dangling like pen-
dulums.

Matyas, the frayed noose on his shoulders like a necklace,
sat. Vaclav lay flat, laughing as his rope collar uselessly
formed a lower case sigma next to him. They could not look
at one another. During that first immobile moment the powerful feelings would have overwhelmed had either sought the
other's gaze. Vaclav rose to sitting. Matyas found himself in
visual confrontation with the officer below.

He masked himself in his Imperial caste as the
bloodstained glove lowered, briefly clutched the swordstrap
across his chest and finally fell to his side. "Take them to the
cell," he called. He smiled at his own forbearance.

"Sir," one of the young soldiers breathlessly addressed
him, "Sir, it's impossible."

He watched as the duo was roughly tossed along the stairs
to the ground. Countenances highly flushed, life having
reentered in full, they seemed children fallen purposely into
the snow. A guard kicked them into standing. They were
dragged from sight into the distant-time refectory. "This is a
modern, new era," he said to the worried infantryman. "The
ancient world is dead. We have been lax, our laws requiring
biblical castigation for biblical crimes. This has been an
omen aimed at me. From this day forward let the technical
prowess of man provide inescapable destiny."

Impatience, a long forgotten affliction, boiled within both

as their guards, not without extra brutality, fastened their iron cuffs once more. With excitement they held their tongues until they were alone.

"Not the work of heaven or hell, did we say? What then, what?"

Vaclav retorted immediately, "But certainly neither mere coincidence nor chance, not after today."

"The hemp was old, decayed—the flash freeze stiffened it and our weight broke it like a man does an icicle."

"Are you offering me a natural explanation?"

"No, you are correct. There is something more."

"I have been pondering this but you will think me insane when you hear my thesis."

"Present it. We will debate."

"I dreamed the night last, the only night I have done thus since my imprisonment began. I saw, or was permitted to see, a greatness well beyond our faculties. Or perhaps it was my fancy, rebelling against my self-imposed strict rationality. . . ."

"An Elysium, a paradise, an afterlife? The Lord's greatness?"

"No, quite the contrary. This was very much a part of our reality yet elevated, on a higher plane, yet still prosiac if not profane. Creatures, ostensibly men and women; I make no scriptural allusions, absolutely none. Not any conception we have of *kakodaimonia* or *eudaimonia* is relevant. These matched us somewhat but were less robust, less of the animal part. Their eyes were very bright and their hands were marvelously agile. They were beautiful as a well constructed, perfectly working clock is beautiful. They were more alive and sagacious than the most intelligent man I could conjure, historic or contemporary."

"How does this phantasm relate to us?"

"I watched these creatures studying me. I was in a frame, in a great mural or tapestry that recorded an unrecognizable swatch of history. I was a figure moving within. Then you appeared, then the diseased Bavarian and next the garden exactly as it . . . but at that point I was awakened by the guards."

"You were given a gift of foresight."

"The prescience was not mine."

"As Joseph did for Pharaoh, interpret this vision of yours."

There was hesitation as the tattoo of a march progressed to their door. There was no sound of departure but the library remained locked. Vaclav spoke in under-breathed haste. "These beings are here, but removed from our perception. Are they from an unknown land, from an Atlantis lost beneath the ocean or are they from another Earth, another sun? Mikolaj Kopernik proved to my satisfaction that Sol is the host of several planets and I have spoken with Galilei about other worlds, other spheres . . . ."

"And these beings saved us? Why?"

"They did not spare us. They are experimenting. We learn by necessity, they by callous, impartial application. Someday we will rise above our fervent desire to convert life and become as they, capable of using life. For better or worse."

A key screeched, the bolt spun.

"But what have they gained?" Matyas hurriedly implored.

"If they can capture the future on a wall, they can send lightning or ice to grant us reprieve."

"Not witchcraft, you say, and I can understand. It is within our grasp."

"Why? To learn. To learn what?"

"Of us, or our captors."

"How diligent will be Habsburg perserverance, how far will the Emperor go to secure our deaths."

"Or what does it take to crush the human spirit."

Vaclav gulped air as the library door began its shrill journey. "We have learned also; is that our test? Our potential is as real as their present. We will not blindly accept, we will always question."

For the first time tears stang Matyas' eyes. "No, not so. Don't forget how easily we surrendered and awaited death. How only such extraordinary measures revitalized us."

"And we shall sink again. We must."

"To what purpose, then? For my faith, my people, my land I have always been ready to die.''

"Why were we given this extension of life?"

A cluster of shadowy forms spilled into the nebulous chamber. One crossed to the fore. Coughing betrayed his identity. Through the boarded windows a glow of late afternoon, the 26th of November, played bizarre tricks. Orange gleaming eyes seemed to pierce from the blackened shapes of troops while the putrid, infested matting mounded ever higher. For an infinite span, to the starvation-numbed minds of the two prisoners, the military figures became complete negatives wavering in a copper aurora borealis.

Forward time resumed.

The courtyard, where the Brothers had studied, meditated, conducted classes or discourse among themselves, extended from the library. The path was short.

The sky had deepened as dusk became imminent. Azure intensity and the fragrance of smoke combined in a suspension of icy air. Evergreens had once grown from squares in the marble; residual torn stumps attested to the needs of an occupation army.

The snow was unclean. Slush and pocks of glass that had once been melt puddles were mixed with rusty, more ominous hues. Frozen mud had been churned. A far wall was splashed, the patterns like stars. A line of soldiers—these with sun-darkened, cracked, veteran faces and dispassionate eyes—opposed that boundary, their musket butts resting in the muck.

With victorious gratification the officer watched fear and finally capitulating somnolence, the drunken look he successfully anticipated, overcome his captives as they were passed before the unmoving squad of perfect gems that would obey a glance or sign. Matyas of Braunau and Vaclav of Moravia were deposited side by side, their shoulders almost touching. The officer approached them, closely insured their proper alignment but also surreptitiously peered into the two sets of eyes, one brown, the other blue, for any spark, any hint of hope. He was somewhat disappointed; an expression of surprise would have suited him. But they had surmised, as he suspected they would, that nothing would stop bullets.

This revelation empowered him, swelled his grasp on fate. He stepped casually to the side of the file, gripped his hands loosely behind his back. Let the Jesuits or Ferdinand take an eye for an eye, he decided, the Lord was served best by disregarding Him. He spoke phlegmatically, ''Present arms. . . .''

The volley was unusually pronounced, it echoed mercilessly. Life was terminated with explosive abruptness. The bodies were not immediately removed; it seemed the officer allowed gloating time to confirm the unmistakable triumph of his undertaking.

What can be said (at this point in time) about R.A. Lafferty? When I first read the following story (for the title, see Macbeth, *Scene VII) and came to the first reference to a time satellite and a time shuttle, I felt my heart sink just a bit—the premise of the anthology, after all, was to get at the past* without *any recourse to such well-used devices.*

I need not have worried. Lafferty's stories, like those of Phillip K. Dick, are not susceptible of being confused with the work of any other writer. And lafferty's time machine is not in the least bit like that of H.G. Wells.

At Moonwick, time is a mulch many meters deep.

These are the centuries and the thousands that we want to explore, and I never saw them piled up so beautifully . . .

BANK AND SHOAL OF TIME

R. A. Lafferty

THE PEOPLE. All are thirty years old except Peter Luna who is somewhat older than that, whatever year it is.

PETER LUNA. The genial and dying proprietor of a time post-house or relay-house. He is a door-keeper of time. "I need a matched set of at least five," he said.

HENRY KEMP, the *"Time-Reconstruction* Man". "You can build time like anything else." Henry is blue-eyed and shocky-haired and pleasant.

ANNABELLA MacBEAN, the *"Clotted Dream* Woman". She is a large young woman, ruddy of complexion and wit.

ETHAN FARQUHARSON, the *"Intuition-is-the-Key-to-Time* Man." "We have *all* walked through time in our powerful moments." Ethan is Scotch, and eagle-eyed and eagle-beaked.

ROWENA CHARTERIS, the *"Did-You-Ever-See-a-Naked-Ghost?* Lady". She is too serious, she is short-sighted, but she is of limitless faith. She is under special auspices.

ABEL ROARING, the *"Time-is-a-Pile-of-Transparencies Man"*. "There is no clear line where archaeology leaves off and time travel begins." He is a rocky and clattering man.

You'd like Abel. You'd like them all.

THE PLACE

Moonwick Estate near Lunel in the Herault Department of the Peoples Republic of France. At Moonwick, Time is a mulch many meters deep.

THE SEASON.

Summertime, summertime, summertime. There's nothing like it for time-travel.

THE PROPS.

Lark song, the noises of contented cattle and sheep, sound of grapes growing, low fidelity radio playing (with all his money, why doesn't Peter Luna get a good radio?), the colors green, blue, gold, yellow, russet, brown, cloud-white, wheat-yellow, water-gray. Sunshine, sunshine.

THE TIME.

A couple of minutes after noon on "Midsummer's Day" of an ambiguous year.

THE MOTTO.

"That Most Intricate of Pleasures, Time."

1

This was the message received by a dozen or so experts in the "time attempters" field:

"I have succeeded in establishing a creeping time-satellite or time-shuttle at my estate of Moonwick near Lunel in the Herault Department of the Peoples Republic of France. If you are really experts in your field, you will appreciate the importance of this. From this time-shuttle, which is just beyond the 'shoal' of all of you to whom I am sending this message, it will be possible for you to launch genuine time probes. I am sending this to a dozen or so and I hope for acceptance from at least five. I must have a matched set of at least five. Some soon. A very little bit after 'soon' will be too late for me to transmit the shuttle to you. Bring ideas only. Everything else for frugal and break-through living is provided. You will receive various transportation chits and enabling papers. Peter Luna.''

The World Courier Service ("No questions asked, Messages carried anywhere or anywhen in the world") delivered these messages to the dozen or so persons who were experts in the time field. And some of the people gave assent and some didn't. So, the next day, the Courier Service delivered airline tickets, train tickets, and International Taxi Coupons to five of the experts who had agreed to go to Moonwick.

So it happened that, on a sunny day in summer, five cabs drove up to the crumbling stone and rusting iron gateway of the estate Moonwick in the Herault Department of the Peoples Republic of France, not far from the town of Lunel. The taxi cabs arrived from five different directions by five different roads (that's right, there were three main roads and two little dog-leg roads that came together there), and they all arrived about the same time.

"Why, this is a marvel," one of the taxi drivers said. "There *is* a big house back from the gate! Why have I never seen anything except a pile of rubbish there before?"

"This is as far as I go," another taxi driver said. "The International Taxi Coupons are specific about this, lady, it's as far as the *gate* of Moonwick. This is as far as I can take you."

"Oh, that's all right," said the lady whose name was Annabella MacBean. "I wrestle a hundred kilograms of luggage a hundred meters every morning just to stay in shape."

"It *is* funny," a third taxi driver said. "I don't remember any big house back there either, but it's there today. The gate is as far as I can go, sir. The fare is covered by the International Taxi Coupons, but you are free to tip."

In another minute, all five of the taxi drivers had driven off, and five persons stood with their luggage at the entrance of an estate named ''Moonwick'' according to the rusting iron letters of the gate over-hang.

"It's Gothic, it's Gulf-of-Lions Gothic," one of the ladies said. "Oh you! I met you at the *'Backward-Turn-Backward-Oh-Time-in-Thy-Flight Convention'* in Ghent. You're Henry Kemp, the *'Time-Reconstruction* Man'."

"Yes, at the Hotel Schamp at Ghent in Belgium. And you are Annabella MacBean the 'Clotted Dream' woman. That was a wonderful meeting! How the minds and their ideas did rattle and bump together! Unfortunately it didn't bear much fruit. How is Gulf-of-Lions Gothic different from any other Gothic?"

"It's Gothic with the bright sun shining on it. All other Gothic is between haunted twilight and lightning riven midnight."

"You, sir," said one of the men to another, "I met you in Dublin at the *'Time-Will-Run-Back Congress'*. You're Abel Roaring, the *'Time-is-a-Pile-of-Transparencies* Man'."

"Certainly, certainly, at the Shelbourne Hotel at St. Stephen's Green in Dublin. You're Ethan Farquharson, the *'Intuition-is-the-Key-to-Time* Man'. I had a feeling that we were very near to a break-through at the Shelbourne. We had it and we dropped it. I pledge myself by all that is in me that we'll not drop it if we hold it so near again."

"I'm Rowena Charteris," said the fifth person of them.

"Oh yes," several of them recognized her name. "You're the *'Did-You-Ever-See-a-Naked-Ghost?* Lady'."

"But what shall we do now?" Rowena asked. "Walk to the house and find out who our strange host is? And see if there is some vehicle to transport our luggage there? Oh, oh, why didn't we *hear* you? Where did you *come* from?"

"I came from my house yonder," said the genial man as he stepped out of his truck. "And you didn't hear me because I didn't make any noise. What are you doing with all that luggage? I told you to bring ideas only."

"These *are* ideas," Abel Roaring grinned. "All of us are very heavy thinkers."

"This truck of mine runs as quiet as a ghost," the man said. "Load you in, folks, bodies and baggage. Yes, I know all your names. In the high and diffuse company of time speculators, you five weren't quite top-rank, until now. But the top-rank people hadn't enough curiosity to come here, so they are put down and you five become the top-rank people in the Time Affair.''

"What kind of truck is this that runs so quietly?" Roaring asked. They were rolling up the weedy drive to the big house.

"It's a Walker," the genial host said. "It's American."

"So am I," Roaring said, "but the Walker Truck refuses to be recognized."

"We will have good hunting here," the host said. "I'm Peter Luna of course. You will already be past the 'shoal' when you begin this hunt, and you will have bewildering freedom and opportunity."

"My watch has stopped," Ethan Farquharson said some while after they were pleasantly installed at Moonwick Estate. With their ears and their eyes they were grazing the fine house and gardens and exploring its excellencies. What a beautiful sunny day in summer! It smelled of new-mown hay and the Hippocrene.

"So has mine stopped," said Annabella MacBean, "and it's a Nicolay Never-Stop Watch. I can take it to any Nicolay dealer in the world and receive one thousand dollars and a new Nicolay Never-Stop Watch because of the failure of this one."

"I doubt that it has failed," said the pleasant host Peter Luna.

"What gives then, Luna?" Henry Kemp asked him. "My watch has stopped also."

"So has mine," said Rowena Charteris. "Have you stopped time itself?"

"And mine has stopped," Abel Roaring came in with it, puzzled. "How far have you gone with things here, Luna? Have you achieved Time Stasis?"

"Not quite," Peter Luna said. "It's a requirement that it be missed slightly. I've put my very local time here on slow-jog. After quite a while you will notice that your watches have really moved ahead slightly, very slightly, a second maybe in what will seem like several hours to you. This is an advantage in several ways. The most obvious one is that we cannot use the excuse that we have not time enough to solve the Time problem. Here and now, in the very-long-drawn-out now, we do have time enough.''

There were all the amenities there, swimming, tennis, golf, walking, eating, drinking. And card-playing, talking on every subject under the summer sun, and talking on their own subject in which, really, all other subjects were contained.

2

''—the Unknown Country upon which reposes this tedious and repetitive world'' —Belloc

"And why, young experts, have you not already walked through time?" Peter Luna asked his five guests as they sat at table.

"All of us have done it, for brief moments," Farquharson said. "We have done it in rapports and transports of unique experience. But none of us is able to do it at will."

"It's quite easy to ramble through time, at unseemly pace, in the future direction," Luna said. "A fairly simple technique will do it. But one comes to his own hour of death all too soon, and he dies. And the thing is not reversible. He does not return from that little jaunt if he goes too far into the future ('You know not the day nor the hour'); and he has a very shallow last-years-of-his-life if he's on a fast-tour survey. Possibly he will live thirty years in three minutes, and there's not a lot of satisfaction in that. So I will not recount to you (though I know them) any of the techniques for travel beyond the normal pace into the future. And there is no way that one may travel into the future beyond one's death. One follows his own ordained future then and not the temporal future of the world.

"But travel into the past! That should be quite simple. Going back before one's birth is not nearly so final a thing as going forward beyond one's death. One can always return from the journey to the time before his birth, if he is able to make a big enough jump. And if he cannot make a big enough jump, he still may come back. I've heard people say 'I've lived this life before: I'm quite sure that I've lived this life of mine before.' And I believe that some of them are correct in saying it. But I'm not greatly attracted to that either. We should go back with a leap beyond, and we should return with the great leap. But as to yourselves and your own attempts, have you found something that prevents your going backwards in time?''

"Of course we've found something that prevents it,'' Anabella said. "There are the years that are interdicted to us. It is my own ghost standing athwart them that interdicts them to me. If we could only get past those most recent years that are barred to us, then I believe that we'd have free sailing. It's like shoal water through which we cannot sail at all. But beyond it there is clear water for clear sailing, if only we could get to it. And the interdicted years (we are able to map them out even if we're not able to traverse them) are not of the same duration for everybody. And yet we have just discovered in comparing our data that they are pretty nearly the same duration for us five.''

"If we had a time-satellite we could take off from a cliff or bank that is beyond the shoals,'' Abel Roaring said. "We could be clear of our own interference and we could make fruitful voyages. You wrote in your message that you had a time-satellite here. That's why I came, Luna. Is there one? Where is it?''

"Yes, I do have one here. It will do what you hope for it to do, and more. It is beyond the shoals and beyond the interference,'' Peter Luna maintained.

"Where is it? When can we see it?'' Henry Kemp asked.

"Oh, you can see it whenever you open your eyes,'' Peter Luna told them.

"You have all guessed that the time journey should be easily made. I believe that each of you has worked out calculations for it, the themes and equations and formulae. You have designs for the hardware. The trip can be made by several different conveyances, and you five have likely hit on the most apt ones. You are able to take all the steps—except the first step. I know that frustrates you. To mix our metaphors, there is a shoal right across the mouth of our harbor and it will not let us come out.''

Peter Luna could have been almost any age. He had truly mastered time, in as far as it might ever have had effect on him. He was not so much handsome as he was deep and interesting. He was attractive, like rubbed amber; he drew people to himself.

''All time travel is highly personal, subjective, and psychic,'' Luna said. ''Whatever the mechanism of time travel is, it always has a preternatural starter or ignition. And we ourselves are the obstacle in going back through those nearest years. We cannot go back where we already are. We cannot occupy the same space twice at the same time; nor can we occupy the same time twice, no matter how far distant those two occupations are in space. It is a personal impediment, and it cannot be waived. A person (the hardware is willing, but the flesh interposes) cannot make incursion back into any time in which he already lives. So a person old enough to have learned the lore and techniques of time travel must hurdle at least thirty years of closed-off time before he begins his exploration. Perhaps we follow the law of inverse squares here; and if so, it will take nine hundred times as much power to go back thirty years as to go back one year.

''The apparent exception, travelers who have hurdled the shoal and got free into the past, but then have come forward through the years of their lives with some mixed memory of the thing, this is no exception at all. These persons are assumed into their own lives, just as reckless travelers into the future are assumed into their own deaths. They merge with themselves. They occupy the same time and place only once.''

''It would seem that young children would sometimes slip back over the shoal accidentally, it being so narrow in their case,'' Annabella MacBean said.

''And young children do it indeed,'' Peter Luna declared. ''And especially do the youngest children of all, those still in the womb, indulge in time travel. As you say, they have such a narrow way to go. Ever since the technique for recording and studying pre-natal dreams was discovered, persons have been startled and unnerved and plain flabbergasted by the contents of some of those pre-natal dreams. These unborn children do often have out-of-the-body experiences that are also out-of-the-present-time experiences. 'He's gone now, for a while,' an understanding mother will sometimes say, and later she will relate 'He's back now, but he's tired. I wonder where he goes?' She knows that the child doesn't take bodily leave of her, but the spirit that is in the child often does take its leave.

"In our own culture we simply ignore this early time travel and the memories that it leaves. In other cultures, those that believe in reincarnation or in the transmigration of souls, these things will be interpreted as memories of previous lives. They aren't. They are memories of early time travel with the young traveler identifying himself with someone he observed on that travel. So we have it in those cultures that children, when they come to the age of six or seven and are able to speculate and wonder and express themselves somewhat, will describe the deaths of children who lived before they were born, for these deaths have peculiar attraction for them. They will identify themselves with the one who had died. Sometimes they will insist that their parents should take them to places where they will call by name persons not known to them in present lives, where they will claim to be a dead child of certain persons there, and they will relate things that apparently only the dead child could have known.

"In our own culture, the same sort of early time travel happens, but other explanations or none at all are given for it. But the thing happens vividly and is remembered vividly by at least one child out of five. There are five of you here, so I suspect it has happened to more than one of you. Maybe to all of you. Maybe that is what has made time attempters out of each of you."

"Yes, it's plain that there is this impediment," Abel Roaring said, "and that we cannot ordinarily travel back into the years where we have already lived, 'where we are already

living,' as a true time attempter would say. And the more
maturity we bring to the problem, the longer is that treacher-
ous first step back into time, over a threshold of thirty years
or more. The shoal is in our way, but what do we do about it?
Can the problem be solved?''

"Oh, I've already solved it," Peter Luna said. "I've
solved it by the time-satellite that I've built here. By it we are
already beyond and previous to a shoal, and by using it you
five are back before you were born. As to myself though, I'm
still in my proper life, right at the end of it, as it happens.''

"You've hinted several times that you have this time
satellite here, Luna," Ethan Farquharson said, "but where
is it? When can we see it and study it?''

"You can see it right now, almost right now," Luna said,
"and I hope you will apply yourselves to its study immediately. Ah, the time-shuttle, it's so close to you that you
can reach out and punch it in the snoot. He who has ears, let
him hear. He who has eyes, let him see. He who has the third
eye, let him intuit!''

A taxi driver of the region had a wife who loved to go
riding in the country. He loved her, so he indulged her in this
love. Now he had gone off shift right after noon on a sunny
summer day, so he took his wife for one of those rides in the
country.

"There's a beautiful big house out in the country that I saw
today and I never saw it before," he said. "Let's go see it
now. You'll love it.''

They drove the taxi out into the country. They came to the
crumbling stone and rusting iron entrance to the estate that
was named "Moonwick" according to the flaking iron letters on the lintel of the gate.

"But where's the beautiful big house?" the taxi driver
bawled. "It was there, right there, not a hundred meters back
from the gate. No, Jemima, I'm not crazy.''

"Maybe it's all those 'No-Doz' pills you take to stay
awake when you drive at night, Jacques," Jemima said. "I
think that's what's making you kind of nutty.''

They drove through the disintegrating entrance-gate and back to where the large and impressive house had been only a half hour before. And it wasn't there. Nothing was there except a weed-grown pile of old rubbish.

"I won't give up," said the taxi driver whose name was Jacques Claxon. "Four other taxi drivers were here and saw it. And we let our five fares out at this entrance here. And here comes one of those drivers, Eustace Merleblanc, right now. We'll see what he thinks about this."

3

Time, a facet of human consciousness felt both in psychic and physical experience, and an aspect of the observed environment metaphorically describable as a one-way flow providing, together with space, the matrix of events. Time can be viewed either as metaphysically ultimate (process philosophy) or as illusory (philosophy of the manifold). For centuries it has been viewed as a significant dimension in the philosophy of history and in the theology of redemption. It can be measured either as an epoch (the moment of an instantaneous event as marked by the clock) or as the interval of duration of a continuous event, and by reference either to moving bodies or to electromagnetic phenomena (atomic time). Its flow has been found, in contemporary physics, to be relative to the observer's velocity and acceleration perspectives, and in biology, to be affected by such factors as environmental rhythms, temperature, drugs, and (perhaps) brain rhythms.

—Encyclopaedia Britannica

"But why do you say it is a one-way flow?" Rowena Charteris asked angrily. "Oh, I'm sorry, people. I was responding to something else that I was rolling around in my mind. Yes, they call me the 'Naked Ghost Lady' because I so often ask 'Did you ever see a naked ghost?' Well, I've seen nine ghosts in my life, but I've never seen a naked one."

Rowena, in that spacious noontime, had played three sets
of tennis with Abel Roaring. Then she had had a shower and a
pleasant nap, but the sun still stood where it had stood before,
a very little bit after noon.

"All ghost appearances are time trips. But time is sticky
stuff, it is tacky stuff, and it is always local," Rowena
lectured them. "We are in a galactic drift of several billion
miles a year, so there is no way we could return to any spot on
earth in any past time according to absolute location in space.
The spot on earth now would be billions of miles away from
the same spot on earth then. But time clings to local physical
objects, like a world, and all physical objects are deeply
imbedded in time. Time is very cohesive and it can only be
moved in quantum hunks, and we can only move out of the
common time stream by quantum pushes. So a ghost has to
bring part of his ambient with him when he comes, and his
minimal ambient is his own clothes. This makes a difficulty
for those who believe that travel in time consists of reconstructing people and things, molecule by molecule, in the
visited time. How much more difficult the clothes would
make it! And yet ghostly time visitants are almost always
clothed.

"And a ghost will always bring a sort of 'datedness' with
him that is easier to recognize than to define. So a ghost
expert is usually able to identify a nineteenth century ghost,
or an eighteenth century ghost. Witches, of course, used to
strip naked, smear themselves with pig-grease, and then slip
through a tight place into another time; but they must have
had a technique that I haven't discovered yet.

"But I do have my calculations as to what it takes to make
a quantum push into clear past time, disregarding personal-
life inertia. If you indeed have a time-shuttle established
here, Luna, then that personal-life inertia and inhibition can
be broken and by-passed, and my calculations *will* work. All
of us here can make a quantum push into clear past time from
a workable time shuttle here. Let's do it right now."

"Oh, you'll do it within a second or two at the most,"
Peter Luna said.

"But your 'second or two at the most' seems like a very long time when things are in an approximate time-stasis here," Abel Roaring said.

Annabella MacBean and Ethan Farquharson and Abel Roaring took a rather extensive foot-tour around the Moonwick Estate. The house itself was an imposing place, loaded with libraries, museum rooms, art galleries, dens, studies, billiard rooms, music rooms, laboratories, machine shops and fabricating *usines*, one very large dining hall and three smaller snack rooms, a big country kitchen and several satellite kitchens, and an even dozen guest suites.

There was a big cellar filled with junk. There was a big attic filled with other junk. There was a morning sun-parlor and an afternoon sun-parlor. There was a swivel telescope up on the highest part of the house, the truncated main gable. It was all a distinguished piece of Gulf-of-Lions Gothic, and one of the big shaded porches had an area of a hundred and thirty square meters.

And everything was open. There was not a locked door in the whole house. There was no place for any hidden rooms. The explorers went into everything, and they didn't find what they were looking for. There was no trace of one, not of a little one, certainly not of a big one.

And the great rolling outdoors of the estate was about a square kilometer in area. It was in the fork of two branches of a small river that rolled chortling the mere twelve kilometers into the Gulf of Lions of the blue Mediterranean. The third and North boundary of the Moonwick Estate was a line of steep and sudden cliffs about fifty meters high.

By anybody's standards, this was a beautiful place. The folded, rolling hills were covered with clover, or they were covered with grapes. Everywhere the three explorers walked the air was pleasantly noisy with bees. There were a dozen heavy white cattle grazing belly-deep in clover, there were exposed rock strata of shale and slate and chalk. There were beech groves.

"I have never seen time piled up so deep in a place,"

Ethan Farquharson said. "Not insufferably ancient time, but historical and para-historical time going back to the glaciations. These are the centuries and the thousands that we want to explore, and I never saw them piled up so beautifully. The banks of the North Border of the estate were once the shore of the Gulf of Lions. What a place to start from! If only 'it' is really here! But there are no hidden valleys on the estate, and we have seen everything big enough to matter."

"No, there's nothing on the estate that could be a time-satellite," Annabella said. "There is just no place here that even a mini-satellite could be hidden."

"I can't imagine a time-satellite smaller than ten meters in diameter and five meters thick," Abel Roaring complained. "Smaller than that it just wouldn't be workable. And it isn't here, it just isn't here. Do you think we are wasting our time here?"

"We're not wasting very much time here," Annabella said, "something less than three seconds since we've been here. And we've had four good meals here and now I'm hungry again. I've had a good night's sleep here, though it was at bright noontime. This is really the most filled-to-overflowing less-than-three seconds that I ever spent in my life."

"Intuition is the key to time," Ethan Farquharson was saying (this was not discernibly later by watch or clock, and yet it was a little bit further along in the time stasis), "which is to say that time is quirky, that it is mental, that it is subjective. There is no such thing as time, certainly not any such thing as elapsed time, unless mentality is present. I realize that this is very near to saying that 'time is illusion'; very near to it, but it is *not* the same thing."

They were all sitting on one of the largest of the great shaded porches of Moonwick Manor, and it was a little bit after noon on a sunny summer day. There was the intricate and genial, and curiously concerned, host Peter Luna. There was the speaker Ethan Farquharson, 'the poet of the time-attempters movement', who was Scotch and who had the hard untrusting eyes of an eagle combined with a cheerful hooked nose that had once been improved by being broken. He was good company in spite of the fits of absent-mindedness in which he acted as if he were the only person in the world.

There was Annabella MacBean ('the *Clotted-Dream* Woman'), a quite large young lady with only enough beauty for a middle-sized woman. So parts of her stuck out from under it and were not covered by that mantle. Her feet and her hands were too big, and her voice was a bit too large. She was entirely too ruddy, she was what is sometimes called raw-boned (nobody knows exactly what that means though). Well, but her hair and her face and her disposition and her wit were excellent. And such largeness-in-reserve as was hers has never hurt anything.

There was Henry Kemp, blue-eyed and thick-bodied, with a shocky crest of hair sticking up to show that he was a Teuton. He was a designer and builder. He believed that it should be asked of the most abstruse idea 'What does it really look like? Why cannot we make a working model of this thing?' And, to a greater extent than with most people, he had built himself, from the inside out; for his thoughts and predilections, coming through his pinkish and translucent flesh, had pretty well determined his appearance.

"As with anything built by an amateur builder, he's a bit lop-sided and rough-hewn," Annabella said about him, "but not really bad, not bad at all."

There was Rowena Charteris, too serious, and always peering intently into mysteries with her myopic eyes. The world itself was such a mystery to her, and she peered into it, taking her glasses off and putting them back on, and not able to see very deeply into it with all her peering.

But she had limitless faith in her chosen field. Limitless hope too. And, really, she had almost limitless love or charity. This time antic *had to* succeed now, if only for her sake. God and all the Jinni will make special efforts to accommodate such as was she.

Rowena was quite pretty. And, to one with eyesight as

poor as her own, she would seem absolutely ravishing.

And there was Abel Roaring. He looked as if he were made out of stratified rock, but that was only his textured complexion. His voice also had this rockiness, like the good-natured clattering of stones. He wasn't a handsome man. He moved with the surety and well-balanced ungainliness of a bear. He looked to be the oldest of the five by some years; but they were all about the same age, all about thirty years old.

You'd like Abel. You'd like all of them. They all had the interior illumination usually seen in people with strong vocations. By their noble vocations, they were the *Time Attempters*.

"Time travel, either into the past, or beyond the set pace into the future, is not a natural human attribute." Farquharson was talking. "Not natural, no. It is unnatural, or it is preternatural, or it is supernatural. But the attempting of it isn't illicit. If it were unlawful, it would not give such a feeling of exhilaration and joy. I am not able to put this into words at this moment in slow-jog time, but I have already put it into calculations. If you indeed have a time-satellite here, Luna (and we have not been able to find it anywhere on your estate), if you do have that take-off bank of time, then I have a bird here that will take-off backwards from it and fly backwards into the past."

"Are these the calculations that you publish in the Spring of 1986 issue of *'Time Returns Again Quarterly'*, Farquharson?" Luna asked. "If so, I'm familiar with them and they will indeed serve for an epochal backwards flight from this bank or satellite of time which I have built here. Yours are really and essentially about the same as the calculations of Rowena Charteris that I perused earlier in the present second. The same, but phrased quite differently. By the way, how long did you look for my time-satellite without finding it?"

"Oh, by your *local* semi-stasis time, it was something less than half a second, Luna."

"That's not very long, Farquharson. But I do have it built here, and I intend to have you all see it and know it very soon now."

Another taxi driver drove into the Moonwick Estate and parked behind Jacques Claxon near the pile of weed-grown trash. His name was Eustace Merleblanc and he had his own wife Ermadine with him.

"Jacques, Jacques, what do you make of it?" he asked as he got out and stood there. "It isn't here, is it? What happened to the large and wonderful house? Was the whole thing a mirage? It looked solid enough less than an hour ago, odd-structured but solid."

"Why don't you fellows just forget about it?" Ermadine Merleblanc suggested. "We all get nutty sometimes and see things that aren't there."

"I'll not forget it," Jack Claxon said. "I'm going to the authorities with the problem right now. I don't care if they do hoot me to scorn. There's something here that's too wrong to let pass."

"I'll not forget it either," Eustace Merleblanc swore. "There's the smell of something dislocated and hellish wrong here. Yes, we'll report it, Jacques, and we'll drive them bugs until they look into it. Something just plain swallowed that big house, Jacques."

4

Complete visual pictures . . . can be reconstructed of anything whose light or shadow fell even indirectly on one of these stones. We can get detailed pictures of animals, of plants, of people as they lived and moved thousands of years ago. We can reconstruct color pictures of the clouds moving overhead, and we can read the spectra of those clouds. We can reconstruct anything that was ever discerned by any of the senses. Give us a dozen good stones from a site . . . and we can reconstruct a complete countryside for any period we wish . . . We can trap sounds and play them back with perfect fidelity. We can play the song of the ancestral cicada that had two more chromosomes than have its descendants . . . And smells! Of course they are even more simple than sounds to lift from the transparencies. We can go back and pick up nearly every scene complete for the past fifty thousand years . . . And patinas and transparency deposits on stones are only one of the dozens of tools that we have available for such historical reconstruction.

—Thunder-Colt

"I'm really curious about how slow a time-jog you have us on here, Luna," Henry Kemp said. "I've shaved four times since we've been here, and we haven't completed the fourth second yet. It seems to me more like a second to twenty-four hours now, but I'm sure it wasn't that slow at the beginning. We had time on slow-jog at a time convention in Ghent last year, but that was mostly illusion and hallucination. I didn't grow a day's whiskers in a second's time there, nor get a good night's sleep, nor get this much of a sun tan. You *are* the original Peter Luna, the grandfather of Peter Bardolf Luna who lives in London now and who also dabbles in time, are you not? But that original Peter Luna is supposed to have died away back in the year 1928. If you did not die then, you would be—how old?—now. How did you avoid your death? And how did you avoid your ageing?"

"I am that Peter Luna, yes. I do not avoid that death. I die in 1928, and this is the very day that I die. That's why I've put this day on such a slow time-jog. It's my death-day and I'm not in a hurry about dying. And I want to transmit this set-up to the five of you before I die. And yet you have to come to the intellectual acceptance of it at your own pace. It's rather frustrating to me."

"What a cover story!" Annabella MacBean admired. "You're quite a spoofer, in addition to other things, Luna. But how do you (alive as you seem to be at this moment) know that you die on this particular day in long-ago 1928?"

"Oh, another time traveler told me. He discovered that I had a time-satellite here and he used it three different times. He had a lot of equipment to move into the past from this easy jump-off bank. In between my visits here he looked me up and found my death chronicled. I had the reputation of 'mad scientist' so I was noticed a bit. My clock, of course, stopped at the minute of my death. And the big house here was taken down or wrecked later. At least there were no signs of it in his day. So I die a little bit after noon today, and it's a little bit after noon now. And it may be that it will take the psychic kick of my death to transmit the realization of this set-up to you.

"You're *here* now. Everything you *need* is here. Dammit, don't bust on it, you five. In all logic, there isn't any way that you can bust on it: but there's an illogical aspect to every time jump and you just might bust."

"Where *is* your previous time-traveler now, dear Peter Luna?" Rowena asked him. "We love you, of course, old father-figure, old father-time-figure, but it isn't always easy to believe you."

"He's still in past time, Rowena. He intended to stay there, in a haven he had picked out and which he didn't disclose to me. He believed that the fewer futurians reaching the past the better it would be for those who did get there. He hadn't any intention of building a time-bridge. But I do wish mightily to build a time-bridge that can be used by all interested persons. I don't have to die today, you see. I could flee into the past alone and forget about today. But if I want to open a workable bridge, if I want to transmit what I have built to you five, then I *do* have to die today: or I have the particularly rank superstition that I have to."

No, Peter Luna didn't look old. He surely wasn't a father-figure to any of them except Rowena. But perhaps a father-time-figure or a master-of-time-figure will not look at all old. Suetonius mentions that "those about to die" sometimes take on a quite boyish appearance during their last moments.

"Are you subject to rank superstitions, dear Peter?" Annabella MacBean jibed him.

"Oh, when a rank superstition seems to be an intrinsic part
of an equation, I don't throw it out. 'Workable irrationalities'
are present in every theory that works."

Abel Roaring and Henry Kemp continued to look for the
time-satellite. Peter Luna was so very cryptic about it, and
yet they still believed that he might have it.

"I can build a time-satellite myself," Henry said. "I can
build anything. I built a human corpse once. Oh, it was
simplified, of course, but it should have been workable in all
its working parts. There wasn't any reason why it shouldn't
work, but it wouldn't. It hadn't the spark of life. Nor would
my time-satellite have it. I've the feeling that Luna's satellite
would have it, does have it, if he has really built it."

"And I projected a human corpse once," Abel Roaring
said. "I suppose that it was simplified, and yet it was consistent. I built it from rock-patinas from a particularly resonat-
ing valley. It was the corpse of a young woman who had
imposed herself with stunning moment upon that valley in
which she lived. But no, I couldn't give her the spark of life.
She was as if she had just died. I'm afraid my own satellite
(and I'm sure I could project one) would be similarly life-
less."

Kemp and Roaring were playing squash racquets. Luna
had a fine walled court there. Imagine anyone having courts
for both tennis and squash racquets. Kemp was the raging
lion on the court, and Roaring was the quick and tricky and
suddenly savage unicorn. They rested when it stood at one set
each.

"The walls of the court are especially resonant," Abel
Roaring said then. "I believe that, from the remembering-
transparencies that form the deep patinas of these walls, I
would be able to recreate a complete game played here in
some past time. There would not merely be the 'pok pok pok'
of the racquets hitting the ball and the 'powk powk powk' of
the ball hitting the walls, there would be everything of sight
or sound or smell. There would be the rumpledness and

hard-breathing of the players and the smell of sweat and adrenaline, there would be the voices and the grunts, there'd be the sunlight warming the courts, there'd be the crows on wobbly wings coming to investigate the sound of the volleys. Ah, there'd even be the bead of sweat on the lip of one of the players."

"Would it be possible to analyze that drop of sweat, Abel?" Henry Kemp asked.

"That's asking a lot. Yes, even that might be possible."

"How is it that your players would be reproduced full of movement and life and the corpse of your young lady lacked the life spark?"

"No, no, the corpse was much more authentic. The reproduction of the game here would still be a picture, a solid, three-dimension moving picture in sight and sound and smell. I could not interfere with the players in the animated picture. I could not touch them, and I could not make them hear my words. But the corpse, I could touch it. It was the more valid. You and I can re-create time sets, Henry. But we cannot enter fully into them. We can picture moments of past time, but we cannot really travel in that past."

"Luna, I remember what the Walker truck is now," Roaring told Peter Luna when they were all back in the manor house some time later in the second. "It was an American battery-electric truck made back in the 1920s and before. It would go twenty miles or so. And then, after its batteries had been on charge for quite a few hours, it might run for another twenty miles. It was clean and quiet. But is there something special about your own Walker truck?"

"Yes, there is, Abel. If it hadn't been special, you wouldn't have been able to ride in it from your year to mine."

"Weren't we in the same year?"

"Peter, Peter," Annabella said, "wherever your damned time-satellite is, whyever did you build it here?"

"This is the place I live in and love, that's why. I built my time-cliff here because I wanted it here. Does not Henry Kemp build his fabrications in his own territory?"

"Henry, dear Henry," Rowena said. "You're an evocative builder. You're a cave-man drawing pictures on the stone walls of a cave. But you draw better than you deserve to. Your homeo-magic (for that's what all of us deal in) *will work*. When we do go out on the hunt, very soon now, we will find that the 'animals' are alive and genuine and infinitely detailed. Aye, and we'll find that the people (for it is really the people in animistic masks that you draw) are master-works of living detail.

"You can build, Henry, and Abel Roaring can project solid representations from old photographs taken by stones; but are the productions of either of you anything more than 3-D pictures?"

"3-D pictures, 3-D smells, 3-D sounds, Rowena," Roaring said, "and I'm not sure that primary life itself is more than that. Or is there something in life that is not recorded in even the most sophisticated pictures?

"What if, within the next stasis-second or so, we *do* achieve time travel? Or what if we only believe that we have achieved it, and we are mistaken in that belief? What if it is only a truer-than-life seance, conducted in a sunshiny summer noontime rather than in a darkened evening room? But then, if we push it too far, may not life itself be only the mottled fruit of a garish seance conducted by larger but perhaps not more noble entities?"

"Peter, when you died here that first time, were we five persons here with you?"

"This is still that first time," Peter Luna said, "and I am still a fraction of a second away from my first and only death. But yes, there is an underlay of you, a premonition of you, but dim. Shadows and voices only in the premonition. But I recognized all of you from them when you came here."

"Peter, in your time-stasis somewhere in the past, in our past anyhow, how are you familiar with the things we have published in our own time, and other things that would be in your future?" Farquharson asked.

"Oh, I get things delivered to me by the *World Courier Service ('No Questions asked, Messages Carried Everywhere and Everywhen')*," Peter Luna said.

"Then does the *World Courier Service* have a time-shuttle of its own?"

" 'Other sheep I have who are not of this fold. Them also—', I forget just how it goes in scripture. And the motto of the *World Courier Service* should be amended to 'No questions asked, and no questions answered either'. I suppose they do have a time-shuttle of some sort. We seldom stumble over anything where somebody has not previously stumbled. But they seem to put their gadget to very limited use. They haven't opened the great portals, nor have I myself done it before I am terminated here. I hope that you five will be able to throw them open, with the impetus I am able to give you. Ah, the semi-stasis is crammed full. It's about to burst."

"What's it crammed full of, Peter?" Annabella asked.

"Of clotted dreams, Annabella. And that's rather your own specialty."

5

Time Reversal—In theoretical physics, mathematical operation of replacing the expression for time with its negative in formulas or equations so that they describe an event in which time runs backwards or all the motions are reversed. A resultant formula is said to be time-reversal invariant, which implies that the same laws of physics apply equally well in both situations . . . and that the flow of time does not have any naturally preferred direction . . . In any case, there is a more general inversion operation that does leave the physical laws invariant, called in its mathematical expression the CPT theorem. It comprises time reversal T combined with interchange of antiparticles and particles, called charge conjugation C, and a mirror-reflection or inversion of space, called parity reversal P. When all these are performed simultaneously, the resultant process or interaction is indistinguishable from the original.

—Encyclopaedia Britannica

"Oh, that's too simplistic," Annabella MacBean growled. "The CPT theorem leaves out something. Maybe it's the RS or Rank Superstition Factor. Oh, I was arguing back against an old definition. I get absent-minded.

"The dreams aren't clotted, Peter Luna. It's just that I have such a clotted time trying to explain them. The dreams I speak of in my work are the entire accumulation of the human affair, and I've found no instruction that they must be reviewed for only one direction."

They were having a sort of party there in the biggest of the dining rooms, and Annabella MacBean had baked a Death-Day Cake for Peter Luna. There was nothing morbid about this. Luna himself was quite willing to be gone, if he could be sure that these five time attempters were able to handle the legacy that he was leaving them.

"I'll be out of this pantomime, out of this token shadow-land, and I'll be in the main show," Luna said. "But it has been very pleasant knowing you five people, even if for less than five seconds."

"Oh, Peter, this *is* part of the main show," Annabella insisted. "It's at least the first act of it. I think it's a full show, five or seven acts at least, and at the end of each of them we die and are then reborn on a more vasty plane. But there aren't any skimpy acts in our main show; surely the first act isn't; and it's criminal for us to skimp any part of it. We must range forward and backward through the act we are living in; we must learn every direction and dimension of it. We have an obligation to understand and to explore, in every way. Life is made up of this compacted emotion and experience and happiness, and if we cut ourselves off from any dimension of it then we live the less. We must unclot it and open it all up. The 'Road to Yesterday' must be one of the opened roads, or we are the less for it."

"It's rather good cake," Peter Luna said as he took a forkful of his own Death-Day Cake.

"For a rather good guy," Annabella told him.

"I'm curious about the corniest touch of all, Luna," Ethan Farquharson said. "Did it, does it, will the clock really stop at the moment of your death? Gah, that sounds like something in a murder mystery from back around—"

"From back around the present year of 1928, Ethan? Yes, I've arranged that the clock should stop at the very moment of my death. The clock is parallel to my own living aura and it has a bascule coil in it; and it stops when my aura expands and then collapses and extinguishes itself. It isn't a very difficult trick. If you'd think a moment, Ethan, you'd see that you could do it yourself."

"Not a difficult trick, friend Peter, but corny. In you, though, it's likeable."

"I keep remembering something about throwing a dead or dying cat through a ring of fire," Abel Roaring said. "It's in some old witches' rite for time travel."

"The cat through the burning hoop, yes, it's another form of my favorite rank superstition. They have it topologically backwards though. I am the dying cat thrown through the hoop of fire, but the hoop of fire is my own aura; and it is the five of you who will fling yourselves through it. And I am the slave killed so that the traveler may step through his expanded dying aura and be back in time for the length of the slave's life. Yes, it is the rankest of superstitions. Cannot you find it likeable in me?"

"I can and I do," Abel Roaring said. "But we do not need either dead slave or dead cat. We'll follow that ritual, though, that all things may be fulfilled. What we have to know now, Luna, is where we can find your time-satellite? Where is it, Peter, where is it?"

"The clock *has* stopped," Peter Luna said with a sort of pleasure. "So I'm in the last second of my life. The clock moved by one-second jumps and it will not move by less. I felt it flick off.

"You five have slightly different ways of phrasing your go-backs, the 'clotted dream break-out', the 'naked ghost impasse', the 'intuition as enabler process', the 'build a world and make it live schematic', the 'time is a pile of recorded transparencies reconstructions'; but the mathematics that all of you have worked out are almost identical, which is to say that they are nearly enough correct to work. There are cautions, of course. How many cautions is a man able to give in the last second of his life? You could enter false worlds that never existed if your reconstructions are too subjective. But you are five correctives to each other in this. You could be an abrasive on the past as some conscienceless travelers are, but you five are surprisingly good people and you should avoid those errors.''

"The time-satellite, where is it?" Abel Roaring asked. "Tell us where it is now, Peter, now, or everything else is in vain."

"Oh, you're inside the satellite. All of us are. The entire estate of Moonwick is a time-satellite. You are all back in the year 1928, many years before your births. You are beyond the shoal, and you have clear sailing now. The 'Road to Yesterday' is wide open to you. 'You will draw water joyfully from the springs of salvation' as scripture says; and it is good to journey back a bit nearer to our well-springs. There are at least five rather furtive and sleazy persons already on the time-roads. Let you five be of a better kind. You could have taken the time-road five seconds ago, of course, but I desired your company for this little while.''

"We've surely crammed a lot into these five seconds," Rowena said. "Ah, those long horseback rides with Ethan!''

"We played golf, Rowena," Ethan Farquharson said.

"And exploring those limestone caves in the north banks with Henry!" Annabella smiled. "How could we have done so much in such a short while?''

"Annabella, we didn't find any caves. But we found mooring holes in the stones where boats used to moor when the banks were the shore of the Gulf of Lions.''

"Was all of it subjective then, Peter Luna?" Abel Roaring asked.

"Not all, but a lot of it. It's hard to cram such a great amount of objective happenings into five seconds. I'm rather proud of this time-satellite. It's more than a million times as large as any time-satellite built or attempted by anyone else. This is one of those rare cases where it's easier to build large than to build small. The house itself here will be pulled down or somehow destroyed within a year or two, so I've been told. But the estate can still be called into service as a time-satellite whenever an instructed one calls. I have sensed that one of you has an aura-amplifier. Which of you?''

"But of course, I'm the one who has it, dear Peter," Rowena Charteris smiled. "I wouldn't be caught dead without one. You others are very robust and have robust auras. But mine has always needed reinforcing.''

"One other thing, Luna," Henry Kemp said. "It's rather a delicate thing to ask, but what do we do with your body if you really do die in this second?''

"Leave it, guys, leave it. Don't worry about it. My doctor has an appointment with me here this noontime. He'll be here in just five minutes, for he's an absolutely punctual man. Doctors are used to certifying dead people. And I drew up and signed all sorts of papers with my lawyer just one week ago.

"Oh, I'm stricken! Death will come almost instantaneously now, but it won't seem so on our slow-jog time. Time here will return to normal with my death though, to a normally-moving 1928 mid-summer day.

"Ah, I cloud over! What are these things around me? Five shadows, five voices? I knew them for a while, but now they dim out.''

The aura of Peter Luna was quite visible, aided by the aura-amplifier of Rowena Charteris. It was a quivering and quaking loop.

It expanded suddenly, and the five persons stepped through it. It collapsed and extinguished itself then, and Peter Luna was dead.

And five happy-sad time-achievers went with lively step down the 'Road to Yesterday'. They could have gone down it five seconds before this, but it does no harm to fulfill a ritual even when it is rank superstition.

ANIMATED BY THE FOSSILS
OF TIME

Robert A. Frazier

Founded in a root system of Rejuvenators and Regenerators,
linked by vines and tendrils of cable,
the Arc 9 Reconstructor creates a hologramatic movie set;
plays De Mille to whole dead cultures.
Through a museum the size of an Athenian city block
you can walk backwards,
as a knife would slide through butter,
dissecting ghostly panoramas of discarded Greek millenia.
Or you can watch in a repeating loop of glassine images
the catspaw entrance of Booth at the Theater
and the rose bloom red behind Lincoln's ear.
Or, if you are wealthy beyond the laws
of Einstein's physics,
you can stroll forever with a dead love
on the sunlit shores of your memory.